Love
Disregarded

Love Disregarded

rachel blaufeld

Edited by
Pam Berehulke
www.bulletproofediting.com

Content Read by
Virginia Tesi Carey

Cover design by
© Sarah Hansen, Okay Creations, LLC
www.okaycreations.com

Interior Design and Formatting by
E.M.
TIPPETTS
BOOK DESIGNS

www.emtippettsbookdesigns.com

Warning:
This book is intended for mature audiences.

For Michelle R., a beacon of light in the reading community.

Michelle, who tirelessly supports, advocates, and champions the romance genre.
For all your yelling from the rooftops, taking time away from your family to help,
and always listening.
Here is to the next time we can drink wine and eat pizza in NYC…the best city
in the world.

Thanks for being with me on this journey.

about
Love Disregarded

When I first met Aston Prescott, I thought I'd be able to let go of him.

I was naive.

He belonged to the country club where I worked, and despite the vast difference in our social status, I still fell for him. I thought he fell for me too, and that our love would overcome any obstacles.

But our relationship was discounted by everyone around us. Our families didn't support us, and our friends avoided us.

So we moved on with our lives, but then everything fell apart.

The man who once abandoned me is now seeking comfort in my arms, and this time, I'm not sure if I can give in.

Because if I do, I may never be able to let him go again.

Prologue

Bexley
Present day

I sat waiting, my butt crammed as far into the bench of the window seat as it could go, flush against the windowpane. With my chin resting on my bent knees, I stared out the bay window into the night, hoping for a sign that I wasn't wasting my time.

My kids had been asleep for hours, but something kept me up. A niggling, maybe…I didn't know what you'd actually call the feeling. A premonition, my grandma would have said, but she'd been gone since I was in grade school.

Most people would dismiss it as black magic or voodoo, or simply plain crap. Yet here I was.

Fourteen years later, I was still in tune with a man, thinking he was going to appear out of the blue, even though he hadn't shown his face here in years. Not just any man, but the man who'd changed me, forced me to love, and then left me—not for something better, but for the life he was destined to live.

If I squeezed my eyes tightly enough, I could feel he was close. Even after so many years, warmth still blanketed my skin when I thought about him.

Nerves flitted in my belly, tickling and scratching, making me uneasy, but I couldn't move from the window seat. I'd waited a lifetime for this night. In this moment, I wasn't a single mom with an overactive imagination, sitting awake in the middle of the night, thinking about a man who wasn't going to show. No, I was a recent high school graduate, waiting for her guy to come by and make me his.

For whatever reason, I was convinced he was coming back to me tonight, and no one could tell me otherwise. Not that I'd dared to share this with anyone.

Afraid to move, I'd waited so long in the window seat, I'd fallen asleep. My hair was stuck in the crook of my neck, drool running down my chin onto my knee, when the sun fully came up. The first rays shone through the crack in the blinds from where I'd been peeking all night.

He didn't show.

I wasn't shocked or surprised.

Not wanting to leave the window, I watched as a kid on an old-fashioned beach cruiser tossed a newspaper onto my lawn and sped off. Guilt had forced me to subscribe; the kid loved his job.

The sound of giggling came from the kitchen, knocking me out of my reverie. Over the hum of the television, I could hear spoons scraping cereal bowls.

Shit. I messed up.

After a long inhale, I swallowed a large lump of humiliation and brushed the hair out of my eyes. Standing on wobbly knees, I decided to grab the paper first.

Pleased for the first time that I didn't drop my subscription for the paper edition, I popped open the door, desperate to stretch my legs, gulping big breaths of fresh air before meeting my reality this Saturday.

As the desert breeze smacked me square in the face, I came to a conclusion...

Aston Prescott was never meant to be mine. He was a dream I should have let die a long time ago, right along with my right to forever happiness.

He was married and had a family with another woman. In fact, he was probably sitting with them at some fancy-ass brunch at this very moment, at his fancy-pants country club with his snotty friends and his pain-in-the-ass controlling father.

In a world where I didn't belong.

Part 1

chapter
One

Bexley

Back then

Three days after my eighteenth birthday, I met *the guy*.

You know…the *one*.

Not to disappoint, but it was your typical *girl meets boy, insta-lust, I'm going to wither away and die if I don't date him* type of thing. The kind of meet-cute story straight out of the movies. The second I saw him, all the mushy feelings swept over me like a sandstorm in the desert.

That particular day was no different from any other, the sun burning hot as hell in Nevada, where I lived and was spending my last few months before college. In a last-ditch effort, I was trying to make some major moolah before school loans knocked me on my ass. Lord knew I needed it.

This was meant to be my last hurrah in this desert oasis before I got the hell out of Dodge, and then I met *him*.

The very moment he laid eyes on me, I knew one thing for certain—he was the gold standard I'd compare every man to moving forward.

That summer, I'd gotten a job working as a sandwich girl at a fancy golf club in our small town outside Reno. My good friend, Milly, and I had been put in charge of making close to 250 sandwiches on any given day for the pickiest, most obnoxious bitches in Reno.

Look, I know, you shouldn't call women bitches. But damn if they weren't to us poor, less fortunate girls.

"One Cunty Tuna and two Bitchy Bacon, Lettuce, and Tomato, hold the mayo, Bexley…on whole wheat, of course," Milly called to me from the counter.

I was in the cold locker grabbing some more turkey bacon, the kind we referred to as *Bitchy Bacon,* and without even looking up, I knew she was rolling her eyes. The women who ate this ridiculous bacon substitute were even bitchier due to caloric deprivation.

"God, don't these women ever have fun? I'm going to dab a little mayo on her damn dry tuna and see if she notices," I muttered to myself, slapping the bacon on my prep counter.

It was stifling in the small kitchen, and I swept a few stray damp hairs off my face with my forearm and set about making the sandwiches. Milly was busy taking an order. She was way better than me at the face-to-face thing, which was why she was stationed at the counter.

"Bex, double that order, but make the last Bitchy open-faced on rye."

I rolled my eyes and yelled, "Okay."

My lackluster dark blond hair was braided to the side, and I could feel it curling in the desert heat. It would be one hell of a mess to comb out later. Sweat dripped down my back and into my thong under my ridiculous polyester uniform.

After Marcus, the waiter, ran our latest sandwich rush out to the tables shaded by a sea of red-and-white-striped umbrellas, I called out to Milly, "I need a breather." Blowing out a breath, I untied my apron and looked to see if she heard me.

Of course, Milly was hanging out of the window flirting with Mike Richards, so I didn't wait for her to answer.

By the way, Mike was a major asshole, and I hated him for her.

"Yeah, go," she finally hollered back as I elbowed the back door open.

I stepped out and took a long swig of my iced green tea before holding my face up to the sun. I let the vitamin D rain down on me and took slow breaths, thinking of how much money I was saving between tips and the cushy salary I was being paid. I was pretty sure the club didn't want us going around and spilling their dirty little secrets, so they overcompensated in our paychecks.

What happened at Sun Rock Golf Club, stayed at Sun Rock Golf Club.

I was occupied with running the chilled bottle down my neck, allowing the condensation to drip down my clavicle into my cleavage, when a deep voice interrupted my moment of solitude.

"You cool?"

I opened my eyes and moved my face out of the sun. "Um, yeah, I'm cool. Can I help you? Milly's around front taking orders," I said, squinting in the bright sunlight.

When I finally took in the person behind the voice, my legs went weak—literally. Conflicted and embarrassed by the jolt I felt from looking at this dude, I swallowed my impure thoughts.

Yes, he was a pompous ass, but his eyes were perfectly blue (like the sky, *of course*), his skin golden from spending time in the sun, and his face was complemented by a mane of light blond waves.

"Nah, I'm not hungry. I saw you sneaking around back, and I came to introduce myself. Aston…Aston Prescott." He said it with authority like he was a senator or something, his voice deep and confident as he arrogantly extended his hand toward me.

"Oh," was all I could croak out. Immediately, I cursed myself like in the movie *Dirty Dancing*, when she carried a watermelon.

"And you are?" Aston asked, staring me down with his heavenly blues.

For the briefest of moments, I felt naked, laid bare in a way I'd never experienced before. I'd never understood what the expression meant, but I did now as I came undone under his gaze.

Feeling my heart in my throat, I swallowed it back down. "Bexley," I said, practically whispering.

"Nice to meet you, Bexley . . . ?" His voice rose at the end as he stuck out his hand again.

I wasn't sure what he wanted me to do. I was a poor girl from the wrong side of the tracks, not a socialite, not even middle class.

"Bexley, I'm waiting for you to shake my hand."

His statement was borderline rude, again pompous, but it made my body quiver.

I stuck my smaller hand in his large mitt. His hands were soft, not a callus anywhere that I could tell, unlike any of the other hands I'd shaken before, which were usually rough and coarse.

"Nice to meet you," I said, my hand still swallowed by his.

"What's your last name, Bexley?"

"Rivers."

"That's quite an interesting name, Bexley Rivers."

"Yeah, it is. I mean, yes, sir. Nice to meet you." I tried to recall some of the training we'd had at the beginning of the summer on how to address and interact with members.

"Oh, you have no idea what that does to me, hearing you call me sir, Bexley, but it's not necessary. Now, tell me about your name."

I gulped down whatever emotion he'd stirred up in me and answered to the best of my ability. After all, my job could be on the line.

"I know, it's a bit much. My mom's maiden name was Bexley, and she was at a loss for what to name me. She thought she was having a boy," I said, rambling, "and was set on Frankie Junior. My dad was Frank Senior, and so when it was time to leave the hospital, she just scribbled down her maiden name and then her married name…and that was it."

His mouth formed a small smirk, and his left eyebrow rose the tiniest bit. It should have felt like he was making fun of me, but he wasn't. At least, I didn't think so. Although I had absolutely zero experience in this area, I could tell Aston was being genuine.

God, this guy—a club member I should *not* be fraternizing with—made my heart speed up and my body feel hotter than it already was from standing inside the sweltering kitchen.

"I didn't mean to go running off with the details, and…I should probably get back to work." I motioned behind me, my thumb making me look more like a homeless hitchhiker than a cool girl.

That's when I realized he was still holding my other hand.

He squeezed my hand tight, not letting me go. "No worries on your running off with details. You should do it some more. Like tonight, we're having a party on the seventeenth hole. Why don't you come by? We can talk more."

"Me?"

He winked. "Yes, you."

"Um…I don't know."

"Why not? You have a better offer?"

I shook my head. Of course I didn't have a better offer. "Can I bring Milly?" Knowing I'd need a wing woman, I pointed back to the snack shack. We weren't supposed to socialize with members, but she was already breaking that rule, so she'd have no problem going with me.

"The more the merrier."

Gulping back my fear, I asked, "What time?"

"Eight." He winked again, squeezed my hand again before releasing it, and walked off.

Anything I'd ever wanted, ever thought I needed, didn't exist after those ten minutes.

After one handshake, all I wanted was Aston Prescott.

chapter
Two

Bexley

"**D**o you think Mike will be there?" Milly asked me for the fourth time in the last thirty minutes.

After finishing our shift, we'd cleaned up, eaten our staff meal, and freshened up in the staff locker room. We couldn't afford to waste gas, schlepping back and forth to home and then back to the club. Taking time to freshen our makeup, pulling combs through our hair, and doing the best we could with what we had at our disposal, we tried to appear like we fit in. Of course, there was no mistaking us for richies like the ones who lived along the golf course.

"I'm sure, Mill, but there's probably going to be a lot of people, and I'm not even sure why we're going. Promise me you'll stay near me, and if we feel out of place, we'll leave, okay? I don't even know why I said yes," I said, my hand shaking the slightest bit.

Milly didn't answer. As we traipsed through the rear parking lot and onto the golf course, she kept her pace steady and a smile on her face, totally excited about the party. My friend acted like she belonged there, but me? I thought about offering to help clean up.

"Listen to me, Bexley." She grabbed my hand and stalled our pace. "We're going because some hottie asked you, and whether you admit it or not, you like him. Plus, we're already out and should have some fun before we drive home to our shit places. Come on."

With a death grip on my arm this time, she dragged me faster down the fairway and straight to the seventeenth hole.

People were everywhere, sitting, standing, crouching. Mansions lined the golf course, exterior lighting showing off their elaborate facades. A large blanket was spread on the putting green near the hole, and bottles of every kind of liquor imaginable were set on it. Small lanterns anchored each of the blanket's four corners, illuminating the amber and clear liquids. A keg was off to one corner, and an enormous bong in the other. Music played from a wireless speaker, filling the air around us with hip-hop. Every now and again, a shriek or a deep laugh rang out over the music.

Despite my immediate acceptance earlier in the day, I wanted to turn around and leave. I felt less than insignificant in my jean cutoffs and white tank. Taking in the other girls, dressed in designer sparkly tank tops and miniskirts, all I wanted to do was tuck tail and get the hell out of there.

"Hey, Bexley…glad you came," a deep voice rumbled near me, sending chills through me. Of course, the owner of the gravelly, absolutely male voice turned toward Milly. "Aston Prescott," he said. Just like he had with me, he stuck his hand out and gave his spine-tingling, cocky introduction to my best friend.

She, of course, knew what to do in response, and tucked her hand in his. "Milly Shump." She said her name with pride, even though it meant nothing to this crowd.

"Nice to meet you, Milly. Can I get you two something to drink?"

"Heya, Milly-girl," Mike Richards said, interrupting Aston as he came up behind Milly and put his arms around her waist. "Whatcha doing here?" He hoisted her from behind and spun her around, her loose blond waves shimmering in the glow from the lanterns.

"Aston *invited* Bexley."

He set her down and shoved his dark hair behind his ear, seemingly searching for the right words. "I would've invited you, but I didn't know if you should come. Know what I mean?"

"Not really, but I'm here now, so you can get me a drink." Milly looped her arm through his and walked off, leaving me with *Senator* Prescott.

"That wasn't weird or anything," Aston said to me.

"They have a thing. I'm pretty sure it's on the DL, or at least it *was* on the DL. Looks like they're outed now," I said, glancing at Milly fawning all over Mike.

"Come on, let's get you a drink." Aston ignored anything related to Mike and Milly, as if nothing was as important as me. Taking my hand, he led me toward the bar-on-a-blanket. "What's your poison, Bexley Rivers?"

"Vodka and cranberry?" I eyed the bottles, pretty sure what they had wasn't the cheap vodka I was used to.

"Coming right up." He knelt on the blanket, his quads flexing under his straight-leg khaki shorts, making it hard for me to tear my eyes away.

My gaze continue to wander over his bicep peeking out from the sleeve of his white polo shirt as he mixed my cocktail. When he stood again, I swallowed a mysterious lump in my throat. Desire? Lust?

Not seeming to notice, he handed me my drink. "Wait a sec. Let me refill mine."

Of course I waited. Where was I going to go? I'd been cast in a spell where Aston was the puppet master and I was the dutiful puppet on strings.

He poured a healthy dose of Jack and Coke and stood again. "Cheers," he said before clinking plastic cups with me and taking a swig of his.

Afraid to miss a moment of this, I took a small sip, forbidding my eyes from leaving his.

Gathering my hand in his again, Aston walked me out onto the golf course and plopped down in the grass, taking me to the ground with him. Although it all felt surreal to me, Aston acted like this was totally normal.

"Are you guys going to get into trouble for this?" I couldn't help but ask, taking in the party happening all around us. People and noise were everywhere, and I was sure it would be a hefty cleanup on a very expensive golf course. I couldn't imagine this flying with management.

"Nope. The club and the homeowners would rather us keep our business in the club than cause trouble outside the place. It doesn't look good for our families or them. So we party here."

"Oh. You live here too?"

"Yeah, though I'm sort of new. Actually, I used to visit on school breaks, so I caught on quickly to the unwritten rules."

"New?" I took another small sip of my drink, the expensive vodka burning my throat and warming my belly.

"I thought you would've heard. I moved here full-time with my dad. My mom was sick of doing the single-parent thing and shipped me off to live here with good old dad at the end of the semester. Apparently, it was all anyone was talking about."

"No. Well, I try to stay out of member gossip…and I don't really know anyone who would tell me anything, anyway. But that sucks, though. Do you miss her, your mom?"

"Not really. I was sick of picking up the pieces. My parents divorced several years ago, but she never bounced back. This last time she lost it, decided she didn't need me around anymore. Said I only reminded her of my dad. She gave me my marching orders—run the company, take all that was owed to me, and get out." He ran a hand through his unruly hair, his gaze drifting over me.

"Wow," was all I could say, not sure if I was referring to his mom or him. It was just simply wow to me—the concept of having money.

"Yep, wow. So I'm new around here. But I'd much rather you tell me about you, Bexley." His eyes continued to focus on me, filled with interest and confidence, as blue as the water in the hot tub by the pool.

I shrugged. "I'm new to the club too. Just working here for the summer and making money for school."

"Where are you going to school?"

"Not too far, just outside Vegas, a small state school, but I'm the first person in my family to go to college."

He didn't look at me with pity or like I was a girl from the wrong side of town. Instead, he smiled, almost as if he were proud of me, and I fell harder for this richie dude.

"What year are you?" I asked, sipping at my drink.

"Almost finished. One more semester in college in Cali, and then I'll be here full time in Reno. Taking over the family biz like my mom wants. Even with her kicking me to the curb, I can't seem to let go of what she asked. Must be all the horror shows I lived through when it came to her."

"I just graduated from high school," I said sheepishly, not knowing what else to say.

"I figured, when you said you were just starting college." His mouth formed that smirk again, the sexiest one I'd ever seen—cocky and endearing at the same time. "I'd thought I'd be going home to La-La Land for one last summer, but my mom seriously wasn't having it. It's all cool, though, because I'm getting down with my dad's shit life now. Like sweet-talking my stepmom into doing what I want."

I laughed and took another sip. *If he thinks this is a shit life, he should come see where I live.*

My feelings must have shown on my face because he said, "Sorry for the bad attitude. She's just…she's not my mom. Nan's sort of bitchy to me, but I don't think it's me. That's all I can say. My stepmother is closer to our age than my dad's, pushing out one kid after another, securing her future with him."

"It's fine. I get it must be difficult. But you know, calling her bitchy…it's just not necessary." I swiped my hand, wet from the condensation on my plastic cup, on my jean shorts, not sure where I came up with the courage to speak up to Aston.

"You know what? You're right, but I'll tell you this. She sucks."

I nodded, not wanting to cause any more waves.

"Let me get you another drink." He motioned toward my empty cup.

When did that happen?

"Actually, it's cool. I'll be the one to drive us home later, so I'm good."

Recently turned eighteen, I didn't need any trouble. My mom had sent me to school early, desperate for full-time childcare, and I'd been fine. But I didn't think it was a good time to mention any of that.

It was quiet between the two of us for a moment, grunge music now filtering around us.

"Listen, Bexley, this is weird, I know. You're not supposed to fraternize with the members, and I can tell you're a rule follower. I'm…I'm probably all wrong for you, but I want to take you out for real. Please?"

My heart pounded so hard, I was sure he could see it.

Aston was right about not fraternizing with members, but not everybody followed the rules. Mike had been screwing Milly for weeks—in the family locker room, no less. Up until tonight, their relationship had been secret.

Sneaking around wasn't really my style, but nothing made my pulse race like the possibility of dating Aston Prescott.

"Are you sure?" I asked. "I don't want you to get into trouble."

He grabbed my hand and pulled me close, cupping my cheek as he kissed me. Gently, not rough or demanding, but tender. His mouth ghosted over mine, grazing my lip gloss and softly touching my soul.

"Oh. I'm. Sure," he murmured.

Three little words, and I was a goner.

chapter
Three

Bexley

After the party on the golf course, Aston came to see me every day. He'd pop into the back entrance of the snack shack, always toward the end of the lunch rush, most of the time shirtless and wearing black Ray-Bans and swim trunks.

Every single time, he'd say, "Aston Prescott, pleased to meet you," with a smirk on his mouth and a twinkle in his eye. Somehow, he knew how his confident demeanor appealed to me, an inexperienced girl smitten with a guy with the perceived power.

There was something else to Aston, though, underneath all the heavy armor. At least, I was young and hopeful and believed so.

Over the next few weeks, he took me on fast car rides and out to eat—neither of which were staples in my regular life. We'd sit, staring googly-eyed at each other over spicy Tex-Mex, washing down the heat and lust with Mexican beer. All the while, I dared to dream of this being my reality.

He told me about college, his fraternity, and wild parties. Reaching across the table, he'd caress my hand, his thumb rubbing over mine as he stared deeply into my eyes. The only times his mood seemed to get melancholy were when he mentioned his mom. He'd get angry again over her kicking him out, but his determination was fierce when it came to taking over his father's company.

If we were in Washington, DC, I'd be the chambermaid and he'd be the president of the United States.

We parked outside one night in one of his dad's convertibles, in the desert in the middle of nowhere, and he put the top down.

As we were looking up at the stars, Aston turned to me and said, "I'm falling for you, Bex. I didn't plan on it, but I am. I don't think I can ever let you go. In fact, I'm not going to. You're the unexpected surprise I never counted on here, this summer. I didn't think I deserved someone like you, but maybe I do. And I'm keeping you."

A meteor shower could have rained down on us, and it would have been less shocking than his words.

Stunned, I said, "It's just a summer thing, you and me. In a million years, no one would ever think there was a future for us."

His lips hovered near my mouth and traced a path to my ear, along my cheekbone and coming to rest on my earlobe. "You need to allow yourself to believe it," he whispered.

We kissed and touched some more, my head and heart muddled.

Desperately, I wished it to be true. Could I believe it? My heart raced at the possibility, but my head ached at the thought of reality.

The divide between our lives was too wide. I'd only met his parents once, and it wasn't planned. Aston had taken me swimming at his house late one afternoon. We hadn't gone inside, only taken the golf cart around back and jumped into the pool, cooling off before stretching out in the luxurious lounge chairs. His dad and stepmom strolled into the pool area, fresh off the tennis courts.

"Son." His father stood looming over our lounge chairs, staring down at me.

"Hey, Dad."

"Aren't you going to say hello to Nan?"

"Hi, Nan," he said to his stepmother, and she held her hand out to me.

"Hi, I'm Nan."

I didn't have a clue how to handle this situation. The handshake? Yes. Meeting the parents? No.

My fingers shook as I offered them to Nan. I wanted to run, knowing I should have excused myself like a good little employee. But for Aston, I didn't.

"This is Bexley," Aston said, interrupting my runaway brain. "Bexley, this is my dad, Peter Prescott, and his wife, Nan."

"Nice to meet you both," I said from my chair. I should have stood, but I was in a bikini.

Absolutely nothing was right about the moment. The only thing I was sure of was Peter Prescott's disdain for me.

Towering over us, looking down his sharp nose at me, literally and figuratively, he asked, "Don't you work in the snack shack?"

"Yes, sir," I said meekly, with no misgivings about my social status. I was lesser than—there was no doubt about it.

"Well, nice to meet you," he said without another glance my way. "Come on, Nan, let's go eat. Aston, I'll speak with you later."

From then on, I avoided any public areas of the club where Peter Prescott may have been lurking.

And I didn't believe a damn thing Aston said about keeping me.

chapter
Four

Bexley

That summer, we spent more time panting like dogs in heat than anything else. For weeks, we survived on lingering kisses and brief touches. As for me, I was falling in love on borrowed time.

Close to a month after the first party, there was another one on the seventeenth hole, and Aston invited me. Just me. Not Milly.

"That's up to Mike," he told me. "I didn't know they had a thing going when I told you to bring her last time. I kind of broke bro code when I said she could come."

I sipped my iced tea while standing behind the snack shack, staring at a shirtless Aston with his swim trunks hanging low on his hips. "I have no idea what you're talking about."

He stepped closer, wrapping his hand around my braid and running his lips along my cheek. "It's one thing if I want to fraternize and only make time for you. It's not for everyone," he whispered in my ear. "There could've been another girl there."

"One who belongs with Mike," I said, my voice hoarse.

"Stop it," Aston said sharply. "That's him, not me. I don't care about that stuff."

Nodding into his chest, I pretended to believe him, but my heart ached all the same. Deep down inside, I knew we didn't belong together.

His hand ran down my back and tightened on my waist, gathering me close. "Not me, you hear me?"

I nodded again.

"Say you hear me, Bex. I mean it. I don't give a shit about anyone else, what they think or do or know. I'm my own man."

"I hear you," I muttered into his rock-hard chest.

Sadly, I was falling so deep in love—or lust—I'd started to believe he was right. I'd finally begun to believe there could be a future for us. A forever.

"Good. So later, why don't you come back with me to my dad's place and change there? He and the stepwitch went to some retreat in Tahoe, and the kiddies are with their grandma."

It was the first time Aston had asked me to go inside his father's house. Up until this point, we'd stolen moments in his car and on the golf course, but what he was suggesting made that all seem like child's play.

"Are you sure?"

"Bexley Rivers, let me introduce myself. Aston Prescott," he said, stepping back and offering me his hand. "Making a difference, not carrying on bullshit traditions. I like who I like, just like how I vote. I choose to vote how I want, not how my dad votes, and I vote to like you."

I smiled huge, could actually feel it spreading across my entire face and swirl around my heart. As my chest burned with an unfamiliar sensation, I said, "Okay."

"Pick you up here around five?"

"Yep."

I couldn't stop smiling.

As promised, Aston showed up outside the snack shack at five, and led me to his car. We drove slowly back to the house, and he grabbed my hand as we made our way down the driveway. Inside the garage, he disabled the alarm and took my hand again.

The house was huge. You could put twelve duplexes like my mom's just inside the foyer.

Leopard-print wallpaper covered every wall, and the floor was a dark polished wood. Twelve miniature crystal chandeliers hung from the ceiling, prisms of light bouncing off the crystal table in the center of the floor. I stood there, looking up and counting the light fixtures, my mouth hanging open.

Aston kicked his flip-flops off in the corner and came up behind me. "Don't get like that. It's just a big old house."

His hand wrapped around me from behind and tightened over my stomach, soothing the butterflies hatching in my belly.

"It's more than a house. It's practically a museum."

"Eh, forget it, Bex. Come on, let's have a drink."

We went into a kitchen built for a master chef, and Aston pressed his hand into what appeared to be paneling until it popped open. It was a refrigerator— of course. *Duh.*

"Water, wine cooler, wine, or beer?"

"Water's great."

He poured a glass of water and stuck a lemon slice on the rim, then grabbed a beer for himself.

"Cheers." He touched his bottle to my glass after he handed it to me. "Sit up on the counter, make yourself comfortable."

I eyed him.

"Come on, hop up." He patted the bright white marble slab, and when I did as he asked, he wedged himself between my thighs.

"Is this what your house in California is like?"

He laughed. "Nah. My mom got the short end of the stick, thanks to a lousy prenup. She has a small ranch house in Sherman Oaks. It's definitely nice, nicer than most," he said, retracting his earlier comment, probably wondering about where I lived. "It's comfortable and lived in, but my mom spends most of her time in bed, wrapped in a robe, yearning for something she'll never have again."

"Sad. She must've really loved your dad."

He took a swig of beer. "She did. Does. I don't know. It may just be the idea of what they once had. The whole divorce was a surprise to her. My dad came home from work one day and announced he was leaving. Months after he left, she was still walking around talking about a trip to Mexico they took. I must've heard it a thousand times."

He stopped, and I watched his Adam's apple bob as he took a breath and a drink.

"They drove across the border, looking for some fun, but their car ran out of gas. Of course, all they had was beer in the trunk. They stayed hydrated on only beer until another car swung by. According to the story, they were out there all day. Apparently, they were once young and carefree and in love, easygoing and full of life. Or so the story goes," he said, his words coming out bitter and sad.

"After that, my dad worked a lot, or said he was working. He rarely came home, and my mom became completely wrapped up in her self-pity."

"Wow, and how old were you when they separated?"

"Thirteen. I remember my entire eighth-grade year, my mom sobbed into her pillow. I used to go to bed at night and wish my dad would come back. Then I just wished she would get up."

"That was a lot for a boy."

"Hey, this is crazy. It's starting to sound a lot like a poor-little-rich-boy story. You, my girl, are strong beyond words." He tipped my chin up with his finger, and I wished for him to lean in and kiss me.

Last week, I'd told Aston my dad had been gone since I was born, leaving my mom and me to fend for each other. It was fine, though. We'd made it work.

I gulped the water, needing to cool off my emotions. Being around Aston brought out every emotion in me—sadness, need, desire, want, lust, pity, and occasionally envy.

"Let's talk about something better," he said, "like school. You ready?"

I nodded. "Getting there. The money's growing in my account, and I bought some stuff for my room."

"I hope you're not planning on inviting any boys to your room." He gave me a pointed look, and I swatted at his chest.

"Come on," I said with an eye roll.

"Seriously."

I stared at the floor, heat burning my cheeks.

How could I take anyone else back to my room, my bed, when all I wanted was him. *Him, him, him.* Dirty thoughts of him pounded in my head as my heart beat an obscene rhythm in my chest.

Aston lifted my chin again with his index finger and his gaze traveled my whole face, his finger tracing my cheek. He took my cup and set it with his beer on the counter and slid his hands under my hair.

With his gaze locked on mine, he whispered, "I'm serious."

He didn't give me a chance to respond, only kissed my lips. At first, our mouths remained closed, until a small moan escaped me. Aston took the opportunity to slip his tongue inside, where it stroked mine.

The kiss deepened, as did the grip his hands had on my neck. With a quick swoop, Aston lifted me, and my legs wrapped around his middle. He rocked his pelvis into me, and another moan came from me.

"Want to go upstairs? Is that okay?" Aston mumbled into my ear as he sucked on the lobe.

"Yeah." My voice was breathy and unrecognizable.

He carried me up to his room and set me on the bed. I took a second to glance around while he shut the blinds. King-size bed, two nightstands, and a desk, all in deep mahogany wood. Some safari-themed border ran around the walls, and I knew this wasn't really his space.

He clicked on the lamp, and soft light flooded the room.

Sliding next to me, his long arm draped across me, he began to run his hand over my side, making me shiver. His hand traveled over my rib cage and over my breast, sending chills up and down my spine, like the kind of shock you get when you take off a sweater in dry heat.

He ran the tip of his finger over my nipple, and it hardened under my tank and bra. He pinched and squeezed it before leaning over and sucking it through my clothes. I'd not done any of this before, yet my back arched and my body begged for more. He tugged down my tank, and when my bra cup came with it, his mouth latched onto my nipple.

"Aston…"

"Yeah, baby?" His lips tickled my nipple as the words made their way out.

"More," I said, my back arching off the bed.

He broke free and yanked my shirt over my head, then unhooked the front clasp on my bra, shoving it off my shoulders in seconds. I slid my hands under his shirt, smoothing them up his abs until I yanked his shirt off.

He ran his tongue over my breast, kissing my cleavage, then made his way to my other nipple, giving it the same treatment he'd given the other moments earlier. He didn't stay there long and soon began to travel south, kissing and licking a path to my navel. I gripped his hair with both hands, pulling, guiding, and pushing.

The room felt like a fiery furnace. My skin was burning, invisible flames licking at it from the inside out.

Aston unbuttoned my jean shorts and shimmied them down. He stood to pull them off where my ankles were dangling off the side of the bed. I watched through squinted eyes as he shoved down his khaki shorts and boxer briefs, fisting his own length, pumping it while staring down at me.

Then he was on me again, his mouth down below, licking places I'd never been touched. It felt good. No, amazing. I couldn't believe how brazen I'd become…I was a virgin when it came to everything. Aston was a man, and I wanted to be every bit of a woman to him.

I squirmed and pushed myself further into Aston's face, surely making a fool of myself, but I'd never felt so hot. All of a sudden, I felt like my body was splitting in half, blistering heat coursing through my veins. I came, shuddering all over his tongue.

He didn't even pause to lick his lips or wipe his mouth. Quickly, he made his way up my body and kissed me fervently, my taste everywhere on him.

I didn't care, couldn't bring myself to worry about that while he was grinding into me, his length touching my sensitive spot, not allowing the tremors to die down.

We kissed, our tongues colliding and playing, our pelvises doing a dance… until he slipped inside me. When he hit the natural barrier, he paused.

"Bex?" His brow furrowed. "You okay with this?"

I nodded, and he slowly pushed inside.

Bringing his hand down to mine while he kept his weight up on the other, he took his time. Languidly, he drifted in and out, the tension heightening, pleasure rising. The pain quickly forgotten, I lifted my hips to meet his, and he picked up the pace.

Maybe he planned it, but it didn't feel that way. It felt like it was supposed to happen like that, the most natural thing that had ever happened to me.

Aston Prescott buried himself deep inside me, taking all of me, making love to me in a way I was certain I'd never have again. We never discussed birth control, other than that I was on the pill to regulate my periods. I didn't care.

At that moment, all I cared about was Aston Prescott being mine.

chapter
Five

Bexley

I wasn't exactly a prude, but until I met Aston, I'd rounded all the bases except two—doing the deed, and letting a guy go down on me. Both seemed to require commitment.

When it came to Aston, there was an intimacy between us I hadn't been quite ready for…my soul was assaulted with lust, love, unnamed feelings. The moment he shook my hand and introduced himself behind the snack shack, I was his. His abundant arrogance and enormous ego should have been a turnoff, but somewhere in there, I found a redeeming man.

I saw through both his ego and pride for what they were—an armor. I'd made it my summer mission to put tiny chinks in that shell until it was chipped away.

When he'd sat me down on the golf course and told me about his life—the true story, his mom, the pain, and the guilt—his drive to succeed made sense. It was all he really had. Despite all the wealth and trappings, his desire to take over the family business and make it great was all that was important to him.

A week after we had sex for the first time, I sat in his lap one night on the golf course, a blanket spread out underneath us and the stars above, while he ran his nose along my neck. He'd pushed my hair to the side, exposing my skin to the evening air, but it was his touch giving me goose bumps and his words making my pulse race.

"I can't stop thinking about you. I want to make love to you every second of the day," he said softly.

My eyes squeezed shut, and a shiver ran down my spine at the mention of making love. Is that what he thought we were doing?

"I want to touch you…all the time." His perusal of my neck stopped, and he nudged my face toward his. "What? I didn't mean to upset you."

"What are you talking about?" The words squeaked out of my mouth.

"You clenched up, went rigid in my arms. Not exactly the reaction I was hoping for."

I slid off his lap and knelt before him, my knees pressing into the soft grass under the blanket. "No, not that. You didn't hurt me or anything. It's just you… you said…make love," I stammered.

"Right, make love. Make no mistake, in my mind I've had you seven ways until Sunday, but when I'm inside you, it's something else. Making love."

A nervous giggle floated from my mouth, and Aston kissed it away.

"Believe me," he said. "I never thought that expression, those words, would come from me. It's all you, Bex."

"I'm falling for you, Aston Prescott. You're nothing like the boys I know. Not like the men my mom knows."

"That's good, because I've fallen for you, Bexley Rivers. You most definitely aren't like anyone I've ever met, and I don't ever want to go back to anyone like that again."

At the end of the summer, he took me home to my house for the first time and saw exactly how different we were. We were complete opposites, but he still acted like I was better than sliced bread.

Aston was gracious to my mom, drinking iced tea from an old coffee mug and shaking her hand in a way that made my heart beat a little faster. He kissed me good-night on my stoop, pretending not to notice the chipping paint and cheap siding. He promised to visit me often, and offered to pay for me to visit him when he couldn't come to me.

And he made good on all of that until he graduated the next semester and began working for his father.

Then all he saw was the cheap facade that was me, Bexley Rivers.

chapter
Six

Aston

Present day

I walked out of the putrid county building, thankful for the dark of night hiding the purple circles under my eyes. Yes, I was vain enough to think of those. Probably because I'd spent so many years being photographed.

Glancing at my watch as I refastened the expensive timepiece to my wrist, I noted how late it was. "Thanks, Patrick," I said to one of my oldest friends, who was waiting for me outside the shitty building.

He'd brought my car over for me without asking a single question.

I didn't dare ask Mike for help. I wasn't ready for him or his inquisition, or more specifically, Milly's wrath. Yeah, Mike had promised to keep everything related to me to himself, but Milly had a way of inserting herself and her opinions into everything. Including my life.

"Listen, you good? You want to talk or something?" Patrick looked uncomfortable as he walked next to me, twisting his wrist inside his French cuff. He was keeping up with my quick pace, yet allowing a significant space between us.

"I'm fine. I need a stiff drink and a hot shower. Maybe a massage. Truthfully, the rest of this shit is up to my lawyers. It's bullshit, so I'm not worried."

"You sure about that?"

I stopped in my tracks, my suit wrinkled and heavy on my shoulders. "Pat, I didn't do a damn fucking thing. I may be an asshole most of the time, a pain in the ass to get along with, and whatever else everyone says about me, but drugs? Really? No. Just no. That's not me, and you know it. Jesus, I hope to fucking Christ you know that. I have kids, who I take care of, by the fucking way. I wouldn't get involved in something illegal."

Not going to lie, the charges humbled me a tiny bit. Everything I'd ever worked for, all the shit, namely Bexley, I'd given up in the name of Federal Stars Hospitality Supplies—a lifetime of sacrifices were on the line. I hadn't spent years sucking up to CEOs to peddle soaps, shampoos, imprinted cocktail napkins, and luxury manicure kits to hotels and resorts, just so I could lose it all because of some bullshit charge.

"It's just you've been off, you know, for a while. That's all. I know you have a shit-ton of pressure."

"Pressure," I whispered to myself and nodded. "I can handle it. I'm a big boy, Pat, made my bed and all that crap. My marriage went to shit, so the fuck what? It happens to fifty percent of marriages. We all knew that would happen to mine. Don't you dare question my integrity, though. All I have left is the company and my kids. Why the hell would I do anything to risk it? Fuck, I have to figure this out because I'm all the kids have." Sweat beaded on my forehead, and I ripped off my jacket and slung it over my shoulder.

Pat nodded. There was nothing left to say. He shouldn't have said anything. Mike had probably gotten under his skin.

"Sorry for losing my cool. Thanks for bringing the car. It's been almost two days in this hellhole. I have to get out of these clothes and get some rest."

I wasn't positive, but it felt like he patted me on my back and then let me go. I'd become so used to not being touched or consoled or loved by anyone lately, I'd forgotten what it felt like.

Anyway, what the hell would Patrick understand about my situation?

He was old money, married to even older money. One richie betrothed to another in a business union—like mine was. His biggest stressor was not drinking too much after eighteen holes, so he could go home, tuck his kids into bed, and fuck his wife. Missionary-style, of course. That was the only thing on the menu with good old Sally Sutton.

Poor Patrick. He should be worried about himself, not me.

Actually, I should shut my inner trap.

I was the saddest sack of them all, carrying a torch for a girl I could have called mine, but tossed aside instead. At least I honored my mom's wishes. She died successful in her pursuit to make my life as miserable as hers was.

Caught up in the past, I no longer cared that I smelled like shit or was shaking for a drink. Once I'd dropped Pat off at his house, it was late, and I turned my car toward the last place I should ever go. Unable to control the urge, I only put her and me at further risk of controversy and speculation.

But all this thinking of sacrifices and past ghosts made me reckless.

I didn't have any fucks left to give, so I put my foot on the gas and went where I'd wanted to go for years. Without hesitation.

I made the drive from memory. I'd done it many times before, but this time I wouldn't only be driving by, slowing as I passed, and moving on. This time I was stopping.

Although, once I got there, I turned into a major limp dick. Not literally. My goods worked fine. Conjuring up an image of Bexley left me at half-mast. Unable to make myself knock on the door, I simply slumped down on her front stoop, in front of the stupid house she'd bought with *him*.

Leaning my head against the door, I remembered her soft eyes and even softer heart. The way she loved me was like no one else ever had, not my bitter mom or my power-hungry dad. Definitely not my often controlling stepmother. Like I said, no one. The closest I ever had was the housekeeper at my dad's place, and she didn't meet me until I was past the gangly stage.

Bexley Rivers adored my condescending ass. She brought out the best in me, and I'd tossed her out like garbage.

God, my mom. Who wants to ruin their kid's life?

If I had to do it all over again . . .

That's how I fell asleep—my head on Bexley's cheap welcome mat, my back to her even cheaper door, wrinkling my suit even more.

It was the best night's sleep I had in over a decade.

As the sun began to rise, my eyes popped open, and my mind was already racing. By some stroke of luck, I didn't get caught sleeping on Bexley's front stoop, and I thanked whatever god there was for that small favor.

Quickly, I hightailed it to my car before someone could see me, my phone buzzing like crazy in my pocket. I waited to answer until I was pulling away from the curb in my car, the call transferred via Bluetooth to its speakers.

"Hey, Mike," I said to my oldest friend, trying to act normal, whatever the fuck that was in this current state of hell. I glanced in my rearview mirror, relieved that the block was still quiet.

"What the fuck, dude?" he yelled. "I've been calling you nonstop. Then Pat says he brought you your car, and you didn't even call me back. What the hell is going on? You don't trust me anymore?"

Daring another glance in the mirror, I took in my bloodshot eyes and bed head. It wasn't a good look. "I needed some time to think, and when it comes to you, everything is tied up with her. You know that. I can't talk to you without thinking of her."

God, I feel like shit. I decided coffee first, shower second.

"Shut the fuck up, man," Mike spat out. "The police haul you off, it's all over the news, and you don't call me? What the fuck, dude?"

"The charges are bogus, and you know it. I may be a greedy ass, but I didn't do what they said."

"You know what? I don't know shit. You've been so off lately, Prescott."

"What the fuck is it to you, Mike? Patrick said the same thing. I haven't been off. Distracted, maybe, but not off."

Flicking on my blinker at the last second—the last thing I needed was a ticket—I turned into the drive-through of the Beanery.

"Pat's right. You're married, and then you're not married, going after loose women in Vegas. And now you're implicated in some major crime. What the hell is up with you?"

"One sec," I told him, then spoke into the speaker. "Large coffee, black." The cheerful voice on the other end gave me the total, and I pulled my Porsche around to the pickup window.

"Where the hell are you?" Mike demanded. "What are you doing out at this time of day, buying coffee? Jesus, dude, you just got out of jail a few hours ago."

"I've been…out," I said, drumming my fingers on the steering wheel while I waited for my coffee.

"Out where?"

"Thinking."

"Aston, please don't tell me you were where I think you were, because that'll confirm what Patrick and I know. You're whacked. Fucking whacked up."

After being handed my coffee, I took a long sip of it as I pulled away from the drive-through and made my way down quiet side streets toward my office. I'd shower and change there and then try to figure out who the hell was trying to frame me, and my fucking company. Anything to avoid thinking about where I'd just spent the night.

"I'm not an expert," Mike said, still ranting in my ear, "believe me. I just know you've stayed away from her for a long time. Why the fuck change that now?"

"It's out of my control. My life is a fucking mess, and she's the only one who can make it right. I'm thirty-fucking-five years old. It's time I made myself happy. I've been chasing someone else's wishes and dreams for way too long.

End of story."

It was the truth. Bexley would make it all right. In the meantime, I ended the call before Mike could argue with me.

chapter
Seven

Bexley

Two weeks had passed since I'd first seen the news, and I still hadn't recovered. From what, I didn't know. Constant exposure to Aston? He was everywhere. The newspaper ran a daily exposé on him. The local television station was featuring him morning and night.

After a few days, I couldn't bring myself to read or watch any more of it. For the last ten days, I'd become a hermit, stuck in my house, staring at a growing pile of unread newspapers and dark television screens, and I didn't dare download the digital version of the newspaper.

My life had become an extended version of the never-ending cycle of trying to block out Aston Prescott.

He's nothing to me—a fling, an obsession, someone who happened to be a part of my life a very long time ago. At least, that's what I told myself.

Yet, every time I glanced at the headlines, I got sick to my stomach. I couldn't stop myself from staring an extra beat or two at his picture. Those eyes, they killed me. Then I'd quickly turn the page before tossing the paper into the recycling bin. *Rinse and repeat.*

Like now, I'd given in to the urge. My finger traced his picture, an expensive dark tie knotted at his neck, a tailored suit jacket snug on his shoulders. He'd aged some, with tiny crinkles at the corners of his eyes and a few laugh lines around his mouth. For a moment, I hoped this meant he was laughing some, and then I wished he wasn't.

I'd wanted all his laughs. They should have been mine to enjoy.

This was how I spent most of my time when I wasn't at work or with the kids—lamenting over what had become of Aston Prescott. What could have been between us, should have been with us.

Get over yourself, Bexley.

The picture was a year or two old, a company headshot I'd seen before during one of my rare Google searches. His smile was similar to the one he wore when he shook hands—half smirk, completely confident, inviting and beckoning. Despite the few wrinkles, he still had thick hair and deep soulful eyes that would sear right through you.

Did he do what they're saying he did?

I couldn't help it, but I didn't believe the accusations. All the way down to my bones, I knew he couldn't, and never would be, capable of what they were saying he'd done. Aston was a lot of shitty things, but a criminal wasn't one of them. He didn't peddle drugs. That wasn't him.

Thankfully, the kids were busy with back-to-school and activities, or I would have been a basket case. I didn't have the strength to do 24/7 with them. Piper was consumed with trying out for seventh-grade soccer, and Tyler was busy convincing me to buy him a drum set and get him lessons. As for me, I was staying afloat of my emotions, working at the women's health clinic three days a week, counseling young women about their choices.

As if I had a freaking clue how to make good choices.

Normally, I was packing healthy lunches, doing laundry, and carpooling every other free minute, but recently anything that wasn't completely necessary fell off the radar.

Typically, I dreaded the one weekend per month my ex graced the kids with his company, but not this weekend. Most divorced couples fought over custody, but not Seth and me. He was happy to give up his time with the kids ninety-five percent of the time.

He had his reasons, and I had mine. Either way, it worked in my favor.

But this Friday, I needed the weekend to get my head right.

A man who I'd carried a torch for—for almost fourteen years—is accused of drug trafficking.

I couldn't wrap my head around that. The very same man I'd dreamed about, night after night. The one I'd convinced myself would eventually come back to me.

In my mind, Aston was nothing short of the most amazing man. If I closed my eyes hard enough, I could picture his large hands cupping my cheek and skimming over my shoulders, caressing my skin before pulling me in for a kiss.

Like he did that first night on the golf course.

I needed to read the articles in the newspapers, the ones stacked up in the garage, and scour the internet for information. I needed to convince myself he wasn't good for me.

Forget the fact he was married, or maybe not. I didn't know. He was probably looking at a conviction, and whether I cared to admit it or not, the idea hurt. It ripped through my heart, my soul, my entire being, like a fire through a dry forest. For other reasons, reasons I absolutely never, ever thought about. I'd buried the real reason for it hurting me way deep in my mind, locked it up, and tossed away the key.

Tonight, though, when Seth sent his mom to pick up the kids after school and I had two days to myself, I dealt in the only way I could. I raced to the liquor store at three o'clock on a Friday.

This was my weekend to drink, study those rags, and drink some more. Forty-eight hours to get my shit straight.

Settled in my garage, I lifted a newspaper, thumbing through the pages until my eyes blurred at the local section, my head going hazy, my hand trembling. I shut my eyes tight and reopened them, hoping and wishing what I'd just read was a figment of my imagination.

Nope, it was still there.

> *Police detain Federal Stars Hospitality Supplies' CEO, Aston Prescott, overnight on drug trafficking charges. Rumors of additional allegations filtering in. His family is well known for providing the highest quality toiletries and custom amenities to all the five-star resorts on the West Coast, and has been known to donate thousands of extras to local shelters.*

I refolded the paper into a neat stack and shoved it back in the pile, walked inside my house, and pretended like none of it mattered.

I wasn't waiting for Aston Prescott anymore.

My phone buzzed early Saturday morning, drawing me out of my stupor. I'd fallen asleep in the damn window seat again, an empty wineglass discarded by my side, my hair in knots, and my heart and mind equally clouded.

Why do I even care about him anymore?

I slid my finger over the ANSWER CALL button without looking at Caller ID. "Hello?" I croaked out, my throat dry and my eyes crusty.

"Bex, you okay?"

I leaned against the glass, the sun heating my back. "Hey, Milly."

"You can't keep avoiding me," she said, coming right out with it. There was no chitchat when it came to Milly. She was a straight shooter, even before her husband helped her perfect the art.

"I need to get my head wrapped around this on my own. Please—"

"That's bullshit. You know it, and I know it. You don't want to talk to me because you know Mike's talked to him. We made a deal a long time ago that what happens between him and Mike stays between them. But I love you, and you love me, no matter what."

I closed my eyes and took in a deep breath. "Say his name, for Christ's sake. Say it!" When she didn't utter a word, I yelled, "Aston. His name is Aston."

"We haven't said his name in almost fifteen years, Bex. I'm following your rules, not mine."

"Forget it. What did Aston say to Mike? Is he okay?"

"I can't tell you that, and you know it. They're friends, and we've always kept that separate. I'm here for *you*."

On weak legs, I stood and made my way into the kitchen, looking for hot coffee, but I knew I wouldn't find any. Seth always made sure we had coffee. Sadly, it was the one thing I missed about being married to him.

"This is why I've been avoiding you, Milly. Because I want to know about *him*. I'm desperate to know about him. I'd gobble up the tiniest of crumbs when it comes to Aston right now."

I held the phone between my ear and my neck, scowling as I stuck the K-cup into the coffeemaker. I hated this kind of coffee. It was never hot or strong enough for me, but it was easy.

And made for singles. Loser lonelies.

"I'm your closest friend," Milly said. "I want to talk about you. Not…Aston. Bexley, I know you're hurting, and I'm here for you."

"Well, in this case, it's impossible to only talk about me and not him. He was in jail, his face and name all over the news, and I can't decide if he's guilty or not."

"It's not for you to decide. You don't have to care or even know if he's guilty. You know that, right?"

"Milly, please. Don't you think I know that? But he must be hurting, and for whatever fucked-up reason, I can't seem to let go when it comes to him. Ugh, I need a tougher backbone, or maybe a steel cage around my heart. If I think Aston is hurting, you have no clue how much that hurts me."

I turned and banged my forehead into the cabinet. "Damn, I wish I'd never met him. Why did I have to take that job at the club? I could've worked at

Wendy's and this never would've happened. What's wrong with me? How can someone spend their whole life in love with someone who doesn't even think they exist in his world? I mean, I'm nothing, the girl who made sandwiches at the club he belonged to. Not a woman. Not a person. Definitely not worthy of being his partner."

"Bex, honey, that was his dad, not him. You existed in his world. But he had to make a choice, and he went with his gut. Or his mom, however you want to look at it. Did you hear me when I said *existed*? You existed for him, but your lives went separate ways. I know it's always been him for you, but you really need to move on. Even with your secrets, which, by the way, are pretty obvious to anyone who knows you."

Blowing out a breath, I said, "Existed. A long time ago, I know. Although he had a funny way of showing it. Now I don't matter at all. You're right. As for my secret, be quiet. I did what I did, and you know why and all that. I can't rehash it."

I poured some half-and-half into my shitty coffee and took a sip.

"Listen to me, Bex, he didn't have a choice. His dad ran roughshod over him, held his dreams in the palm of his hand, and made it clear he'd squish them if Aston didn't bend to him. The company was his future livelihood, the retribution his mom wanted him to have. This is how rich people act."

"Blah, blah, blah." I slammed my coffee mug down on the counter.

I thought about my good friend, my lifelong sister from another mother, and how our lives had veered down separate roads. Milly had bought into the high life, with her glossy hair with highlights, big houses, and expensive jewelry. Her weekends were filled with fancy events and activities at the club.

"Milly, I thought you wanted to talk about me, and now you're taking up with him? Defending Aston, taking his side. Why? Because you're one of them now, the rich people?" I couldn't help it, the last part came out on a sneer, but I was hurt and defensive.

"It's not that. I'm trying to explain how things are on the other side."

"You mean the richie side. Do you forget you used to be like me?" I leaned my hip into the counter and prayed for the call to get disconnected.

"If that's what you want to call it, the richie side, then fine. And no, I didn't forget. You can live in both worlds. I do." A small laugh escaped Milly, but I barely heard it as it floated in the dead air between us on the phone.

I resisted the urge to laugh. Milly wouldn't survive a day in my suburban subdivision.

"Well, I'm glad you got a chance to cross over to the other side, Milly. Really, I am. Sorry I had to settle for a middle-class existence after growing up dirt poor. It's not all that bad. At times, it seemed pretty damn good to me."

Milly sighed. "We're getting sidetracked. What I mean is, Aston didn't have a choice. His whole life, he was groomed for that damn business. He'd be nothing if his father took it away from him. I suspect he always wanted to grow the business himself, sell out, and come and get you."

"Still not about me or how Aston is actually doing right now. I gotta go . . ."

"I'm in the car. What if I call Mike and tell him to deal with the kids, and then come and be with you?"

Of course, Milly snagged her perfect guy and tied him up in a nice big red bow. Like in a fairy tale, she married Mike Richards. She fell for him, and he fell back. Now they lived a good life in Tahoe, where he owned a large construction company. She had the dream house and the kids to fill it when they weren't at private school.

"No, Milly. Don't. I'm fine. Honestly, this doesn't even affect me."

"Bexley." She growled, and I heard her honk her horn as she muttered, "Bastard."

"Don't get into an accident."

"I'm not. Some ass cut me off."

"You can't come here. All I'll end up doing is begging you to tell me what Aston told Mike, and we know how that went after your wedding. Not good. I shouldn't have even asked you if they'd spoken. So, no. Let me be, and I'll be fine in a few days."

It was hard to keep the relationships separate, but I'd done it for a long time and I'd continue to do it. Milly was my oldest friend…I owed her my loyalty. This time around, though, I needed to deal with things on my own.

"I'm calling you later," she said.

"Okay, I gotta go now." I ended the call and dumped the crappy coffee in the sink.

I needed to make up my mind, for good, that this thing with Aston was over. *This* being something that never was.

On my way to the shower, I tossed my clothes in the hamper and considered calling Seth to see if he wanted to have dinner with the kids and me.

It wasn't until I washed the conditioner out of my hair that I remembered what a bad idea that was. After all, that's how I ended up married to him.

He was available, and Aston wasn't.

chapter
Eight

Aston

"I didn't do it. Again, let me repeat, *I had nothing to do what they're saying I did.* Drug trafficking," I said, then laughed out loud. The words had already tumbled out of my mouth so many times. Each time, they sounded almost as ridiculous as I felt.

I stuck my hands up in the air, mocking the district attorney standing in front of me.

"Stand down," I said to him as if he were a threat to me. "Drug trafficking is an insane accusation. I appreciate you stopping by my office, pretending to be here on a goodwill mission, but my attorney isn't present. You can either wait for me to call him, or you can leave. Oh, and if you could tell the reporters hanging around outside that I didn't do jack shit, that would be fantastic."

Standing up behind my desk, I stuck my hand out.

I was guessing he'd leave at the word *attorney* and I'd shake his hand, sending him on his pitiful way. Poor sap, he earned shit money doing civic duty. But he wasn't going to win this one. I'd greased enough county officials' palms to learn about the skeletons he had in his closet.

I'm guessing that's why he made this little visit—to see what I had in my back pocket.

No one bested me at poker. Not to mention, I had a lot of issues, but shipping and receiving drugs certainly wasn't one of them. Whoever planted that shit and set me up was going to pay…big fucking time.

The idiot, I mean the district attorney, continued to stand there, staring me down.

Although I'd perfected the tough-guy outer shell, I really wanted to slump down in my chair. But I knew better than to let my composure crumble. I'd been groomed all my life to keep my poker face securely fastened on.

Of course, I'd been faced with a shit-ton of problems over the years, but my lack of business integrity was a new one. Not my personal integrity, though. That had been attacked for years, although not in the newspapers.

"So, you admit that two years ago, you were—"

"That's not why you're here. Now, if you don't mind wrapping this up, I have a business to run, and I need you to leave." I stood a little taller, puffing out my chest out as I stared down at the short, bald district attorney.

"Mr. Prescott, it's not going to be that easy. Someone has to take the fall here, and it's not going to be me with a dead-end case. I know you've got yourself some hotshot lawyer who has you walking around like a free man, but I'm telling you, it's not for long."

"You should've never searched my factory, but you were in such a hurry to take me down. The rushed search-and-seizure bullshit you tried, for real? But, honestly, I'm done with you, Myers. Don't let the door hit you on the way out. And next time, make an appointment before you show up."

That's basically how I'd spent the last two weeks. Telling every Tom, Dick, and Harry that I didn't do shit. But the DA? The sucker was ballsy as hell showing up at my office like that.

Worse, as a condition of my bail, I was restricted to staying in Reno, where I have my office, and Carson City, where I now live. Originally, it was a vacation place, but since the divorce, it served as my full-time humble abode. No more weekend trips to Santa Monica or Vegas for entertainment or stress relief.

I'd had to let go the private investigator who'd worked for me for years, so I no longer had his weekly report. That was my own freaking doing. Two fucking weeks, and no updates on *her* other than my own nighttime stalking, which had proven unfruitful.

I was crawling out of my skin from lack of information, but I couldn't risk keeping official tabs on her for all these years seeping into this, or any of my other legal affairs. If questioned, the investigator would be bound by law to admit that I hired him to look after the love of my life, so I cut ties. The less I had to do with him, the better.

Just thinking about all of it made me laugh out loud—again.

I'd been tethered to this stupid town since I came back the summer of my senior year. Yeah, I'd left again to go to business school, but guilt and family politics brought me back to a place I'd come to despise. Now I was really stuck here, and the only thing that actually made it all worthwhile…well, I had to let go of that too.

You'd think it would finally be time for me to get what I deserved, but it wasn't working out that way.

Who the fuck is importing drugs through my company?

I leaned back in my chair, propping my feet up on the desk, and made a mental list of my enemies. I didn't think I had many.

Milly, maybe? But she was a stay-at-home-mom, not a drug lord.

After wasting most of Friday afternoon thinking and plotting what I'd do when I found out who used my warehouse for their illegal operations, I went home and poured myself a whiskey on the rocks.

The house felt emptier than usual. I should have relished the quiet, but it ate away at my soul, nibbling at every cell in my body.

As I watched the ice melt and condensation drip from my tumbler onto the couch, melancholy set in. Typically, I'd tamp those feelings down with a young woman and a long night.

Not tonight, though.

Tonight, I cuddled up with my good friend, Jack.

Sometime in the middle of the night, I'd taken myself up to bed.

The next morning, I woke up, naked and twisted in the sheets, a burning pain in my chest and an even bigger ache in between my legs. My morning wood throbbing, I stumbled into the bathroom. Desperately trying to keep my dick in line with the toilet, I held my length in one hand and braced the other on the wall in front of me.

Neither a shower nor a double shot of espresso brought me out of my funk.

For fuck's sake, I was an innocent man until proven guilty…that's how I got dressed and ready for the day.

With one foot in front of the other, I made my way to the garage and into my SUV. It was time to go to war, and I needed a tank, not a sports car.

I didn't need to put my destination in the GPS; I knew exactly where I was headed. It had been my preferred spot to wallow for days now.

Years, actually.

Reversing out of my driveway and onto the narrow street that sliced through my development, I pointed the truck toward the main road and went back toward Reno.

With the window rolled down, the dry desert air funneled inside the truck. Drying my damp hair was about all it was accomplishing. It certainly wasn't cooling my emotions.

Parked out front of Bexley's house, I shut the car door quietly. Finally where I wanted to be, there was no need to make a grand entrance. I would just sit with my back to the door and my ass on the concrete like I'd been doing.

At least, that's what I told myself right up until I reached the front door and started banging on it like a tiger at mealtime at the zoo. If the surface in front of me were mirrored, I was pretty sure I'd see claws and teeth in my reflection.

No one came to the door, so I pounded again. The idea of her kids being home didn't even bother me. Nothing did. Not when it had been two freaking weeks since I'd last met with the investigator.

I needed a fix, and for some reason, after waiting so long, I'd convinced myself that nothing other than face-to-face contact would satisfy the urge.

Lucky for me, I knew those newspaper people didn't like to work weekends unless they were being paid overtime, or they'd be camped outside my house when I left and probably would have followed me here.

My fist met with the wood again, and for a fleeting moment, I thought about leaving. This was risky. Why would I gamble dragging Bexley into this equation when I'd hidden my dealings from the investigator?

The urge was too fucking strong. I couldn't leave. I'd wait. Now that I knew she'd tossed out her sorry sack of an excuse for a husband.

And I'd keep waiting.

More pounding in my head. And on the door.

"What?"

The door flung open, and my eyes first met with her bare feet.

"No…no…absolutely not," or something of the sort came out of her mouth as my gaze roamed up her body.

Tight yoga pants hugged Bexley's legs—capris, because I could see her bare calves. They were just as muscular and tanned as back then. She had on a sheer pale blue tank and some lacy thing underneath, the straps sticking out from the tank. Her golden hair was drying in wavy lengths around her face. She looked how I remembered, but better. Way fucking better.

"Shh," I whispered as I studied her face up close. It was the first chance I'd had in fourteen years, other than grainy photos and the very rare run-in.

A few fine lines radiated from her eyes as her brow furrowed. She wore no makeup, other than on her lips. They were glossy and smelled like cherries.

Old habits died hard, I guessed. Obviously, since I was standing at Bexley Rivers' front door with my words stuck in my throat and my heart thundering in my chest. My confidence was long gone, my mouth dry, and my mind a frazzled mess.

"Aston," she said, her voice raw.

"Can I come in?"

I stood on ceremony at the threshold, waiting for her to invite me in. I certainly didn't think our little reunion was meant for broad daylight.

"I don't know."

Leaning in close, I asked, "Are your kids here? Your family?"

She shook her head. "I have to hold on to something. I feel kinda faint," she said as she pressed her hand to the doorjamb.

"Let me come in. We'll sit down. You'll feel better." That familiar confidence surged back in my veins.

"Why are you here?" She kept her gaze on my shoes.

Immediately, I wanted to shove off the designer loafers. They were a visible reminder of the divide that ultimately separated us.

"Why?" she said again.

"I needed to see you."

"After all these years? Or because you're in trouble and you need something. Am I a last resort, a last-ditch effort?" She stood there, her body vibrating with anger, refusing to let me in. There was a time when she wouldn't have let me leave.

"Please, just let me in." I hovered close, the cherry of her lip balm burning my nostrils and making my dick hard.

This wasn't the time for that, though. My hand itched to run its fingers through her silky hair. It was longer and thicker. Her breasts rounder, fuller.

"Aston...I don't know. I've spent the last two weeks agonizing over the news, but now that you're here, I'm speechless. Honestly, I don't think it's a good idea."

I'd had enough and decided to make a move, slipping by her narrow frame and through the door. "I'm coming in," I said with my hands in the air, an all-too-familiar gesture lately. "I can't stand outside your house and have a private conversation with you."

Giving in, she closed the door behind me. "Did Mike tell you where I live?"

"Yeah." I lied, pretty sure that now wasn't the time to tell her I'd employed a private investigator since Mike and Milly's wedding, whose main responsibility was keeping tabs on her.

My dad thought my PI was being paid to keep an eye on untrustworthy employees and shady sales reps. I'd thought those half-assed jerks were a rarity. Clearly not, in light of my current predicament.

"Let's sit," I said with a wink.

"Not now, Aston. It's been a long time…years of nothingness. You abandoned me. You can't just barge back in here and act like we're back on the seventeenth hole, winking and flirting."

She started walking toward the back of the house, a small Craftsman-style house. A starter home, by any definition, and nothing like any of the houses I'd lived in lately. To Bexley, it was probably a palace. It looked comfy, lived in by her and her kids. A pair of socks was balled up in the corner, and remotes were scattered on the coffee table.

"So, would now be an inappropriate time to ask if you have underwear on underneath those pants?"

She spun around and glared. "Don't be crass, Aston. It's beneath you, especially considering you're the one with a criminal indictment. Your confidence and flirting may have worked on me when I was eighteen, but I'm a grown woman now."

What did she expect? I'm a man staring at the woman of his fantasies, all lush and improved since the last time I laid eyes on her—in person.

Impatient, I forced myself to wait to speak.

"Yes," she finally spit out.

"Yes, now would be inappropriate? Or yes, you're wearing panties?"

"Aston, seriously, what do you want?" She leaned a butt cheek on the arm of her couch and crossed her arms over her chest.

Bad move on her part.

I chose to behave and not point that out. Instead, I skirted around her and sat down.

"Sit," I said.

For some reason, she actually listened. She sat there, hands in her lap, dutifully on the other end of the couch.

"I'm in trouble."

"I've seen."

"I didn't do it."

She waved her hand back and forth. "I don't want to know about any of that. I don't want to get mixed up in this. Does your father know you're here? How about your wife?"

I shook my head. "That would be a negative. And she's my ex-wife."

That got a reaction. Bexley's shaky hand rose to shove her hair behind her ear. "I'm sorry to hear that."

"Really?" I raised my left eyebrow…a move that used to make her wild, but she sat there unaffected, still and silent.

"You have kids, right?"

"Yes," I said. "A girl and a boy. Honestly, they're better off. It was never happy at home. I was never happy, and now when they see me, I'm at least halfway happy."

"I guess it's just sad when any home breaks up."

"You? Are you happy?" I asked, already knowing the answer.

"Seth and I split over a year ago."

"That's too bad." Lies spilled from my mouth like it was nothing.

"Honestly, it's fine. For the best. I haven't been happy in a long time."

My hand physically hurt from me holding it back, keeping it from reaching out to her. A lifetime of feelings—most of them sadly negative and harsh— swirled around us, but I yearned to reach for the good stuff.

"I always wanted you to be happy, Bex."

chapter
Nine

Bexley

"I always wanted you to be happy."

God, the nerve of the man, sitting in my family room spewing lies.

"Don't," I said, interrupting him. "It's not necessary to say that garbage. Meaningless words you know you don't mean, just because you want to fill up the space between us. What do you really want? Why are you here?"

He inched closer until his thigh grazed mine, making me feel as if we were young lovers again. But we were a long way from that. Butterflies swarmed my belly and a cold sweat lined my neck. None of this could lead to anything good.

"I can't explain it, Bex. I needed to see you. My life's pretty much in the shitter, although I guess it always has been. Before you, it was, and definitely after. You were the only person who made me feel like…I wanted to get my shit together. Like my life could be better. As though I could leave my dad and all the doom and destruction he left in his wake. I didn't, though. I had to get the business. Shitty excuse, I know, but—"

"But you didn't…or couldn't. Whatever you want to call it. Instead, you left your own path of destruction trailing behind you, starting and ending with me."

When I looked closely, Aston seemed tired, as though he'd aged a few years in a couple of weeks. My hand trembled to smooth his hair back, to tuck a longer strand behind his ear. His curls were longer than usual, and there was a cowlick begging to be patted down.

"Please, Bex. I can't go through this now. I need you. That's all I know."

"It's been a long time, Aston. I'm not that person anymore. Not going to listen to your gripes and make them all better. I'm not the one, the one you idealized as being strong and capable. I'm no longer that woman. Haven't been for a long time."

I tried to form full sentences, but it wasn't happening. My brain was overwhelmed, firing with fractured memories and thoughts. My mouth spewed whatever it could get out as self-defense mechanisms kicked in. I had to protect my heart, and my kids.

I didn't confess how much time I'd spent over the years devoted to thinking about him, and what could have been or should have been. I didn't say a word about the knots in my belly when he was arraigned. How I'd been trying not to obsess over the case…and failing. Horribly.

Obviously, I left out the part about how his memory broke up my marriage. Aston didn't know how much Seth hated him, or at least the ghost he'd left behind.

I went on, standing up for myself, quite possibly for the first time when it came to Aston. "You can't use me like that anymore, as your person. It was one thing when I was eighteen, and you were a slave to your mom's ambitions and your dad's disinterest, and well, we thought we were in love."

"Not thought. We were in love," he said stubbornly, and I rolled my eyes.

Shutting him down, I said, "Let's not argue over it, 'kay? It's in the past. Like us."

Every therapist I'd seen over the years pointed one thing out to me. Beneath Aston Prescott's hard and overly confident exterior shell, he was a hurt little boy, confused about what his parents really thought of him and expected from him. He was looking for acceptance.

To diminish his feelings was like dragging a rake over his already scuffed heart, but I had to worry about myself.

Unable to move, I watched Aston's hand cover mine in slow motion, as if I weren't inside my body anymore. With one tiny statement—*let's not argue*—I'd let him in. Completely in.

Maybe it was the alcohol from the night before. Or maybe it was Aston being here in my living room. But I felt like a fly on the ceiling, watching his fingers close over mine. I needed to stop him, but I couldn't.

More than anything, I wanted to pull away. Even more, I wanted to lean into his chest.

His eyes drew me in, the warmth of his palm smoothing over my trembling hand was a burning fire I couldn't escape. I had an overwhelming desire to give in, an idea as crazy as wanting to run straight into a burning building. All of it was too much.

"Bex, I don't want to use you. I never meant to make you feel used back then. For me, it was always you, only you, and…it's still you. The situation was so fucked up, but—"

"But what? All of it was fucked up." I yanked my hand back and stood up. Pacing the floor, I refused to look at anything but the gray shag carpet—which probably looked cheap to him.

He stood and clasped each of my biceps, steadying my frantic steps and forcing me to look at him. "Slow down. I'm not here to hurt you. I'm here to make things right. I was going to say, 'Back then, my dad hung everything over my head, and I wasn't smart enough or strong enough to tell him to go fuck himself.' But now I am."

My gaze dropped to the carpet again. I couldn't get lost in him, especially after those words. Even though they made my heart beat a furious pace, my head needed clarification, and my body required space. "You're what now?"

"Strong enough. I know what I want, and I'm going to get it."

Somehow, I managed to meet his eyes. "And this isn't about your legal troubles? Maybe you don't have anyone else in your corner. Are you looking for a shoulder to cry on or a character witness? Or maybe since your marriage fell apart, I'm the likely replacement? By the way, your divorce is old news. It's been going around town like Shirl Betts getting knocked up the summer we met."

"Neither. I'm innocent, so I don't need a shoulder to cry on, and I don't need a replacement wife. I only want you, the one woman I've ever loved," he said, his voice confident and strong.

"I promise you, I'm not going to soothe your aching heart over a broken marriage."

He nodded, that cocky, arrogant, full-of-himself nod.

"Did you do it?" I blurted, unable to help myself. "I've been walking around here for two weeks thinking, could you do it? Why would you do it? And stupidly worrying if you were okay if you did it."

"I thought you didn't want to get mixed up in it?"

"Stop. Don't play games with me."

"I didn't do it." His breath tickled my cheek as he held me tighter in place. His fingers dug into my biceps, his gaze serious and soulful all at once.

"Then why are they saying you did?"

"I don't have a goddamn clue. That's what I'm going to figure out."

"Don't you think you should be doing that instead of wasting time here? I mean, it's a little late. Four kids between the two of us, two broken marriages, and let's not forget the elephant in the room—your dad. By the way, how is the old guy?"

"Don't ruin this. Don't bring him up. He's the way he's always been. In love with himself, his legacy, and Federal."

"Then what do you want from me? I mean, Milly could've asked me. You talk with Mike, and that's all hush-hush."

"I want you. Not Mike. Not my dad. You."

"It seems too coincidental. All these problems dogging you, and now you're here. I've waited a long time for this day, and now it's here and I don't believe it."

His lips came close, grazing my cheek as he whispered in my ear, "You need to allow yourself to believe it."

I pulled away.

After all, I'd heard those words before.

chapter
Ten

Aston

I'd never been much of a liar, but the fibs started coming naturally a few years ago. They would roll off my tongue with ease when it came to my wife, Cass, currently my ex. Sadly, it never felt wrong.

Now, as I dropped breadcrumbs of little white lies with Bexley, it felt horrible.

There might have been a huge divide between us, financial and otherwise, but I'd always told her the truth. At one time, Bexley was like a truth serum for me. I craved that, wanted it back, that time when I could tell her anything and know she wouldn't judge me.

"Remember when we first met? Christ, we were young." I ran my hand through my hair, feeling it stick up at the ends. Cass would have sneered and told me I needed a haircut.

Bexley, who was standing right in front of me, didn't say a word. We were facing each other, but she left enough space between us so I couldn't touch her. My hand shook, wanting to close the divide.

"I was a kid then," she said. "A foolish, smitten girl looking into a window of a world I knew better than to think I'd ever belong to."

"Nah, you did belong. Do belong. The only foolish person was me. What I mean is, you were the first person I'd ever come clean to, been honest with, you know? I'd never really told anyone about my mom before and her antics. The endless lying in bed. The pining-away bullshit. At least, I thought it was bull, but she was the one who knew what was up. I chose to believe my dad, and that's on me."

"You can't beat yourself up over that. Not your dad, but your mom. Each of them tried to pit you against the other."

Bexley finally moved toward me and ran her hand down my arm. Her fingers ghosted over mine, and I grabbed hold of them before she could pull away. My grip might have been tighter than necessary, but the fear of her slipping out of my grasp attacked my heart.

"Look, I know he did us dirty, but back then, he held the keys to everything I wanted. *Thought* I wanted. Money, prestige, power. I'd been raised to think that's what made life worth living, but I was wrong. And when he took you away from me, it was a loss like I'd never felt, a sacrifice I shouldn't have had to make. Or you."

A small tear formed in the corner of her eye. I waited for it to fall, but it floated on a precipice—like the current status of my life.

"I can't go over all of it again. It hurt like hell then, and it still hurts now," she said, sniffing back more tears. "I tried my best to move on, and that's all I could do."

"I know, but I hate that it happened. That I allowed it to happen at all. And to think I did this to you. My dad took you from me and me from you, and with the way he was, I thought you were better off. It's no defense. Believe me."

My heart and head pounded in synchronicity from the stress of dredging this all up. The fact I was here…with Bexley. It was all too much.

"I can't. I said I can't. Let's not talk about it anymore," she begged.

She moved back toward the couch and sat down, dropping her head in her hands. Her separation was an immediate shock to my system.

"I want a chance to make it right." I knelt at her feet, my jeans cutting into the back of my knees, and I welcomed the pain. "Look at me. Please."

This time, her tears fell heavy and hard. "Why now? I can't believe this. What are you doing here? Now, of all times?"

"You can believe it. I'm here." I brought a thumb to each cheek and wiped the wetness away.

"You're probably going to go to prison. Then what? We'll have our second chance with me visiting you behind bars? Oh, that's so romantic, Aston."

With my hands on either side of her head, I laughed. "I'm not going to go to prison, because I didn't do anything wrong."

"Are you sure?"

"I'm sure, Bex. I fucked up with us, but I'm not a criminal. I would never do what they're saying. Although, I don't think it's going to be a cakewalk proving it. Good thing I've kept my own counsel over the last few years."

"How can you sound so confident? I've spent the last two days poring over articles and information. Crying and obsessing and more crying." She leaned back. "Ugh, I can't believe I'm admitting to that."

"Sitting in front of you, I have to believe it. This is the best I've felt in fourteen years."

"Don't, Aston. Just don't. I told you, we can't play games. You have kids, and so do I. We have responsibilities and grown-up lives and a whole lifetime of baggage between us, and it's not right. We can't do it."

I'm getting to her.

"I'm not playing any games," I said. "This is what I've wanted for a long time. Cass was never right for me, and she knew it. More importantly, I knew it. My feelings for you haunted our relationship, and before you interrupt, I know it wasn't fair. I tried. We had kids, bought a house, went to Orlando, drove the Amalfi coast, scheduled date nights, did all the shit we—you and I—should've done, and it was never enough. It didn't work because she wasn't you."

My heart came back to life with each word leaving my mouth.

The truth will set me free.

Bexley looked up at me with tear-filled eyes. "I've spent every day since you left me wondering what we could've been like. I wanted you like a foolish schoolgirl. Do you understand that? I wasted the last fourteen years wishing for you, Aston! That's the cold, hard truth. Seth was a poor replacement, a nice guy who wanted a wife and a family, and I took the position. Then I ruined him. Destroyed him. I filled an opening and fell short doing the easiest job ever. It was a role I couldn't play because I was too hung up on you."

There was no answer, no right response to Bexley's honesty, so what did I do?

I leaned in and kissed the woman I'd waited a long fucking time to kiss again. When my lips touched hers, I was twenty-one all over again, hormones raging, my pants biting into me, and it felt fucking great.

I was soft at first, taking her lips in a gentle kiss, saying with my body what I couldn't verbalize. Then I was on my knees, wedged in between her curvy, muscular thighs, and I kept her close.

She could have pulled back if she really wanted to, but she didn't. Instead, she moaned into my mouth, and I swallowed her ecstasy like medicine for the soul. Becoming unglued, I threw all my tenderness out the fucking door and pushed her back on the couch. Lifting myself over her, I ground my hips into her, my tongue seeking immediate entry into her mouth.

With my weight braced on one elbow, I slid my free hand through her hair. Pulling her head back and exposing her neck, I ran my tongue over her creamy flesh, goose bumps rising in my wake.

"Slow," she murmured. "We have to slow down, Aston. This is crazy."

But her pelvis continued to lift to meet mine, seeking friction, her chest rising and falling with heavy breaths. My hand stilled her hip.

"Okay, Bex, but you've got to stop that grinding. I'm going to do something I've never done if you keep that up. I swear, I never even blew in my pants when I was a teen. Christ Almighty." The last part was a whisper, but she eyed me anyway.

Her hand ran through the hair at the back of my neck, and she gathered me close for a closed-mouth, yet sensual kiss. It felt like a promise, but I didn't want to get my hopes up.

I'd made a lot of promises at one time too.

chapter
Eleven

Bexley

Aston and I lay there together on my couch like his world wasn't potentially crumbling. This was Nevada, and I'd read drug trafficking convictions came with a stiff sentence here. But in this moment, that harsh reality didn't touch us.

Somewhere in the recesses of my mind, I knew he could be taken away from me all over again, and this time I wouldn't survive. Yet I shoved it way down, ignoring that possibility.

We were playing a dangerous game, or maybe only I was? In my mind, for this one fleeting moment, we were back together as if we'd never been separated, and all was good and right.

I knew none of it was reality, but I couldn't let that permeate my brain. My heart was the stronger of the two organs.

Longing glances, gentle caresses, our fingers exploring, our lips tasting… our passion was still there, hanging heavily in the air.

Finally, we both stilled, taking in our surroundings, and I spoke first.

"This is surreal."

Aston rested on his side, cramped in next to me on the couch. "Yes."

"I'm not sure what's happening, if there's something even happening. It may not be such a good idea . . ."

He brought his lips to my neck, sliding my shirt away and kissing the top of my shoulder. The heat from his lips prickled against my chilled skin.

"It's—" was all he said before his phone rang. "I've got to grab this."

He rolled over me and stood up, swiping his finger across the phone. "What's up, boo?"

His gaze glued to the carpet, his expression was serious as he walked back toward the front door. In a matter of seconds, his demeanor changed and his voice turned gruff.

"What? Put your mom on the phone." A few seconds later, he stepped into the adjoining room, sputtering, "You're kidding, Cass? You can't be serious."

I wasn't sure what I should do. Should I stand and go to him, or hang back? Instinct begged me to wrap my arms around him, but experience told me to stay away. These were his kids and wife, his *ex-wife*, matters I wasn't involved in.

"I have to go."

Aston walked back into the family room, looking his usual nonplussed self in his dark-wash jeans and white oxford rolled up at the sleeves. He didn't look rumpled or shocked or overwhelmed like me, didn't appear to be stressed like I was.

"I'd like to come back, but I'm not sure how long this will take."

I swallowed a cocktail of confusion and regret. I'd let him back into my life and my heart like nothing had ever happened, as if he hadn't rocked my world in the worst way possible years ago. If we'd gone on a few more minutes, I probably would have been on the floor, carpet burn on my back. *Crass but true.*

Cass, his wife, ex or not, needed him, and he was going.

Cass, who came with all the trappings and the right family name.

Cass, who wasn't me.

"I don't think you should," I told him. Protecting myself came first. "Come back, I mean."

"Don't do this, Bex. I have to go. This isn't a choice. Someone pulled Mara's hair at school and told her that her dad was a criminal. Cass is freaking out, and when she does that, she hits the bottle hard. I gotta go get my kids and make sure they're okay."

Shame washed over me. I didn't even occur to me that the phone call could have been about his kids.

"I can't leave Mara and Little A there."

Mara and Aston Junior were his kids. I knew that much from Milly, one of the small morsels she'd fed me over the years. All this time, they'd seemed imaginary, but now when he said their names aloud, they felt real.

They were innocent souls, like my own kids, caught in a nasty web of bullshit and years of deceit. I couldn't fault them or hold them accountable for ruining this moment.

"Is that okay, Bexley? Say it's okay. I don't want to leave, but I have to. Say you understand. I have to get my kids and see if Denise, the nanny, is at my dad's house and can go watch them." His expression softened, and he pleaded with me while his fingers lightly ran down my forearm. "Then I'll come back."

"Okay," I mumbled. "But we can't fall back into bed with each other like the last fourteen years haven't happened. Like there isn't this huge divide between us, and we didn't both move on. There are a whole lot of other people involved now."

He kissed my forehead, his lips lingering one second, then two. "Of course. I'm on your pace, your terms, whatever you want. And all those people are important, but none are as important as you. I know I haven't shown you that in all these years, but give me a chance to prove it?"

I nodded, unable to form a response, and Aston hurried out.

Sliding down to the floor, my back against the couch, I whispered to myself, "I'm not even sure what I just agreed to."

I was still in the same place, the seam of the sofa digging into my back as I stared down at my wrinkled tank and bare feet, when my phone rang. For the second time in twenty-four hours, I answered without looking at the screen. This wasn't my real life.

"Hello?"

"Mrs. Miller?"

"It's Ms. Rivers now. Who's this?"

"This is Doug Pyle. I work for Peter Prescott's attorney. We've been keeping an eye on Aston for Mr. Prescott, and we noticed he paid you a visit this morning."

"I'm sorry, I have to go. I don't know what you want with me, but I don't have anything to do with this."

"Please, one second."

"Does Aston know you're watching him?" I asked, hearing the tension in my own voice.

"No, ma'am."

"Then hang up the phone and stop, or I'm going to tell him."

"Please don't. Mr. Prescott thought the two of you could come to some arrangement. It's what's best for Aston."

"Tell him he tried that once before, and I didn't bite. I'm not going to this time either."

"For Piper, even?"

I hit END CALL before I begged and pleaded for him to never mention her name.

chapter
Twelve

Aston

*F*ucking *Cass.*

As expected, I found my hollow shell of an ex-wife laid out on her chaise, with a bottle of expensive vodka hanging from her hand and a glass of wine on the table next to her. Three freaking sheets to the wind, she stumbled over her words and tripped over her feelings.

"I won't be embarrassed at the school like this. I mean, really? I d-d-don't deserve that shit. Or at the club either," she shouted, stuttering.

By embarrassed, she meant the accusations against me, both current and past. Plural. Not only the most recent one.

Ironically, she'd never considered her drinking and pill use to be cause for embarrassment.

"All I ever heard was about you and your wandering eye and cock," she spat out. "Of c-c-course, your heart always belonged to that poor bitch, and now you're free to run around sticking your dick in any willing hole. And you still fuck up."

I didn't bother to respond. Cass would eventually tap out. Or pass out.

Whichever came first.

"I was a catch, came from a good family, the right kind of people. Your dad's wife handpicked me," Cass said, her arm thrown over her face, her voice slurred from the alcohol. "You had me and then let me go...and for what? A memory? Of a fucking good time on the golf course when you were a freaking kid?"

Against my better judgment, I said, "Cass, don't talk about shit you don't know anything about. Especially when you're drunk." I couldn't let her disparage Bexley anymore.

She pulled her arm from her face to glare at me. "And now it comes out that you're nothing but a coldhearted criminal. Ha!"

I didn't answer this time. The kids had already packed a bag and were waiting at my car. They saw me as good, and that was all that mattered. I walked out on a half-passed-out Cass and gathered my two kids in my arms and squeezed them tight before depositing them in my SUV.

I'd planned to take them to my dad's, where Denise would take care of them. She'd raised my half siblings for Nan, and now she was a personal assistant of sorts to Nan, but she adored my kids and took any chance to be with them. Then I hoped to hurry back to Bexley.

Until I walked out of my dad's house after leaving the kids with Denise and found Doug Pyle waiting outside in his car. As I made my way to my SUV, he got out of his car and approached.

"You can't go back there," he said.

"Where?" I played dumb. Who the hell did he think he was, my keeper? I paid people like him to do my bidding.

"You know the fuck where. Aston, you're playing with fire."

"Bullshit." I stared him down, despite him having at least twenty pounds of muscle on me, and then I turned to go.

I was halfway into my SUV when he said, "Your dad knows all about your extracurricular activities. He's watching you."

Yeah, I figuring that out for myself, you dipshit.

Doug was a loyal employee of my dad's, but also a longtime buddy of mine. We'd gone to camp together every summer as kids, until his dad lost everything in the stock market. Doug ended up doing grunt work for my dad after graduating from the police academy. My dad took him in with big promises and ended up exploiting his time and skills. Occasionally, Doug took pity on me.

"So, you know," Doug said quickly before I could leave, "I called her and made her the same offer your dad did years ago. Maybe even sweetened it up a bit, considering the circumstances, but she didn't accept."

Pulling in a deep breath, I tried to tamp down my fury. "She didn't the last time either. And she's not going to—"

Fuck this. I didn't have the time or patience for it. Jumping into the SUV, I cranked the engine and got the hell out of Dodge.

I didn't make it back to Bexley's until dusk. Her blinds were drawn, and her car wasn't out front or in the carport.

I waited an hour, watching for any signs of her.

Nothing.

With my tail between my legs, I went to get my kids and took them home with me, playing both mommy and daddy for the evening instead of reunited lover.

chapter
Thirteen

Bexley

I didn't know what to do, so I ran.

In a matter of hours, I'd regressed from a competent, resilient adult to a needy young woman. I needed perspective and information, and there was only one place to get it.

Bringing my kids home would have only been a Band-Aid to my pain. Instead, I grabbed a box of cheap wine and hightailed it to Tahoe.

"Mike home?" I asked when Milly answered the door, the box under my arm.

"He's out back with the kids, pretending to watch them, but really checking baseball scores on his phone."

"Great. I need to ask him some questions."

I barged inside and made my way to the patio, dramatically throwing open the French doors. It was one of those perfect backyards surrounded by perfect trees to match their perfect life.

Their kids were splashing in the pool, floodlights illuminating the idyllic scene.

"What happened?" Milly chased after me, trying to calm me down. With her hand wrapped around my arm, she tugged me to a stop.

"Take your hand off me. I've been manhandled enough today. Take the kids for ice cream. I need Mike. When you come back, we'll talk."

"Bexley, I don't think I should leave you here. I don't think Mike will like that."

"Go, Milly. I need this. Just go." I pushed a strand of hair out of my eye, careful not to drop my wine, and yanked free from her grasp.

I didn't wait for an answer before I stomped toward the pool. "Hey, Darcy! Hey, little buddy," I said, smiling at their son. "Mom's gonna take you for a treat. Go dry off!"

A trail of *hoorays* and dripping water followed them into the house.

"Bexley?" Mike looked up from his phone at me, one eyebrow raised.

"Put the phone down. We have to talk."

"Huh-uh. Not doing this." He stared me down and started to stand.

"Guess who showed up at my house today?" Without pausing, I spat out, "Aston—that's right. So, sit down. We're going to talk for once."

"I didn't have anything to do with that," he said, raising his hands in surrender before he sat back down.

I set the wine box on the table next to him, then crossed my arms over my chest as I towered over him. "When he showed up at my door, I asked if you gave him my address, and he said you did. Told me about his innocence, his divorce, made a move on me, and then hightailed it out of there to rescue his kids from his wife. His ex, or whatever she is."

Mike shook his head. "I didn't give him your address, but that's easy enough to google, Bex. I didn't have anything to do with this, so what do you want from me?"

"I want you to give me the SparkNotes on the last ten years."

Mike let out a frustrated sigh. "No can do."

"You can and you will." I tipped the nozzle of the box into one of the plastic glasses out by the pool and took a healthy swig of wine.

"Stop standing over me and bossing me around, Bexley. I told you after Milly and I got married, when you woke up hanging over the toilet, barf stuck in your hair, your pregnant belly hitting the floor, that I was never getting in the middle of you and Aston."

When he tried to stand again, animosity surged through my veins. Furious, I pushed him back into the lounge chair.

"Listen to me, Mike. I need to know what the hell is going on. Is the guy a criminal? Is Aston, the only man I've ever loved, a criminal? Was he happy with this wife? Is he happy now? Why would he show up at my house like that? Didn't he think Seth might be there?"

Mike shook his head at that.

"So, you told him we split? The rule didn't work both ways? Milly respected his silence and confidence, but you betrayed mine?"

He shook his head again, and I felt like tossing his stubborn ass in the pool.

Slamming the end of his chair with my foot, I jostled him. "Wake up and answer me!"

"You have to calm down, Bex. Sit down."

Closing my eyes, I counted to ten in my head. When that didn't calm me down, I took another gulp of wine, letting the alcohol coat my soul. Like a wet noodle, I flopped into the chair next to Mike.

"Breathe," he told me, and I did.

In and out, in and out, my lungs gasped for fresh air.

Finally seeming convinced that I'd calmed down, Mike said, "I never wanted to have this conversation, understand me?"

I nodded, leaning forward in the chair. With sweat dripping down the back of my neck and my hair a frizzy mess, I waited for him to elaborate.

"I wanted Aston to make a life for himself, and Milly wanted you to be happy. But neither of you did that. After he ended things with you, he thought you'd wait for him. He'd planned to convince his dad you were the only choice for him. But you married Seth and pushed out two babies, so Aston married Cass. His stepmom picked her, and he agreed to it."

Stunned, I dropped into the chair. My lungs hurt from trying to breathe. "I didn't know. He was so mean, leaving me like he did, just waiting. Nothing but a phone call telling me he'd moved on like his dad wanted him to."

"When you showed up at our wedding, pregnant for a second time, he went crazy. He spent a week drinking and destroying everything in his path. The next month, he took Cass to Vegas and married her."

"We always wanted to get married in Vegas," I whispered to myself.

"In less than two years, you made a life. He had nothing, so he grabbed what was available. Except the fucker was never happy and worked all the time. He couldn't hire enough people to be with the kids, and Cass drank all the time. It was a clusterfuck."

"Why didn't you tell me?"

"We had an arrangement, or did you forget? We didn't talk about Aston, and he and I didn't talk about you."

"Seems like that didn't really work out. Did he ever ask about me?"

Mike shook his head, his brow furrowed, and closed his eyes.

"What? What are you not telling me? How does he know so much then?"

Rather than answer, Mike kept shaking his head.

"Tell me." I sat forward again, my head cocked to the side as I watched him.

"He didn't have to ask. He kept tabs on you."

"What? How? That's nuts. I wasn't his to keep tabs on."

"That's where you're wrong." Mike raised an eyebrow at me and waited for me to clue into what he meant. When I squinted at him in confusion, he explained. "Aston had a private investigator on you, so he pretty much knew everything. When you split from Seth. All the fights. The money issues. Piper's appendix…and the hospital stay afterward."

"No, not Piper," I whispered to myself, shaking my head. "No, no, no."

"He'd stayed away from the kids until that incident," Mike said, trying to calm me.

"I have to go. Tell Milly the wine's all hers."

"Bexley, don't do anything stupid. Stay the night. You're a long way from home."

I didn't answer, just hightailed it out of there, much like Aston had left my house.

A half hour later, I ended up in some motel outside of Tahoe near the highway, and I didn't even have my box of wine to keep me company.

When I arrived home the next morning and saw Aston sitting on my front step, I was so conflicted.

I wanted to run to him.

At the same time, I wanted to run far, far away.

As soon as I got out of my car, he was at my side.

"You okay?"

Ignoring his question, I held up a hand. "Don't get too close. I stink."

He surveyed me, his gaze taking me in from head to toe. "Where have you been?"

"I went to see Mike."

"Last night?"

"Yeah. He had some interesting things to say."

"Shit."

My eyes felt as dry as the desert air. I didn't have any more tears left in me. Or feelings—maybe. "Shit, exactly. And now I have to go shower, change, and get my kids."

Stepping around him, I made my way up the walkway.

"I want to talk." He walked next to me in flat-front khaki shorts, running shoes, and a ragged white Polo shirt.

It infuriated me that I couldn't help but notice that he both looked and smelled great. I needed to get inside, far away from him, put some physical walls between us.

"Make an appointment, Aston. Stop showing up at my house. My kids'll be back, and I can't explain you to them right now. Plus, you've been on TV every other second. I really don't need them seeing you here. They'll be all over school blabbing about it."

"*Your* kids? Don't you mean yours and Seth's?" Aston's eyes narrowed as he glared at me, lit with anger more blinding than the Nevada sun. He wanted me to come clean, and knowing Aston, he'd push until I did.

Glaring back at him, I said, "You tell me. You're the one with all the inside scoop."

I opened the door, slipped inside, and slammed it in his face.

chapter
Fourteen

Aston

The son of a bitch broke his own damn rule. Mike was the one who'd said he wasn't going to discuss me with Bexley. Then he went and told her about the PI I'd hired.

That was messed up. Fuck bro code…this went beyond that.

It wasn't until Mike clammed up that I'd hired Bill to watch Bexley. It was right after Mike finally married Milly after a long-ass party-filled engagement and one of those big fancy weddings, close to two years after their original engagement party. Bexley was pregnant again, hanging on to that asshole Seth, her belly huge.

Seth was drunk, and I was loaded. Poor Mike spent a good part of the evening making sure we didn't get near each other. Bexley apparently didn't feel well, and after Seth took off without her, she ended up spending the night hanging over the toilet in Mike and Milly's honeymoon suite.

I'd wanted to kill Seth for leaving her there alone. My need to comfort her was at an all-time high.

That's when Mike had said, "No more, man. Milly's got Bexley, and she's not going to discuss you with her. And vice versa."

As soon as I'd gotten to work the following Monday, I'd set up a date with Cass and hired Bill to watch Bexley. He'd been watching her for over a decade.

Now the jig was totally up.

After Bexley slammed the door in my face yesterday, I went to my office to collect myself to call Bill and let him off the hook for good. I'd put him on hold after the police detained me, wanting to protect Bexley, but I needed to set him free.

Then I could explain him to Bexley. And find out if she meant what I thought she meant by *inside scoop*.

Back in my office again with my feet propped on my desk, I texted the number I knew to be Bexley's. It was Sunday afternoon, and I was hoping her kids might still be with her ex, even though she'd planned to pick them up yesterday.

ASTON: *It's AP. Can we talk? Grab a coffee? Please?*

I watched the bubbles float over the screen while she typed. Damn, I didn't think I'd ever done that. I was too old for that shit.

BEXLEY: *Kids are back. It's going to have to wait.*

ASTON: *How about tomorrow? Monday?*

BEXLEY: *Don't you have work? And more pressing things to worry about?*

ASTON: *Not more pressing than this. How about nine at the Beanery near you?*

It was wiser to meet near her side of town, since the only thing near my office was trouble. Reporters, lawyers, and bullshit.

I stared at the screen, willing the floating bubbles to appear, but nothing.

Frustrated, I slipped my phone in my pocket and headed out. Passing the factory floor, I looked around, wondering how someone had infiltrated my business. So I called Bill back and told him to look into this current mess rather than watch Bexley.

Of course, he was already bitter about just being fired.

"Isn't that Doug's job?" he said snidely.

Yeah, except he's watching me for Dad…instead of trying to get this all cleared up.

Someone was fucking with my business. It should have been my priority, but Bexley had been waiting longer.

Just as I slipped into my car, my phone buzzed with a text.

BEXLEY: *At the Beanery. 30 minutes.*

I started my car, feeling like a winner.

chapter
Fifteen

Bexley

"Mom, you okay? You look tired," Piper said as she finished her toast. The kids were home, and as much a salve to my bleeding heart as they were a knife.

And now I looked like shit to meet Aston. I'd wanted to have the upper hand, or at least feel like I did. A quick glance down at my jeans revealed a hole in the knee. Whatever, they'd have to do with my plain white tank and pale blue cardigan.

My outfit echoed how I felt.

Blue. Pale blue. Neither bright nor vibrant. And bland with a gaping hole in the middle of my heart.

"I'm fine, baby. Just a lot on my mind. Don't you worry."

"Love you," she said, her blue eyes blazing back at me, taking me in, deciding whether to believe me or not.

I brushed her dark blond hair behind her ear and kissed her cheek. "Right back at ya, doll. Swear, I'm just tired."

She seemed to buy it, because then she hollered from the kitchen down the hallway, "Let's go, Tyler. I can't be late."

Poor Tyler, he was slower than a turtle in the morning. It took him longer to pee and brush his teeth than it took Piper to go through her whole teenage-girl beauty routine.

"Coming," he called, clunking into the kitchen.

I walked the two of them to the bus, the sound of my flip-flops slapping against the concrete mixing with their sibling banter, distracting me from my yo-yoing thoughts.

After waving good-bye, I ran to pee again—it was a bad habit of mine when I was nervous, especially after having kids. Laughing at myself as I pulled up my jeans, I wondered what Aston would think of this. Surely, he'd be turned off.

I wouldn't be so hot after all...*ha*.

I dreamed up a thousand excuses why I couldn't meet him while washing my hands and grabbing my tote. Then I got in my car.

Wanting to arrive after him, I drove around the block at least ten times, killing time and making excuses not to go at all. Finally, I parked and went into the Beanery.

"Hey," Aston said huskily, waiting inside the door wearing a navy suit and a light blue shirt.

He looked dapper, except when I took another look at his face. Up close, he appeared about as tired as I felt, maybe even more. For a moment, my heart shattered for him.

"Hi," I said quietly.

He took my elbow and guided me to the counter. After I ordered a triple Americano and he got a black coffee, he asked, "Something to eat?"

I shook my head. It was awkward and stilted between us. How could I eat?

"Did you take your kids back home?" I asked while we waited for my beverage.

"You mean, to my ex's place? That's what became of my home."

"I guess. I'm sorry that happened. I always think about my situation and the kids being with me mostly full time. I don't think they feel their dad's place is home, but I suspect your situation is different."

"It doesn't matter right now. They're staying at my dad's place with the nanny. Denise will drop them with Cass after school, if she's sober enough to keep them. Another big secret in a long line of family secrets."

"That's a lot of shuffling back and forth for them."

Aston nodded, looking defeated. When my drink was slid across the bar, he picked it up and carried it to a corner table with his.

"It's not ideal, but Denise is about the only constant they have. She's been watching them occasionally since they were born, when I traveled or worked late. Cass has made her way through a parade of daytime nannies, who all ended up hating her. When the police showed up at my door, Denise was right behind them to take the kids for me."

"That's odd." I took a sip of my drink, the liquid burning my throat, a welcome discomfort compared to the pain in my heart.

"Maybe they alerted my dad to what was about to happen. I don't know. It was such a blur. But thank God for Denise. The kids were set to spend the weekend in Carson City with me, which meant Cass was off the grid. Literally and figuratively."

Silence filled the air around us, along with the whoosh of the espresso machine frothing milk and the scent of freshly ground beans.

"They're fine for now. It's not them I'm worried about. They're both strong little creatures, and resilient. What I need is to talk with you, explain a few things, although my explanations will never be enough."

"What do you want to say?"

"I assume Mike told you I had someone looking after you?" Aston cut to the chase, his hands settling on the table in front of him. He didn't flinch or fidget, just asked with no remorse.

"You betcha. I wouldn't exactly call it looking after. Maybe spying? Stalking?"

My body was burning hot, my heart beating through my bra and delicate tank, despite the chilly conversation. Sitting across from Aston brought my body to life, no matter what we discussed, but this was unacceptable. My cheeks blazing, I slid my cardigan off my shoulders and hung it on the back of my chair.

"You didn't seem yourself at the wedding, and Mike told me how you slept in his hotel room, on the bathroom floor, sick as a dog. After that, he swore he'd never tell me anything else about you, so my hands were tied. I didn't have a choice."

"Um, you did have a choice. You chose to give me up, remember?" I said, not afraid of the man in front of me, despite his larger-than-life frame and squinting eyes. "It still seems a bit off to me. After all, you ended it. You *never* called me after Mike's engagement party. It was all you, and pardon me for saying it for the millionth time, but you're being accused of something criminal. So, why now? Don't you have more important things to worry about?"

"Because I don't really care what's going on. I've wanted you back since that night, at Mike and Milly's party. Look, I'm going to do right now by you and… for everything."

"I'm sorry." I closed my eyes as the apology floated in the air between us, and he took my hand.

"For what?"

"For not waiting," I murmured, waving the white flag, admitting defeat way before I was supposed to. "I went and made a big mess."

The hard part was, Aston didn't know the half of it.

My eyes were still squeezed shut at the prospect of coming clean. As little electric waves coated my nerves, I could sense him rise to his feet and stand next to me.

"Come with me." His hand tugged on mine. "Open your eyes and come with me. I'm not going to hurt you. Come on, you know that."

I wanted to believe him, even though I knew I shouldn't listen to him. My head at war with my heart, the latter won, and I went with him. After all, hadn't I just sat in the window waiting for him only a couple of weeks ago?

"Leave the cup. They'll get it," Aston said as he handed me my cardigan, then led me out of the back door of the Beanery as I slid it back on. In the alley, he stopped and turned to me. "Bexley, I know I've done a bang-up job of ruining everything, but I'm going to make it right," he said with confidence oozing from his words. "I swear to you."

Before I could respond, his lips came down hard on mine. He'd backed me into a brick wall—literally and figuratively—and took over my soul with one touch of his lips.

With the brick biting into my spine and his mouth assaulting mine, I hadn't been this hot for years. Never with Seth. Maybe halfway with my own hand and memories from long ago.

"I made so many mistakes," he said into my mouth. "But you were never a mistake."

His tongue swept through the *O* my mouth had formed, and his hand slid up my side, his thumb caressing my breast over my bra. A shiver ran the length of my body, despite my cardigan.

His hand wrapped around the back of my neck, under my hair, his thumb continuing to caress my nape. Back and forth and back and forth, the pad of his finger moved. My back arched and my pelvis rocked forward, both desperate for contact.

"I should've said fuck it all," he said as he broke free from my mouth. "Told my dad to go fuck himself. You were all I ever fucking wanted. *Fuck*."

I should have been turned off by his crude language, but his f-bombs only took me higher, made me hotter. I was fire and his body ice. Together, we smoldered, smoke pouring off of us.

"Oh God," I said, meaning his closeness, his words, everything.

"I fucking mean it. I need you." His lips came close again, his hardness grinding into my semi-softness.

The back door swung open, nearly hitting us, and a hipster with a beanie on his head stepped out and lit up a cigarette without making eye contact. "Sorry, dude."

Aston ran his hand over the side of my face and held me close, protective and dominant. "It's cool, but watch where you're going, buddy."

I leaned closer and sniffed, inhaling Aston's scent. Cologne permeated his suit, and I remembered the smell from years ago. It was a special blend imported from Europe.

"Let's get out of here," he murmured against the top of my head.

He led me to a black sports car, a manual, of course, as if I weren't turned on enough already. "We can grab your car later," was all he said before the engine purred like my libido, and we took off.

As he drove us toward my house, I watched him, trying not to overthink what was about to happen. At least, what I thought was going to happen.

The itch between my legs—the one that dared me to scratch it—won.

My brain turned to mush and my pulse quickened as Aston parked in my carport. He was at my door before I could open it, and he took my hand and tugged me out.

"Wait!" I said, looking down as I blew out a breath. "We have to stop."

Aston backed up slightly but still held my hand.

Finally meeting his gaze, I said, "I told you, we can't just hop back into bed like we don't have history between us. We just can't. It doesn't solve your current problems or erase all the bad memories."

He nodded, looking more like a scolded schoolboy than a cocky businessman. "Let me walk you in."

Knowing better, I shook my head. "It's fine. Go. I'll see you soon," I said before turning and heading to my house.

Alone and realizing I needed an Uber to get back to my car.

chapter
Sixteen

Aston

"What's up, Doug?" I said as I picked up my phone.

I was back in my office, my assistant finally calmed down, happy I wasn't in jail. Wasn't a man allowed to get busy without justifying it?

"I've been trying to reach you all morning," Doug Pyle yelled into the phone.

"You mean you weren't watching what I was doing?"

I shouldn't have pushed his buttons, but I was furious with him. I sat back in my chair, a smug look on my face. I didn't trust this guy, and my mood was already foul. He was going to be on the receiving end of my nasty side.

"No, you ass. I was talking with your other guy, Bill, after he got a text from you."

I leaned forward. Doug had my attention now.

"Yeah, we chatted, and now I have some interesting theories."

"Good. Are you going to enlighten me?"

"In person."

"Okay, when? Tonight? The Bull Lounge at seven? Should I bring my lawyer?"

"No, and you tell Bill," Doug said before he disconnected.

Sitting forward, I rested my head in my hands, wishing I could still smell Bexley.

Cognac swirled in my tumbler as I set it down and waited for Bill. I'd arranged to meet with him first, needing us on the same page before Doug showed up.

Fucking Doug. He was so full of hot air and inflated self-worth. He should remember that without me, he'd be nowhere.

"What's happening?"

A hand tapped my shoulder and I turned to see Bill, all two hundred fifty pounds of him, his shiny bald head looming above me. A retired Marine, he was always looking to scare off the demons of other people's problems, but I was pretty sure one look in the mirror would do it. That freaking glass eye got me every time. It didn't move like the other, remaining in place like an old lady kneeling before Jesus at church.

"A holy mess," I said. "That's what's happening. Doug got himself involved in all this on my dad's side, but he's playing double agent. I don't know what he wants. Probably money."

Bill sat across from me and lifted his chin at the waitress. She promptly appeared; he had that effect. "Scotch on the rocks…and a beer to wash it down."

When the waitress left, Bill turned back to me. "Dude called me about a month ago. Said he knew I worked for you. Told me the old man was keeping tabs on the girl you've had me watching for years, and told me I should back off."

"Why the fuck didn't you say something?"

"Because I didn't." Bill leaned forward in his seat, trying to intimidate me, but I'd been dealing with him for a long time.

"Because doesn't cut it. Why the fuck not?" My voice was almost a growl, yet low enough that no one else could hear. My manners had never quite left me.

Bill shrugged. "Wanted to see what his angle was. My prerogative, been watching her long enough. I care about the lady. Anyway, I'd known for some time the dick was watching me watch her. It'd been a little game we'd been playing, and I was winning, letting him think I didn't know. 'Course, he thought if I knew, I'd come at him, gun blazing, demanding he stop."

I took a swig of my drink, the alcohol chasing away my anger for a moment. "Still. I hired you to watch the only woman I ever loved, and you let this twisted fuck watch her too?"

"Aston, you're one sick fuck. You got a wife—I'm sorry, ex-wife—who can't put down the bottle. You got two kids with the damn woman, who spend most of their time with your stepmother's old nanny…mind you, the same woman you looked down your nose at for hiring a nanny to raise her kids. You can't keep your dick in your pants since you got shot of Cass, and you got the sickest relationship I ever saw with your father, some weird hero-worship bullshit, and the guy's nothing but the king of all assholes. All the while, you obsess over some teenage flame who has her own freaking issues, two kids, and a loser ex-husband to deal with. I'm no fucking shrink, but *let it go*, I say. Let it go. You won't, but you should."

"That's Disney to let it go, and good thing I don't pay you to shrink my head. I pay you to watch the woman I love, the last woman I ever want to stick my dick in, the same woman who I've wanted to stick my dick in instead of every other lonely hole I was filling." I spoke with a smile on my face. To any Tom, Dick, or Harry, we were just two businessmen having a friendly chat.

Bill shook his head. "So, you finally bedded the blonde? Thank fuck. What do you want from me now? You pulled me off, said we couldn't go near her. Never mind, you fuck her."

"You're speculating, but whatever, you're gonna know eventually. Listen, I want you to watch Doug. He's coming to meet with us, supposedly full of goodwill. Take his intel and whatever he's dealing, and watch every move he makes. And don't play this cat-and-mouse game. Don't let him know you're watching."

"Incoming." Bill smiled and took a swig of his beer as if we'd been shooting the breeze.

"Doug." I stood and greeted our guest.

"The Bull Fucking Lounge? Should've known you never really slum it, AP."

"Aston," I said, correcting him. AP was for friends and Bexley. "You want something to drink?"

"Hell yeah."

The Bull Lounge was an old establishment, a small mahogany-paneled bar attached to a steak joint. Like a private club, it was exclusive, all male, and reeked of old money. Bill came and went as he pleased, since we always met here, and quite frankly, I was pretty sure the maître d' was scared to death of him. But this was a special treat for Doug.

"I'm sure my dad's brought you here before. No need to cream yourself," I said, my voice still low.

Doug shrugged. "He brought me here once, when I signed on to work with him. Never again."

"Well, do yourself right. Order an old-fashioned, it'll put hair on your chest, and grab a cigar while you're at it. And then tell me what the fuck is going on."

Bill lifted his chin again for the waitress, and she appeared like magic.

"You got a thing with her?" I whispered while Doug ordered, but Bill didn't answer.

"Refill, Mr. Bill?"

What the fuck is that? Mr. Bill?

His voice soft, Bill said to the waitress, "Not now, Red. But bring me a cigar, doll."

Red?

Doug ordered a drink and a cigar, then turned to me when the waitress left. "As you know, your dad's been having me watch Bexley." Cocking his head toward Bill, he said, "And he knows you've been watching her."

I stared Doug down, hoping he promptly washed his mouth out with soap. I didn't even like her name rolling off his tongue.

"Your dad has an interesting theory," Doug said.

I scoffed. "All the way from his vacation in Hawaii? The ass picked up and left the day after I was arrested."

"Well, he and I have been talking. Yes."

"Please enlighten us."

Red appeared with the drinks and smokes, making a big show of cutting Bill's cigar (not Doug's), and lighting it for Bill (again, not for Doug).

After taking a puff, Doug continued. "Your dad thinks Bexley is somehow involved with the drugs. Her and that cheap whore, Milly."

Furious, I glared at him. "Hey, no need to call anyone a whore, Doug. She's happily married to Mike. Remember him? You two used to be friends a long time ago."

Mike let out a dark chuckle. "Since when are you Mr. Reasonable? She's been fucking a guy up in Reno for a year, Aston."

"What?"

"Yep. She's unhappy, underserviced or unsatisfied by your man, and she's porking some medical sales rep every day and freaking night she can. Every chance she can get it, she's hopping on it."

"How do you know this?" I asked, not wanting to believe it.

"She meets Bexley for coffee and then hightails it out of there to fuck this dude."

"Okay, enough," I said sharply. "There's no way either of them did this."

I denied their involvement, even though Milly had crossed my mind. But he was talking about Bexley, and she wouldn't do this to me.

Memories swept over me of Bexley crying . . .

At Milly and Mike's wedding. When I let her go for good.

When Piper needed surgery, tears streamed down Bexley's face as she waited at the hospital all alone.

For just a moment, the idea had legs. I'd hurt her, more than once. Was this a revenge scheme? After all, I didn't know Milly was screwing around, so how could I be so sure about Bexley?

"It's likely, Aston," Doug said smugly over his cigar.

Looking at my guy, I said, "Bill?" but Doug interjected.

"What the fuck does this guy know? He's been eye-fucking the redhead for ten minutes."

Bill glared at him. "I'm hearing every single bullshit word coming outta your trap. How the hell would two bitches turn Federal into a drug trafficking operation?"

"I never said they were dumb," Doug said with a smirk.

I didn't correct Bill's use of the word *bitches* before he abruptly stood.

"I smell a rat. Text me when you have a job for me, AP," Bill said, then stalked out.

I knew him well enough to know he was doing this for Doug's benefit, but I played along.

"So, you going to get me proof or what?" I asked Doug, leaning forward in my chair.

"Yep, but you've got to stay away from her."

"Bexley?" I asked.

I imagined what he saw when he looked at me, with my cocked eyebrow and a smirk, but it was way different from what was happening on the inside. Anger roiled deep inside me—dark red anger, hot and violent. Toward my dad, and Doug, and even Bexley.

Doug nodded.

"No way," I said. "Keep your enemies even closer and all that. You know the saying?"

He just didn't know I was referring more to him than to Bexley.

chapter
Seventeen

Bexley

"Bexley, let me in," Aston yelled as he pounded on the back door.

I sat with my butt firmly planted on the kitchen floor, my spine against the door, feeling each of his blows vibrating in my back. Thankfully, the kids were at school.

"I know you don't work today," he shouted.

How?

"Please," he said. "I had to look into some shit last night about the case, and now I'm making a scene. I can't afford to have a scene."

I couldn't let him in. *Shouldn't let him in.* And I wouldn't, because if I did, we'd sleep together.

Allowing him to come inside wouldn't help anything. It would only make things worse. Somewhere deep in my heart, I'd known Aston and I were on a collision course, and the only place we collided and worked was in bed.

"Come on, Bex," he called through the door. "I'm embarrassing myself, and I don't do that."

"Pretty sure when you got arrested, you did that," I mumbled.

"I heard that. Come on, you never used to make me wait."

My head clunked back against the door. I never made him wait. Maybe that had been the problem. No one ever made the great Aston Prescott jump through any hoops, except for his dad.

It quieted, and I could sense him on the other side. Somehow, he knew I was crouched down on the floor. The pounding ceased, and I closed my eyes.

"I'm sitting right behind you. I can hear you shifting around the floor through this cheap piece-of-crap door."

That does it. I stood up and swung around to open the door, and the ass fell backward onto my feet.

"Guess the apple doesn't fall far from the tree, *AP*." I spat out his nickname as he scrambled to his feet. Looking him in the eye, I said, "You never used to call me cheap or make fun of my stuff. That was always your dad."

Aston stood with his arm braced against the door frame. "Bex," he whispered, "I didn't mean that. It's just that you could have had better with me, and this pisses me off." He flicked his finger against the siding.

"This . . ." I mimicked him, plinking my finger against the siding, "is far better than anything I ever had before."

"I know. I didn't mean to marginalize that. It's just…my head is so messed up. I'm being accused of something I didn't do, and the more I look for answers, the more I'm not liking what I find."

"What does that mean?" I stared up at him.

"Can I come in?"

"Why? So you can get me back in bed?"

"So we can talk." He brushed past me, not waiting for an answer, and sat at my kitchen counter.

Slamming the back door shut, I said snidely, "How's that cheap stool treating you?"

"Stop. I didn't mean what you think."

"Well, what did you mean when you said I could have had better with you?" I twisted my hair back into a messy knot and raised an eyebrow. "To me, it seemed a lot like you let me go."

"I didn't have a choice."

"No, you did. You chose the company."

He looked tired, his eyes dull and deep wrinkles at the corners. "It was all I ever worked for. You know that," he said, sounding defeated.

Guilt dripped from my heart into my veins. It shouldn't have, but it did.

I walked to the cabinet and pulled down my old coffeepot. It wasn't a good time for the one-cup thing. I poured in the grinds and water and set it to percolate while Aston sat quietly at the counter, his head in his hands.

"Did you eat?" I asked, my tone softer now, and he shook his head.

This time, I walked to the fridge and pulled out the eggs and a handful of veggies. I set an omelet pan on the stove top, drizzled in some olive oil, and turned on the burner.

I needed to be busy, to make work for my idle hands. In reality, they yearned to smooth their way down Aston's back. My mouth ached to place kisses along his neck and across his cheek, all the way to his mouth.

Instead, I sliced an onion, diced a pepper, and halved a few cherry tomatoes.

"You don't have to cook for me," he said, his voice scratchy, gruff, and oozing sex.

I scurried back to the fridge and grabbed some spinach. I needed to do something, and that something was *not* kissing him.

"Omelet okay? You still like it without cheese and your eggs mixed with milk?" I kept my gaze glued to the stove and my back to the man in my kitchen.

"Bexley, look at me."

Ignoring him, I tossed the veggies in the frying pan and gave them a stir with the same concentration as if I were solving the national debt.

"Bex, turn around. Now."

Reluctantly, I did.

"What're you doing?" He wasn't on the stool but walking toward me. "Huh?"

"I don't know. I really don't know."

"You need to calm down." He pushed a stray hair out of my face and ran his knuckles down my cheek. "I should be asking you if you ate."

I shook my head because I hadn't eaten, but he didn't need to ask me that. That wasn't his job anymore. Or ever, really.

"Come on." He guided me toward the stove and stood behind me as he picked up the spatula and brought it to my hand. Together, we stirred the vegetables, his large hand cupping mine. His lips tickled my ear as he whispered from behind me, "I want to take care of you."

I felt elated and saddened, all at the same time. How could I be so excited over him wanting to care for me...after he left me all those years ago? Chose his dad over me?

"Let's get the eggs."

He set the spatula down and guided me toward the sink where I'd left the eggs. He repeated the whole hand-in-hand cooking business, cracking eggs and dumping them in a bowl, adding milk, and whisking it all together.

Back to the stove we went.

He nudged the burner down a bit, stirred the vegetables one last time, and poured the eggs over top. Then he turned me, setting my butt on the counter next to the stove.

"Aston," I whispered, "I don't think I can. I've been waiting for this moment, it seems...all my life. But I don't think I can now. It hurts. The memory of what we were, what we could have been, what later happened. There are too many sides, too many lies," I said, rambling as my eyes began to sting.

He held my face close, looking deeply into my eyes. "Love isn't scripted. It's not a movie or a book where there's a formula. There's no plan. In real life, it just happens. This is our story, and it's my time to come back into your life. We may have had a messy middle, only to get a little messier with this shit going on. But the ending is going to be perfect."

I felt weak everywhere. My heart, my knees, even my toes. "How can you be sure?"

Ignoring my question, he said, "Now we're going to eat, and then I'll tell you what I learned. Go sit."

Somehow the tables had been turned. I was now sitting on my kitchen stool, and Aston was walking toward me with half an omelet.

"Coffee? Pancakes?"

I could only nod. He poured me a cup of coffee, and I couldn't help myself. "You make pancakes?"

"Damn straight." Without another word, he started rifling through my cabinets, apparently looking for pancake mix.

chapter
Eighteen

Aston

"Here, take this, and we'll talk." I handed Bexley the coffee and took a plate for myself.

As she took a long sip, I watched her swallow. It was a beautiful sight. Bexley had always thought she was plain, had never realized how stunning she truly was. She was natural and real, everything I'd never been exposed to, and all I ever wanted to have.

It hadn't been possible years ago, but now it was. I was through with being a pussy. Through bending for my dad. And definitely through with being accused of something I didn't do.

I grabbed my plate and a cup of coffee for myself and stood next to where she sat on the stool, leaning my hip against the counter. "My dad thinks you and Milly had something to do with all of this."

"What?" Bexley jerked as she looked up, almost knocking her coffee off the counter.

"He does, and now I have to prove him wrong, in addition to proving my own innocence. So I need to ask you...do you think Milly would do something like this?"

"How dare you!" Bexley went to get up, and I eased her back onto the stool.

"There's a lot going on with Milly that you don't know about. Try not to get your panties in a bunch."

"Oh yeah? Are you spying on her too?" Bexley chugged the rest of her coffee, never taking her death stare off me.

"No, but the guy my dad had watching you couldn't help but learn some stuff about her. A casualty of the job…we'll call it."

Bexley's mouth hung open, and I couldn't help but want to shut her up with something on her mouth—like my own. But I knew better than that.

"I thought you had someone watching me. Now it's your dad who has someone? Who else will you blame in all this?"

"It's both of us, actually. He had someone watching you, which is how he found out I was keeping tabs on you. It's a bit of a sordid affair, if you ask me."

Bexley's eyes narrowed. "Damn straight it is."

"Listen, the heat is going to be on us. Mostly me, but you as an unintended casualty. You know my dad's like a bulldog when he gets his teeth into something, but this time I'm going to outsmart him and fix this."

Her head tilted to the side, and she looked at me in the compassionate way I craved like a starving man at a buffet. "Do you know what you're doing?"

I started to nod, words of affirmation about to spill from my mouth, but then she leveled her gaze on mine, a truth serum if there ever was one. Eyes as green as the grass on the golf course pinned me, her dark blond hair swirling around her face.

"Don't lie, Aston. It's okay to say you don't know. It's okay to look for help. It doesn't make you any less of a man to ask for help. Seriously, take it down a notch."

She was right, but I'd never let my guard down. I'd been the strong one, resilient, and had developed my take-charge attitude after my parents' divorce.

Unable to stay away, I made my way closer and turned Bexley's stool so she was nestled between my thighs. "I wasn't man enough years ago to fight for you. Now I have to be double the man. Understand that? I need to fight for you, my freedom, and my family."

Her forehead met my chest, and I listened to her uneven breathing. "I've lost you once, twice, but a third time will kill me, and I have kids now. I can't get them mixed up in this. The last few years haven't been easy on them. Seth, he…he's not always there for them."

"Listen to me, Bex, nothing is going to happen to me. You have to know what I'm like. In a dog fight, I'm always the toughest, strongest mutt in the lot. My mom made sure of that." I tilted her head with my finger and looked her dead on. "She wasn't the best mom, nothing like you, but she made sure I was tough. Speaking of kids, I want to meet yours, and maybe you'll meet mine. I'd like that."

I didn't call attention to her swallowing hard. She could pretend I didn't see her do it, or wonder why I'd notice it at all.

"We'll see," she said, and then went back to eating her eggs.

Later that day, freshly showered, shaved, and suited up, I went to see my lawyer. After scouring hours and hours of security tape from my factory, his team still had no new leads. Nothing but a host of my employees coming and going, in and out of the factory.

Aidan, the lead lawyer on my case, paced back and forth. "There has to be something else we're missing. The Feds claim their case against you is airtight, and there's no way it is."

Turning to his associate, he said, "Sniff around and see who fed it to them," and then he looked at me. "You gonna go behind my back and put your guy on that too?"

"No, he's back on Bexley."

He blew out a long breath. "Aston…we've discussed this. She needs to stay out of this. And you need to stay away from her."

"No can do."

"No can do what? Keep your guy off her? Or you?"

"Both. My dad's got his own guy on her, and I need someone on his prick. Stupid fuck thinks Bex has something to do with it, which is bullshit. And now he's telling stories about her friend Milly fucking around and being a part of this. I need to watch what they're doing."

Aidan gave me an incredulous look. "For Christ's sake, when did your life become such a soap opera?"

"The day I gave up Bexley for my dad."

He nodded as if I'd made my case. "And that's why you need to give her up."

Shoving my hair off my forehead, I noted to book a haircut. "Are you my lawyer or my therapist? I'm not giving her up, and you know better than anyone why. I should've never walked away in the first place. Christ," I said, slamming my fist onto his desk. "Why do I have to keep repeating myself to everyone? I have a shitty ex, my kids are a mess, and I've never loved anyone but Bex. Oh, and I'm being accused of a crime I didn't commit. Back off of my love life and get me cleared."

Aidan dropped into the chair behind his desk. "I'm doing the best I can. I have a whole team working around the clock on it."

"Just fix this." I slammed my fist onto his desk again. "Fast."

He looked up, rattled. "Get a hold of yourself, Aston. Calm down," he said, using a tone meant for a mental patient.

"No can do. This is as good as it gets."

I didn't have anything left to say to him, so I pushed out of my chair and headed back to my office, wishing I had eyes in the back of my head.

Every person who walked by my office in a suit or a warehouse uniform was a suspect. As if my day wasn't shitty enough, my dad stopped by, knocking his knuckles on my door frame as he paused, giving me a salute.

"What's up?" I smiled at him, his face still tanned from Hawaii. If I'd learned one thing from the Bexley situation, it was to never show my hand to my dad. Ever.

"Just running in to grab something from my office, then I'm heading to Vegas. Since you can't go, I'm taking the meeting with the new hotel going up in Red Rock. They want to do all private-label soaps, men's grooming kits, napkins, and possibly exercise towels with gold embroidering, mostly standard stuff, but also have an interesting idea for their exercise machines. Could be a big account. They have deep pockets, you know?"

"Good luck with that. And don't think for a minute that I wouldn't be there if I could. My hands are tied. Luckily, yours aren't." The last part came out on a sneer. Fuck if I cared. He'd micromanaged me long enough.

Dad gave me a smug look. "Yeah, pretty lucky I can do it. I'd hate to see the business go to shit too. How would you support yourself?"

Closing my eyes, I leaned back in my chair. "Get out," I said through gritted teeth. "I don't have time for your guilt trip. I know I'm forever indebted to you, Dad. But right now, I need to put my life back together, and while I don't expect any help from you, you could let me be."

"Help?" He scoffed. "I'm closing accounts you should be handling."

"Lots of luck then. Oh, I'm moving Denise in with me. Cass is in no shape to take care of the kids, even part time, and I don't like having them over at your place all the time."

"You'll have to pay her more and take over her benefits," he said before he turned away.

Typical Dad. All he cared about was the bottom line.

"Yeah. 'Bye," I said to his back.

chapter
Nineteen

Bexley

When I walked into the women's health clinic on Tuesday, a sense of calm washed over me. The kids were in school, where they belonged, after a good breakfast, lunches packed, and after-school activities planned.

My clogs clunked on the floor as I made my way to my small office and flicked on the light. It would be a busy day—it always was—and I welcomed as many distractions as possible. The kids came home on Sunday night, and at least Aston had the decency to text, asking if he could come over. I'd said no, and then he protested for a while, explaining that he'd hired a full-time live-in nanny, so he could leave his kids at home.

After Mike spilled the beans, it was pretty obvious Aston knew my secret, but I didn't know why he was staying quiet about it. Aston was always direct, so I expected him to confront me about Piper. Then again, I didn't know him all that well lately. Either way, I still wasn't ready to have them meet.

"Bexley?" Maria, my supervisor, called from my doorway.

"Oh yes, sorry. I was going over my to-do list in my head," I said while looking up. Busying my hands with twisting my hair in a tight bun at the nape of my neck, I wondered what she wanted.

"I have a sensitive case in my office. A young girl, only fifteen. She's here with her mom. Dad isn't aware of her situation. I was wondering if you might take them. It's going to be a long morning for them, I fear, and I don't want to rush with her."

To me, it was manna from heaven—a long case, a dragged-out decision, a laborious morning. *Check, check, check.*

"Sure, no problem. Do you want me to come to you? Or do you want to bring them here?"

"I'll just show them to your office. I have a grant visit later, so I need to keep my office open."

"I'll be ready," I said, turning on the desk lamp and standing to turn off the overhead lights. Over the years, I'd found that soft light was comforting.

I also lit a lavender candle, refilled the tissue box, and replaced the hard candies on my desk. Noting that none of my family pics were up, I ticked through some of the touches I'd added over the years. This was about making it easier on the client, not me.

As expected, this client did take several hours, and by the time I finished up some paperwork and checked my schedule for the next day, it was after two o'clock. My stomach let out an angry growl, and my head pounded for some caffeine, so I decided to take a quick walk to the coffee shop around the corner for a sandwich and a cup of joe.

But as soon as I entered and the bells jingled above the door, I wanted to turn back around. Sitting in the middle of the coffee shop, waiting like a king, tanned and glowing, sat Peter Prescott.

About to turn and leave, I paused when he crooked his finger at me. Not wanting to make a scene so close to my work, I went.

"Are you going to order?" he asked me like we'd planned to meet up like two old friends.

I shook my head. "What do you want? You do realize I'm in the middle of my workday?"

"You mean that liberal do-good job?"

"Yes, that's what I mean. It's honest, unlike you." I didn't have any goodwill toward the man, and I was beyond pretending I did.

"Please sit," he said, like I had a choice.

I'd also come to realize he knew my secret too. Everyone did, apparently.

Sliding into the chair, I asked, "What do you want?"

"You know what I want, the same thing I've always wanted—you to stay away from my son. We don't need you sullying our good name. We have enough problems right now."

"I'd say you do," I said, my hand itching to fidget with my bun, but I silently commanded it to remain on the table.

"Look, take my deal. Take the money for Piper. Lord knows, your loser of an ex would take the handout. He doesn't want to pay for her."

"Stay away from Piper," I said sharply. "She doesn't need any of this to fall onto her. She's a kid. She didn't ask for any of this."

"No, you did." His eyes bore into me. A very familiar shade of blue, but they didn't have any of the fire or passion of Aston's…or Piper's.

"You asked for it when you didn't take care of things. You could have ended the pregnancy, but instead, you kept the baby—or insurance policy, as I would call her. You held on for a moment just like this, when my son could come crawling back to you, like we all knew he would. Can't blame the guy for coming back. You must be one hell of a lay."

"How dare you call my daughter an insurance policy?" The sex comment was the least of my problems. My blood gurgled and boiled in my veins, and if I didn't spot two coworkers in the coffee shop, I feared I'd topple the table over on the asshole's lap. How could he speak about Piper like that?

"My granddaughter," he said, not flinching. "Don't forget, she has my blood too. You know, if I wanted her, I could get her."

"Look," I said, trying to reason with him when I knew better. "You've left me alone for all these years. I didn't take your money way back then, and I don't want it now. I don't want anything. I don't hold you or your son responsible in any way for Piper. She doesn't know who you are, or what you do, or how much you're worth, or that you even exist. She doesn't know Aston exists. She thinks my ex is her father, and he is, for all intents and purposes."

"Bullshit. You'd tell her in a minute if it would benefit you," Peter said, glaring at me. "I want you to let go of my son, because when he finds out about all this, he'll lose his mind. He'll learn about Piper, and it will all be over. Everything I've built will be for nothing. He won't be able to stay away from you or her. He's a sucker for a happy ending, like the one his mom never got."

Taking a deep breath, I decided to use the dagger I knew would mortally wound him. It was more about self-preservation, having the last word and getting away from him.

"He already knows. Guess he played you too, old man."

Standing, I decided it was time for my coffee. The asshole stood too, staring at me with his mouth hanging open, speechless in a way I'd never seen.

What? He didn't think anyone would ever play him?

Stepping around him, I went to the counter and decided a cookie was in order too.

chapter
Twenty

Aston

"Do you get what I'm saying? This isn't a punishment for you. It's actually something special, okay, guys?"

During my regular business day, I closed million-dollar deals, but when it came to parenting, I was way out of my comfort zone. All I knew was I grew up with bitterly divorced parents, and I didn't want the same for my kids. They also didn't deserve a broken lush of a mother, so they'd have to settle for divorced parents who did their best not to be bitter.

Aston Junior nodded, and Mara asked, "Will you be able to braid my hair in the morning?"

"No, but Denise will do it before you go to school. I promise. What's important is that both of you know Denise will be in charge. Your mom's not feeling well, and so you'll stay with me all the time, until she gets better. But now I have to go to work."

"You mean, when she's not drunk, we get to see her again." Little Aston spoke of his mother's problems so matter-of-factly, like no child should ever have to do.

A shudder ran through me. To say I'd fucked myself royally wasn't harsh enough. "Don't worry about that, okay, buddy? Just worry about having fun and being seven."

We were sitting in my car outside the kids' school after I'd picked them up, both of them in the back seat, and me twisting around to see them from the front seat. We could have had this conversation once we got home, but I wanted to get it over with. I had too many things to tick off my to-do list, but this was the most pressing.

"Most days I won't be able to pick you up, so Denise will come in this car. You don't ride with anyone else, especially Mommy. You get in this car with Denise."

"Because she could be drunk. Mommy," Mara said. She was six going on twenty-five. "That's what Denise told us one time. To have a teacher call you if Mommy was drunk, or acting funny, when she picked us up."

"Right. It's bad to drink and drive. Denise is right. But now you don't have to worry about it."

"You drink coffee and drive," Mara said.

"That's right, baby. Coffee doesn't have alcohol. I mean a drink like wine or beer, a special-occasion drink. Those don't mix with driving."

This discussion was way above my pay grade. I fumbled with my words and needed to get this conversation over, and I still had to get in touch with Bexley and my lawyers.

"Oh." Mara tilted her head as she considered what I'd said, setting her braids swinging.

"What if you're drinking?" Little A asked, eyeing me from the back. "Mom said you drink, and you know, the other kids at school said their parents are talking about you. Is it because you drink?"

Facing the front to collect my thoughts, I took in a few deep breaths before turning back to the kids. Of course, Aidan had warned me about all this before I pulled this power move. It didn't take more than threatening Cass with her access to funds for her to convince the kids that they might lose both of us. I'd reminded him that it was his job to keep me free, and not behind bars.

"Don't listen to them. They're gossiping, and gossip is for old ladies in church and people on the golf course. You're both future CEOs or lawyers or doctors, so you don't need to gossip. You hear me?" I said, and they both nodded. "Let's roll."

Of course, they picked that moment to go in for the kill.

"Can we get ice cream? We're hungry," Little A said on a moan, and Mara chimed in. "We are."

"Ice cream it is, but don't pull this with Denise, kids. Got me?" I said it knowing they would do this exact thing several times a week, and she wouldn't say no to them. But there was nothing else I could do. I needed Denise so she could help me keep my kids safe.

Steering the SUV into traffic, I decided to go to the ice cream shop in the shopping plaza in case they needed anything else, although I'd sent Denise to pack their stuff today while they were at school.

She'd move into my pool house tomorrow. Her husband, Hank, ran a training base for the Army, and was only home a few months here and there. They'd never been able to have their own kids, and he liked that she was close with mine. It made me feel a little better knowing that my needing her wasn't interfering with her own family.

As I parked the SUV, the kids talked excitedly about how much they loved this place.

"There's an arcade next door too. Can we go?" Aston Junior asked. Of course he knew there was an arcade.

"Let's eat the ice cream and see. Do you have homework?"

"Dad! I'm in first grade," Mara said, rolling her eyes.

"I do," Aston Junior said. "But I promise I'll do it if I can play a few games… please?"

"You're going to go cross-eyed with all the video games your mom lets you play," I said without thinking, immediately wishing I could take it back. *Shit.*

My son shrugged. "Well, you weren't there, so she said I could."

Fuckup number ninety-nine by me.

"I know, I know," I said with a sigh. "Okay, ice cream, video games, then home for homework and dinner."

Who was I to say they couldn't be a little hedonistic?

The bell rang over the door as we walked into the shop, and Mara ran straight to the cooler, running her finger along the names of the flavors. Little A looked up at the chalk-covered boards on the wall, and I took a moment to check my phone.

I was supposed to be working. After all, someone had to pay for all this shit. Two houses, multiple cars, country club memberships, private school tuition, vacations, and fucking alimony. It took a lot of money to keep the Prescott machine running.

"Dad! Can I get bubble gum? I promise I won't swallow the gum!" Mara shrieked from the other end of the store, causing me to look up.

I caught a glimpse of Mara's braids swinging in the air, and three other pairs of eyes on me, one of them the same blue as mine.

I'd never seen her other than in pictures.

I knew she was mine—*learned too late*—but I'd never been brave enough to get close. The thought of losing her now, when I'd never really had her, scared me more than meeting her.

A few feet away, Bexley's mouth open and closed. She looked like a fish—a stunning one—with no sound coming out. Seated between the two females was a gangly boy, all limbs and curly strawberry-blond hair, his eyes the same green as Bexley's. There was no chance he was mine, but then again, he was all Bexley, and therefore held a piece of my heart.

As I approached, trepidation and anxiety coursed through my veins in equal measure. I noticed Bexley give me a small shake of her head. I didn't know if she meant for me not to approach or not to say anything. I wouldn't do the latter, but there was no way I wasn't saying hello to her.

Or meeting my daughter.

Mara saw me and ran over, swinging from my arm like a monkey, distracting me. "Daddy, did you pick?"

Thank God for little things.

"Hey, baby," I said, squeezing her hand. "I see a friend of mine, and then I will. Let me say hello and introduce you."

Mara had been raised in a country club, so there was no argument from my little girl. Glancing back for a second, I saw Aston Junior was busy trying out different flavors.

Swiftly approaching before she could run, I said, "Hi, Bexley."

"Hi," she said, keeping her eyes lowered.

"Aston Prescott," I said, this time extending my hand to her son. This got Bexley's eyes on me. "I'm an old friend of your mom's," I said when he stuck his hand in mine, and gave it a gentle shake.

"Tyler."

"I'm Mara," my daughter—my younger daughter—said politely.

"Hi, Mara," Bexley said, meeting Mara's eyes.

Piper remained in her seat, watching the whole scene unfold with thoughtful eyes. Eyes that were exact replicas of my own.

"Aston." I repeated my name, offering her my hand.

She stood and slipped her small hand in mine, holding my gaze. "Piper."

"Nice to meet you." I tried to say more, but I couldn't find the words. I had to actually force myself to let go of her hand.

This girl was my daughter. She was beautiful, the image of her mother, except for having my eyes. She stole my breath away.

"You're so pretty," Mara half whispered to Piper, interrupting the moment. "Do you play princess?"

Piper looked down at Mara and smiled. "I used to, but not anymore. Now I have a lot of homework and school stuff, and I play soccer."

"See, Daddy? She has homework and still goes for ice cream after school. He said we couldn't come if we had homework, and Little A…my brother…his name is also Aston, but it's too confusing with my dad. Anyway, he wants to go to the arcade, and we can't because Daddy has work," Mara rambled, ratting me out.

Piper laughed, and all of a sudden, the air didn't feel as heavy.

"Well, my brother," Piper said, pointing at Tyler, "has karate near here, and we usually don't go for ice cream. But my mom had a rough day."

The minute the words were out, I snapped my head toward Bexley. Another swift shake of her head forced me to school my expression, which I'm certain wasn't a happy one.

"Well, ice cream fixes everything. What flavor did you get?" Trying to lighten the mood, I turned to Tyler first.

"Chocolate and caramel swirl. Two scoops in a sugar cone."

"Mango sorbet," Piper said.

"That's what Daddy always gets," Mara said, and I was pretty sure Bexley turned a little green. "It's his favorite."

"Mine too," Piper said with a big smile.

I laid my hand on Mara's head. "You know what, baby, let's go order. If not, we'll never get to dinner."

"Yay! Come on, Daddy."

She grabbed my hand, and if it weren't for that, I might have never walked away. I had so many questions. My palm itched to run to touch Piper's face, her hair, to know that our blood was the same.

Not now, I told myself. I'd waited this long, so a little longer would be okay.

While Mara ordered a sugar cone with bubblegum ice cream, I couldn't worry about her having too much sugar. I was too busy tapping out a text to Bexley.

ASTON: *Text me as soon as you're free and tell me what happened.*

She didn't reply.

Little Aston ordered a waffle cone with two scoops of chocolate peanut butter, and I decided an hour at the arcade was in order. Mostly so I could clear my head.

chapter
Twenty-One

Bexley

Back then

Seth was a nice enough guy. Sweet when he wanted to be, and fun (sort of). He'd put himself through college because his parents insisted. With no resentment, he worked hard, chipping away at his college loans and making a living. We weren't from the same side of the tracks, but a whole heck of a lot closer than Aston and me. We were a better fit.

Except when it came to Mike and Milly. From the first time I introduced them, Seth decided they couldn't get along. "He's too rich for my blood," Seth would say about Mike.

As I'd sucked down drink number three at Milly's engagement party, I admitted to myself that Seth had never wanted to come. He'd said yes, but then he caught a cold. Here I was solo, Aston staring me down from across the room, and I needed a human shield. Like a magic potion, his eyes drew me into his bed every time I saw them. I couldn't go there tonight. Wouldn't go there.

I liked Seth all right. He was nice enough, and he liked me for me.

"Aston Prescott."

I'd been so deep in thought, convincing myself Seth was the one, I hadn't noticed Aston making his way toward me. Now he stood before me, giving me his campaign-worthy greeting, and my panties were exploding.

"Hi, Aston," I said, trying to sound calm. All of a sudden, I was burning hot in my little black dress. I tried to touch my cheek without him noticing, to see if it was warm to the touch, and wondered if it was pink.

"Looking good, Bex," he said, putting his arm around my back and drawing me close for a soft kiss on the same cheek I'd just checked. If it wasn't red before, it absolutely was now.

"Thanks." I maneuvered out of his light grasp for my own sanity. Being in Aston's arms brought back too many memories, most of them good, but too hurtful to think about.

"Having fun?" he asked, never taking his eyes off me, even while signaling something to the bartender. A fresh Scotch, I presumed.

"Oh, you know how much I love this club."

Milly just had to have the party at the club where she met Mike. Never mind it was the same place that marked both the beginning and end of my love life.

I have Seth now rattled in my brain.

"I know, it's bittersweet. We had a lot of good times here. But I'm running Federal now, and I think my dad may trust me soon to really take over."

"So, you want me to wait? Wait for your dad to decide I'm good enough for you?"

Looking at him in his dark slacks, his white shirt open at the collar and its sleeves rolled up, I decided I could. Wait, that is.

"I know it's a lot, but I want to be able to support us, you know? I need the business to do that."

It was always the business. "You know, Aston, I've told you a million times—and not that it matters now—but that door is closed. Slammed shut. But I never cared about the business, or you supporting the two of us in the way you grew up. I cared about you. I'm sure anything you did would be successful, and if there were bumps, there'd be bumps. We'd survive."

He gathered me close again, and I silently cursed Seth for not being here. To protect me. To protect himself from what I knew would happen with Aston. My heart and body were unable to resist him. A few more minutes in Aston's arms, and I'd be his.

"I appreciate that," he said, "more than you can know. But my dad ruined my mom's life and their marriage over this business. It's my cherry on top, and my mom wants—no *needs*—me to have it. I have to do this for her."

"I get it, you're still a pawn in their game. Your dad pulls and your mom pushes you. You're going to have to grow up sometime, and I can't say I'll be here when you do." They were my words, but I was only brave enough to share them courtesy of the alcohol.

Aston's eyes squeezed closed. He looked hurt, as though I'd physically struck him, and I couldn't deny how that wrecked me. And that empathy for him would be my downfall.

"I'm sure it looks that way, Bex, but I have to see this through. Let's not let it ruin this night for Mike and Milly...or us."

His lips brushed my cheek again, this time lingering, his warm breath cascading over my skin, his invisible grip holding tightly to my heart.

"Another?" he whispered into my ear.

I didn't know if he meant a kiss or a drink. Either way, I nodded, wanting to whisper *yes, both please*, but I bit my tongue. We'd been down this road before, and it didn't matter if we were older or wiser.

We ended up avoiding any further serious conversation, and danced and laughed the rest of the night.

All the way up until we landed between the sheets...my legs twisted with Aston's, his lips hard on mine, his tongue working its way inside my mouth. Our hearts beat a furious rhythm, in sync, like our hips as we moved together as one.

Later, when Aston snored softly into the pillow, I left. Ran with my tail tucked between my legs, back home to a hot shower and a sleepless night.

We hadn't used protection. He must have assumed I was still on the pill, but I wasn't. I'd had some weird hormonal surge recently, and my doctor had told me to take a break. Mostly, I was panicked over catching a disease. I was sure Aston had been sleeping around, and I didn't need that kind of complication. I had a boyfriend.

After a few weeks of worrying, I went to the doctor for a round of STD tests and a checkup. I was ecstatic when the nurse called to say the results were clean, and I almost hung up as she was saying, "One more thing, though . . ."

It had been the same day Seth had asked me to move in with him, and I thought, *I have two things to celebrate.* Until I heard, "Good news, you're pregnant."

That's when I committed my biggest sin and told Seth we were having a baby.

Being a nice guy back then, Seth asked me to marry him, and I said yes. He hadn't been ready for kids. Or taking on a woman in love with someone else.

He tried, though.

chapter
Twenty-Two

Bexley

Present day

"Mom, who was that man we saw today? Aston?" Piper asked later when we were alone in the kitchen.

Good thing I was wearing long sleeves, despite the Nevada heat, because goose bumps broke out all over my arms, and probably red blotches too.

"I knew him when Milly and I worked at the country club. He lived on the golf course. Remember I told you I worked in the snack shack? We made a lot of money that summer."

"Oh. He looked kind of familiar . . ."

Like every time you look in the mirror?

"I don't know why. I haven't seen him in a long time. Since Milly got married," I said, trying as usual to be as honest as possible when it came to my kids.

"Hmm? Maybe at the club when we've gone with Aunt Milly?"

"Maybe that's it."

I tried to avoid going to the club, and on the few occasions Milly dragged me, she assured me Aston wouldn't be there. Now that I knew he knew about Piper, I wasn't so sure he hadn't been lurking somewhere in the corner. If it were me, I would have been.

"I have to go read for English," Piper said. "God, I can't stand this book. Blah, blah. I wish we could read *The Fault in Our Stars.*"

And just like that, the conversation was over. Piper jumped down from the counter where she'd been sitting and grabbed an apple.

"Probably because I'm the only seventh-grade parent who would approve that book."

"Oh, Mom, stop it."

She walked out of the kitchen, and I finally took a moment alone with my phone.

ASTON: *Text me as soon as you're free and tell me what happened.*

ASTON: *Bexley, I'm not joking.*

ASTON: *Either text me back or I'm coming over.*

The last text had come in fifteen minutes earlier, and I decided it was time to answer Aston before he stormed through my front door and tore apart my carefully constructed life.

BEXLEY: *Take a chill pill. My kids are older, they're around. This is my first free moment. I'm fine. Nothing happened.*

The little bubble filled with dots appeared, and I decided a glass of wine was in order. I wasn't sure of too much, but there was no way Aston was letting me off scot-free tonight.

As I stuck the cork back in the bottle, my phone beeped again.

ASTON: *Yeah, older. Let's discuss that, shall we? Do you want to come clean?*

BEXLEY: *For obvious reasons, I kept things to myself. I understand you've been snooping, so I don't have to say much. You know.*

I gulped my wine, not able to down it fast enough.

ASTON: *I understand. But my understanding is over. I'll have my lawyer draw up some papers for your ex, thanking him for what he did, but having him relinquish all ties.*

Oh boy.

It didn't take Seth long to figure out what had happened. As Piper got older, she looked exactly like Aston. Seth only had to see Aston once to assume, and the appendix surgery made it official. One look at our blood types, and it was clear we weren't her biological parents. At least, Seth wasn't.

Once again, being the bigger guy, he forgave me and never spoke of it again. When Tyler was born, I believed I'd redeemed myself. I'd given Seth a boy.

After the split, he stayed close with Piper. He knew he couldn't be upset with her. She was an innocent party in all of this.

Picking up my phone, I walked out the back door and toward the carport.

Aston picked up on the first ring. "Don't think you're changing my mind on anything. I've been nice and stayed quiet. I let that ass raise my daughter because it was what you wanted or needed. Now I'm done. Especially after today."

"Well, hello to you too, Aston." Leaning my head back, I rolled my neck and closed my eyes.

"Cut it out, Bexley. I gave you plenty of latitude when it came to this. But she's mine. Look at her…Christ. She's mine, and I've missed all of it," he growled through the line.

"You didn't want me." A tear rolled down my cheek, and I swiped it away while trying to keep my wineglass steady in my hand. "How could you want her if you didn't want me? You had a plan, needed to get that business for your mom. Without Federal, you were never going to be happy. A baby was never going to be a fair substitute in your mind. It was Federal or bust, and everything your dad wanted for you to do. How's that working out for you now? You're in trouble…what will happen to the business if something happens to you? Your mom's plans will all be destroyed."

Years of rage spewed from me. Unable to stop the verbal diarrhea, I said, "Thank God your mom passed. At least she's not here to witness this. You getting arrested, the company crumbling…all she ever wanted for you. Not a life, a family, a good marriage."

"Nothing's crumbling. I'm innocent, Bexley. I don't lie; I've never lied to you. At least I have that to hold on to. These charges won't stick…you'll see. I was wrong, okay? I didn't realize it until my mom died. She died happy to be a grandma and see me all grown up, but I wasn't happy. She didn't know that, though. Or maybe she did—I don't know. Point is, I have to tell myself the job could have been with anyone, any damn job, anything would have made her happy because I was her son. Otherwise, I can't breathe. What kind of woman sets her kid up for failure and heartache? By the time she was sick, she didn't care about the company anymore. She was consumed with her own destiny and my dad not by her side while she was dying. But by then, I'd already fucked up my life for it. Fuck," he yelled into the phone.

The sound echoed in the background, and I assumed he was in a garage talking with me, away from his kids. The ones he'd always known about.

My mom had warned me I was playing a dangerous game when I met Aston and brought him home way back then. Unfortunately, she'd passed away in a bad car wreck while I was pregnant with Piper. I missed her terribly, but honestly, I was relieved she never had the chance to see me for the liar I was. She would have known what I did, how I'd lied, and called me out on it.

"Fuck, Bex, I'm sorry. I don't want to talk about this over the phone. I want to hold you and cherish you and tell you I messed up. I ruined so many years of our lives, and I need to get that time back. At the very least, your heart. I need you."

Aston shook me out of my memories with his soothing words. No matter what he said, it was a salve for all that ailed me.

"We can't get the years back. That's not how it works, Aston. We can only move forward. I get that you want to know Piper, and I'm sorry I kept her from you. I need to talk with Seth, and then we can move ahead with it. I owe him that much. So do you."

"I don't owe him shit. He should've manned up and told you to tell me. That's my daughter."

I wasn't going to argue with Aston. I knew better than to think I could win.

chapter
Twenty-Three

Bexley

"Everything okay?" Seth said after he picked up on the second ring. "I'm real busy."

I'd called him at work. Admittedly, it was a chicken move, but first, I knew he'd pick up, and second, he couldn't yell at me.

Seth was a senior account executive in an advertising agency where they worked in one of those open floor plans. With no doors or walls, creative juices supposedly flowed free amongst the air particles. Seth had worked his way up through the ranks, reminding me every few days of our married life that nothing had been handed to him.

"Everything's fine. Kids said they had a good weekend. Thanks." I didn't owe him my gratitude, but as always felt compelled to give it.

"Well, they're my kids."

He had a comeback for everything these days. Although he was once a nice guy, Seth's contempt for me poured out of him lately. Not wanting to make it worse, I didn't bring up how often he'd tried to get out of having the kids with him. I assumed they cramped his dating life.

"Well, you know what I mean," he said, this time a tad more quietly.

He wouldn't yell at the office, but that didn't stop him from lobbing jabs at me. Over the years, he'd had plenty of opportunities to call me out, to force my hand when it came to Piper, but he'd cared for her from the moment she was born. He often rocked her to sleep when she was little, and on the first day of preschool, he'd held her hand.

Even if he'd done those things because it was what he'd thought he should do or had to do, he didn't have the right to be resentful about it now. I'd given him some of my best years…and a son. Plus, he'd been able to save face among his coworkers at his beloved advertising agency by me not exposing the truth.

"Funny you mention the kids…being yours. I was hoping to meet you for a coffee. Maybe sometime tomorrow? I have to discuss something about Piper with you." I was trying to be vague. Seth could pull a tooth from me if I wasn't careful. He had this way about him, his *I'm such a nice guy, poor me, I need to know right now* routine.

It had been three days since Aston threatened me with blowing the cover off my full-of-shit life. I'd dragged my feet for two days and spent most of today spoon-feeding myself courage. I'd held Aston off, but he was coming over tomorrow, "with pizza and all the kids," he'd told me.

Seth sighed. "I'm in the middle of putting together a big presentation. Can it wait? I lost a lot of time last weekend with taking the kids around, you know."

"I wish it could wait, but I think it's best to discuss quickly."

"Okay, well, why don't you tell me now? Just rip the Band-Aid off. Did she get her…you know? Is she a woman now? She's about the age." He whispered most of it, but I heard him.

"No, she didn't get her period, and if she did, I would probably let her decide whether to share that with you. Anyway, how is tomorrow morning, right after I drop the kids off at school? I'm not at the clinic."

"Bexley, I don't have time for a long thing today or tomorrow. You're already interrupting my workday. You know, how I pay for the kids you want to talk about? So, out with it…what does this have to do with? I send the money, you kept the house. Is there anything else?"

He spoke softly. I pictured him at work with a smile painted on his face, appearing as though everything was fine and dandy.

"I can see you're making me talk now. Look, there's no sugarcoating this. Piper met Aston; he ran into us in an ice cream shop. He knows. And he wants to tell her."

"That's what you want to talk about? You can do whatever you want. Call the lawyer, though, and make Aston pay up for all the years he missed. You know, when I was raising Piper like my own, and then you kicked me out. Honestly, I was a good guy. I fell for you and your scheme. Don't be mad at me over this."

That's not exactly how it went. After Seth had an affair at work, we decided there wasn't any love left between us. In exchange for my keeping quiet about his workplace infidelity, he'd agreed to my terms.

"She has a right to know," I said.

"You took that away from her. Not me."

"Yes. I'm taking all the responsibility. I wanted to make sure you knew, for you to understand. I didn't plan to diminish how important you were to her."

"Listen, Bexley, I'm at work. I knew this day would come, especially after we got divorced. Reunite our daughter with her *criminal* father, do what you must. Remember, Tyler is ours, and I'll have a say in everything that pertains to him. I have to go now."

He disconnected the call without allowing me to even say *good-bye* or *thanks*, or *go fuck yourself.*

Taking a deep breath, I rested my forehead on my desk at the clinic and continued to breathe. I had five minutes before sprinting to school to pick up the kids, and all I wanted was to take a nap. Or a giant coffee.

I'd just decided to settle for a few minutes of meditating when there was a knock on my door.

"Come in," I called, sitting up in my chair and shuffling the papers around on my desk.

"Heya, Bex." Aston opened the door and stood in the doorway, wearing what I assumed was a very expensive suit and holding a coffee in one hand.

"What are you doing here?" I asked as an array of emotions caught in my throat.

"Delivery with a smile," he said, setting the coffee in front of me.

"Um, I have to go get the kids from school. But thanks. I was just craving a coffee."

"With whole milk, dirty blond, just the way you like it."

He waved his hand in front of the large to-go cup, and I couldn't lie. My mouth watered.

"Thank you. This right here, right now, is definitely the way to my heart. Although, I don't think I should give myself away like that."

He raised an eyebrow, and I looked away.

Anxious about what came next, and unsure of what to say or do, I stood to walk out. I was at work, and this visit was unprecedented.

"Walk with me?" I finally asked after grabbing my bag and taking a sip of my coffee.

"How about I drive you to get the kids?"

It was my turn to raise an eyebrow. "Isn't that a little odd? My car is here. And what about your kids?"

Could I have any more excuses?

"No, it's not odd. I plan to do it a lot more after our night tomorrow. When we come clean. Notice how I said we? I don't plan to throw you under the bus, Bex. You did what you had to do. I'm not a bad guy. I may have acted badly, but I'm not the enemy."

I felt my head shaking. Standing by the door, I said in a hushed tone, "I'm at work. We can't have this discussion here, where anyone could listen. It's not fair to me."

"Okay, let's roll. You can tell the kiddos we got together for coffee after running into each other the other day. By the way," he whispered, "you look sexy. Are you sure you're working?"

I was wearing a black jumpsuit with short sleeves and a plain zipper up the back. "This is hardly sexy, but thank you."

"I want to tell you about my lawyer. He's drawing up some papers for Piper, but also, we have a new witness in the case. It's top secret right now, but I want to fill you in. Also, I spoke with my dad. I know he came to see you, and I won't tolerate it."

We were outside by the time he finished, and Aston was unlocking his SUV and ushering me inside.

"Do you have more hours in your day than everyone else? Wait just a minute—you talked with your dad?" I swiveled in my seat and stared at him. Aston seemed to work at a speed I couldn't keep up with.

"Yeah, one sec." He handed me back my coffee, shut my door, and ran around the front. Seated in the driver's seat, he said, "I have just as many hours as everyone else, but I have a staff that helps, and I also want to get my life back together. As for my father, I told him about Pipe—"

"Wait a minute? Pipe? Her name is Piper…don't give her a nickname. You haven't even formally met her."

"Yeah, I know. Piper. I'm just a little wound up. So my dad…of course he knew about her, the slimy fucker. He finally admitted to paying you a visit, and said he was working on things, so I didn't need to worry about my little problem. That's what he called Piper…the fucker. He actually said he was working on making it so Piper wasn't my concern."

Grimacing, Aston went on. "I almost punched him, but I'm working on remaining calm, so I didn't. I had plenty of harsh words with him, like threatening I would walk into every CEO's office on the Strip and tell them what a cocksucker he is, disparaging Federal along the way, until they took their business to the cheaper outlets with less customer service and quality, but I didn't care."

"Take a breath, Aston. You're going to faint. Slow down. You don't need to defend me to your dad. He's not going to make any problems go away, because I don't do business the way he does, with payoffs."

Aston ran a hand through his thick hair and then dropped it to take my hand in his. "Don't worry. He'll stay away now, especially after I brought up his wife and her tennis pro. He's so fickle. The business, Nan, he doesn't want his legacy disrupted. Well, he'll have to accept a granddaughter born out of wedlock and kept a secret."

Then Aston actually winked, like this was fun. Like telling a teenage girl she was a long-lost secret daughter of your teenage love affair...was *fun*.

"This isn't my life," I said, staring out my window as he pulled out, cocky and confident. "You don't even know what school we're going to...oh, wait. Of course you do. Anyway, you can't just keep threatening people. First me, and now I got involved with Seth after your threats, and now you and your dad. Oh, and by the way, you're still being investigated."

We sped along the correct route while I ranted and Aston let it roll off of him, staying calm as he drove.

"Bexley, I'm protecting what's mine. Get used to it," he said, but I didn't respond. "And before you go down the whole path that I didn't protect you back then...I wasn't a man yet. But now I am."

"I'm going to need some time alone with Piper to sit down and explain everything. I did some reading on how to break sensitive topics to teens. I'm going to be as honest as possible with her. I thought about how I may leave your dad's part in this out of it, let him save face—"

"Absolutely not!" Aston turned his head for a second to glare at me. With his eyes back on the road, he spoke firmly. "No, he doesn't get to be absolved of the role he played. I'm never going to be close with him, and I doubt you will. Piper will know the truth."

As we neared the school, I moved on. "I'm not sure whether Tyler should be around or not. I would ask Seth, but he barely had time for me when I called about Piper. He was thrilled you're stepping up—"

Aston interrupted again with a quick flash of his smug expression. "More like me letting him off the hook financially."

"It doesn't matter now," I said, trying to reason with him.

"It does, and don't defend him."

"Listen, I wronged him first."

"No, you wronged *me* first—"

"Aston! That's not fair."

Glancing at me, he sighed. "You're right. Listen, why don't you let me take Tyler to the arcade with Little A? And you can have time with Piper."

As we pulled up to the school, I asked, "How would we pull that off?"

"Simple. I need a helper."

My eyes rolled on their own. Aston had an answer for everything. As usual, he ruled his world.

I opened the car door and walked toward where I met the kids when I picked them up. The lower school and junior high shared a campus, which was great for a single mom like me. They took the bus when I couldn't be here on time, but I tried to pick them up one or two days a week. Today, I wished it had been a bus day. As the kids ran out of school from all directions, I wondered how I would explain Aston's presence.

"Hi, Mom!" Tyler called to me first.

Piper came up shortly after. "Hey, Mom, why are you out of your car?"

"Hi, guys. Um, actually, I met Aston—you know, from the other day? We had coffee and we ran late, so he brought me over here."

"Aston?" Piper waggled her eyebrows at me.

It was a little startling. I didn't think she'd be doing that until she was much older.

"What kind of car does he have?" Typical Tyler.

"You know what? I don't even know. It's an SUV, but I don't know what kind."

Tyler gave me an annoyed look. "Mom, you need to pay attention to these things."

"You're right. Totally right," I said as I slung my arm around him. When we stopped next to the black beast, I said, "Here it is."

"Mom, it's a Range Rover," Piper whispered. "That's a fancy car."

I nodded, letting her know I heard her.

Was I shocked it was fancy? Of course not.

"Hi," Tyler said, jumping in the back seat.

"Mr. Prescott," I said quickly, correcting my son, and Aston gave me a quick glare.

"It's Aston, just Aston."

"Hi," Piper said with less excitement, sliding in next to her brother.

As soon as I was seated, Aston pulled away from the curb and drove toward my house.

"What about your car, Mom?" Piper asked, never one to miss out on details.

"I'm going to send someone to get it," Aston said, answering for me.

I watched Piper's brow furrow in the rearview.

"Who?" she asked. "Who would do that? Get our car?"

"One of my guys, someone who works for me," Aston said matter-of-factly. He was going to have to adjust to the way my kids had been raised. I hoped he didn't expect to turn "Pipe" into a spoiled brat.

"Well, I can make them cookies," Piper said. "I'm going to bake when I get home."

That's my girl. She'll never be a brat.

Aston glanced at the kids in the rearview mirror. "I'm sure they'd like that. Baking sounds like fun. Since you're busy, Tyler, do you want to come with me to the arcade? I need to take Little A there, but he's a handful, and I need some help chasing him around."

"Mom! Can I, Mom?"

I could feel Tyler's excitement vibrating all the way from the back seat. "As long as you do your homework as soon as you're back."

"Yes! Yes, I will."

With that, we pulled up in front of my house, and both kids bolted inside to grab a snack. By the time I got out of the car, Aston was in front of me. His warm palm came to my hip, steadying me.

"It's going to be fine." His lips tickled my ear as he whispered his words just for me. With his index finger, he pushed a stray hair behind my ear, then kissed my cheek as he said again, "Bex, it's going to be fine."

"I don't know," I said, shaking my head. "This is like some weird dream I'm living in, and now it feels like it's turning into a nightmare."

"It's not. I'm here for you. And like I told you, my dad isn't an innocent party in this, and you can tell Piper what you want on that. And yeah, I listened to him, and so neither am I. But first and foremost, you need to protect yourself . You did what you thought you had to, and I stand behind that."

His thumb caressed my hip over my jumpsuit, making me wish I was wearing a regular shirt and pants so I could feel his skin on mine.

"Where did this all come from?" I asked. "One minute I'm so in love with you, and then *poof*, you're gone for what I thought was forever. And now you're back."

"Hey, let's not dwell on it," he said softly. "Today's about Piper."

I nodded, and he tipped my chin up so my gaze met his. His lips brushed across my eyelid, then made their way to mine. On a closed-mouth kiss, he mumbled, "It's always been you, Bex."

"I don't think we should do this here. For anyone to see."

He stepped back from me. "You're right. Soon," he said, making it sound like a promise. "Soon you're going to be fine. More than fine."

"I've done a lot of reading the last two nights. Hours of reading on the best way to talk with Piper. Apparently, honesty is the best policy. I need to own my actions without seeming defensive. I had my reasons, and they weren't to hurt her."

"Exactly," Aston said from next to his car, which felt like too far away.

Sadly, I already missed his touch. I'd made this mistake once before. When it came to Aston, I couldn't stop myself.

"I'm going to go. Time to do this," I said, more to myself than to him.

He nodded. "I'll text when we're on our way back. Tyler doesn't have a phone?"

"Not yet...and don't get any ideas."

"We'll see. Send him on out. Little A's going to be ecstatic," Aston said.

But Piper certainly wasn't going to be.

I turned toward the house without another word.

chapter
Twenty-Four

Bexley

"Piper, can we talk?" I said, interrupting her as she pulled down ingredients to bake cookies.

"Mom, I should do this. Aston said the car would be here later."

My heart cracked in two over what I was about to do.

Piper's world had already been destroyed once because of the divorce, and here I was about to shatter it all over again. Funny that Seth asked about her period; Piper and I had the talk about eight months ago. What to expect, what it meant, and all of that. She knew how babies were made and where they came from, but this conversation would be on a whole different level.

Fuck.

Out loud, I said, "Piper, honey, we'll get it done. I promise. We need to talk for a few."

She turned toward me, her face pinched with concern. "Is everything okay? Are you okay?" Running over to me, she took my hand in hers. "Mom? Say something."

I hated how much worry she was filled with—how she felt she had to mother me.

"I'm fine, sweetie. This is good news, I swear. Come on, let's sit."

With my arm wrapped around her, I guided her to the window seat. Seemed appropriate, considering how much time I'd spent thinking about Aston in that exact spot.

"Piper, this isn't easy for me to tell you," I said. "But it's good stuff. It may not seem that way, but it is."

"Are you and dad getting back together?"

Drawing on every bit of my self-control, I kept my expression schooled. That wasn't where I thought her head would go, but I should have expected it. "No, we aren't getting back together, sweetie. But this is sort of what I wanted to talk with you about. Your dad and me, and you. There's some stuff that you need to know."

"Oh." She dropped her gaze to our hands, our fingers entwined.

I had to get on with it. Period.

"First off, I love you. So much. You're my whole world. And Dad loves you, and what I'm about to tell you doesn't change that," I said, taking some liberties when it came to Seth and his feelings for Piper. "Here's the thing. I knew Aston a long time ago, before I met your dad. And at one point, we were really in love."

"So, you can be in love again now. You're divorced, and you said you and Dad aren't getting back together. I get it. I watch TV."

I tried not to squeeze my eyes shut in pain. Piper wasn't making this easy on me.

"Well, yes. That's true. We could love each other now...maybe we never stopped. But there's something else. When we loved each other a long time ago, we couldn't be together. There were reasons . . ."

"What reasons?" she said. Of course my smart little cookie would ask all the right questions.

"Well, Aston's dad didn't care for me. We were from two different worlds. As you know, he's very rich, and that doesn't make him a bad person, but...not Aston . . ." I started to stumble over my words. "Not Aston, but his dad felt as though wealthy people should fall in love with other wealthy people, and he forbid us to be together."

"Oh." Piper squeezed my hand, and the small gesture made me feel like I could continue.

"It hurt a lot back then, and I was really sad. Then I met your dad and thought I could love someone else. And I did. I cared for your dad, Seth, very much. But you know how we talked about how babies are made?"

She nodded, her cheeks pinking a bit.

"Before I met Seth, Aston and I were very much in love—so much so, that we made love. Like I told you adults do. We—Aston and me—shared something very beautiful, and that's how we created you, my beautiful girl. Aston is actually your father, but he didn't know. I never told him. Seth and I raised you because I thought it was right. It's not Aston's fault."

"What?" She jumped up from the seat, a lone tear rolling down her cheek. "Mom!"

"I didn't want to risk Aston losing his company. His father would have taken it away from him. And I didn't want to risk losing you…his father could have taken you too. Money makes people do all kinds of crazy things. Seth was, *is*, a good man, and he loves you. There were too many risks in telling the truth. But things have a way of twisting around, and now Aston is here and back, and he met you, and, well . . ." I stopped ranting and took a breath.

"Well what? I have two dads! Who is my dad?" Piper fell to her knees at my feet and laid her head in my lap. "I'm so confused."

"I know," I said, running my hand over her hair. "And that's the last thing I want you to be. I want you to know this is my fault. Not yours, or anyone else's. I decided to keep you from Aston. That was a choice I made as your mother. What I thought was best. Aston says he's not mad at me for it, because he understands why. I'm not saying you have to understand. I just want you to know that Aston wants to be in your life. Now, no matter what happened before."

She lifted her head. "He has his own kids now. He loves them. Why does he want me?"

"He has a big heart, and there's room for him to love you. I promise."

At least, I prayed it was true.

"What about Tyler? So, he's not really my brother?"

"Of course he's your brother. Always has been, and always will be. Little A and Mara are your brother and sister too. I didn't think about that; I've just been wanting to tell you this. I hope you understand…someday…why I had to do this. Your grandfather isn't always the nicest man, especially when it comes to me. I wanted to protect you from that. But I can see it was a mistake."

Her head fell heavy back on my lap.

"I love you, Piper. I'm sorry. I didn't mean to hurt you."

"So, who do you love, Mom? Aston? Did you ever love my dad? Not my dad-dad, but Dad. Seth. Do I still call him Dad?" She raised her head and looked at me with sad eyes.

My heart split into shards over the pain I was causing her.

"Honey," I said, pushing her damp hair off her face. "You can call him Dad. Seth helped raise you and loved doing it, and I'm grateful for that. He's still going to love you. At one time, I cared for Seth very much. I loved him, but it wasn't the kind of love I had with Aston—your biological father. I do still love Aston, but we need to get to know each other as adults. We haven't spent much time together over the years."

Suddenly, Piper's eyes widened. "Wait! Am I rich?"

"Piper!"

"What? You said Aston was really rich, and he's sending your car here with some guy. If he's my father, does that make me rich?"

"I don't know. But that's not a reason to reconcile all this. Money doesn't make everything better. Look what happened with me. And you. Money made things worse."

"Reconcile?" she asked, staring at me.

"Make sense of it all. That everything checks out. Money doesn't make this better. What I did, or what's ahead of us now."

"Aston does seem cool," she said, tilting her head to the side, taking me in. "You know, he looked familiar to me the other day. Probably because we look so much alike, now that I think about it."

I could practically see the wheels turning in her head, firing off questions like neurons.

"I'm going to get to know him," she said slowly. "He's not going to replace Dad. But he's also my dad, I guess. So, yeah. But…I don't think I want to tell anyone at school."

"That's fine, sweetie." It wasn't until now I realized the nape of my neck was damp from sweat. Taking a deep breath, I said, "You don't have to tell anyone anything you don't want to. We'll explain this to Tyler. That it's your choice."

"Aaack, Tyler, what if he doesn't think of me as his sister anymore? Or he thinks I'm different because I'm rich?"

"Piper, stop with the rich stuff. And that's impossible. You'll always be Tyler's sister."

"Okay. You know what? I'm going to make Aston some cookies too."

And just like that, my baby girl stood up and walked into the kitchen, leaving me a jumbled mess of feelings and tears while she digested this all with grace.

"Mom! They're back!"

My car had been returned an hour earlier. With cookies in hand, the delivery guy made his way out to a Ford pickup waiting for him, and Piper settled in the window seat. She'd been waiting for Aston to pull up, and truthfully, I'd been hiding.

"Oh, look, they're in a sports car. Tyler must be excited!"

Piper ran to the front door and yanked it open before they even made it up the walkway.

"Hi," she said quietly, shyness replacing her exuberance from earlier.

"Move, I want to show Mom this," Tyler said as he pushed past her, and I frowned at him.

"Tyler, say it nicely."

"Excuse me," he said automatically, and then held up a video game. "Look!"

"Oh, I'm looking. Where did you get that?"

"Little A and I won enough tickets for us each to get a game! Can you believe it?"

"Oh, I can believe you probably spent a fortune in tokens to get those tickets." I shot Aston a dagger-filled look, and he rolled his eyes.

"Mom, don't ruin it," Piper said. "They had fun. Plus, you know…you didn't pay for it."

"She's right," Aston said with a smug grin. "This was my treat. We went for a good time."

Freaking Aston, spoiling everyone already.

"Where's Little A? And Mara?" Piper asked.

"We dropped Little A at home with Mara, who stayed home with Denise to do her nails."

"Oh, is Denise your wife?"

Freaking Piper, pumping for information.

"I'm going to get some water. I'll be right back," Tyler said, oblivious to the tension.

"Denise is my nanny. Well, not mine, but the kids," Aston said, looking directly at Piper.

"Oh. I bet she's nice. We don't have a nanny, but my friend Ashley does. She does all their laundry and cooking. Mom does that here."

Smoothing my hand down the front of my shirt and clearing my throat, hoping to buy myself an hour, I only got ten seconds. "Piper, sweetie, calm down. No need to ramble."

"It's okay," Aston said, bending a little to see eye to eye with her. "You can ramble, and I'll answer all of your questions."

Piper nodded, studying Aston's face. "We have the same eye color."

"Yes. Yes, we do." He reached out to touch her, maybe to stroke her cheek or hair, but he pulled back with a slight tremor in his fingers.

Now my already shattered heart was dust. I'd done this, caused this pain.

"Can I give you a hug, Piper?"

His voice didn't waver, but I knew it took a lot for him to be so hesitant. Gone was the cocky attitude, and in its place was a nervous dad meeting his daughter for the first time, thirteen years too late.

Piper nodded, and Aston pulled her in.

Tyler took that moment to reappear. "What's going on? Piper! What's wrong with you?" When no one answered, he turned to me. "Mom? Why is she hugging Aston?"

"Tyler, let's give them a moment, and I'll take you in the other room and explain."

Aston looked up and mouthed, *"Thank you."*

I led Tyler to the kitchen. I wished I could report he took the news as well as Piper.

"What? You mean, he's her dad? Why don't I get him? He would take me to the arcade. Dad never takes me to the arcade."

My son was young, immature, and bruised from the divorce. I didn't know why I expected him to react any other way.

"Tyler, listen. You can be close with Aston," I said calmly. "He's going to be spending time with Piper, so you can see him too."

"Whatever." He slid down in the kitchen chair, sulking, his video game forgotten on the counter.

"Tyler," Aston said from the doorway. "Your mom's right. She didn't have a choice in how this all happened. But you're Piper's brother, so guess what? You're going to be part of my world too."

Tyler eyed him warily, and I couldn't blame him. This was a lot for me, let alone an eleven-year-old kid.

"Yeah. Dad always says he's going to do stuff with us too, and then he never does. Now Piper doesn't have to be upset with him because she has you. And

I'm stuck…and Mom gets upset. She doesn't think we know, but we do. Right, Piper?"

Tyler glanced at his sister, who looked up and nodded. Then they both turned to look at Aston. Up until this moment, they'd only seen jovial Aston, but now they saw his hard-as-stone expression. He didn't try to hide it, even when I gave him a death glare.

"Now, that doesn't work for me. I don't like to hear your mom was hurting."

"Well, what about when your dad hurt her?" Obviously, Piper couldn't help herself. Then again, I'd always encouraged her to speak her mind.

"Piper, I don't think this is the time for that—"

"No," Aston said sharply, interrupting me.

Sweat once again lined the nape of my neck, and I wished the air was blowing a bit harder.

"Piper, you're right. My dad did hurt your mom, as did I. I hate to admit it, but this was before I knew what being a man meant. I thought I was a man, all grown up, but I wasn't. Now, as adults, I don't want to hear of another adult hurting your mom."

This was all still taking place in my tiny hallway. The four of us in a standoff—a motley crew—trying to make sense of what we meant to one another and how we all fit together.

"Whatever." Tyler shrugged, scowling. "I'm fine. You have a new dad, Piper. Good for you."

Piper moved close to her brother and wrapped her arm around him. She was such a giving soul. If Aston hurt her, I'd kill him.

"Tyler, listen to me," Piper said softly. "We're in this together, okay? If Aston's not going to be nice to you, then I'm not going to spend time with him. Yeah, Dad isn't always nice, but now you can share with me. 'Kay?"

Tyler nodded but refused to look up.

Aston didn't look up either, too busy watching his daughter with equal parts adoration and wonder.

I couldn't blame him. She was pretty freaking amazing.

chapter
Twenty-Five

Aston

Back then

A s my body slid in and out of Bexley's, my blood had never felt so heated. My skin prickled from being near her, on top of her, inside her, everywhere.

I wanted her for forever, but I'd take this one weekend. It was the fix I'd been jonesing for.

I'd had a lot to drink by the time Bexley arrived at Milly and Mike's engagement party. Mike and I had started the evening with a round or two of shots, and then I switched to my old standby, Jack and Coke.

She'd shown up by herself, sexy as fuck in a skimpy black dress and matching heels. It was probably some bargain-basement special, but on her it looked like couture. At least to me.

They'd told me to bring a date because Milly expected Bexley to bring some loser, Seth. Unlike her, I couldn't convince myself to bring someone who wasn't important to me. For the last four months, all the someones in my life were nothing more than a warm body and a release. I was beginning to hate every woman I met.

When Bexley showed up alone, I knew I'd made the right choice. Although it might have been the alcohol talking. My dad had just signed me on as a full-fledged partner in the business as an early Christmas gift. Not saddling myself with a poor girl like Bexley had been my dad's demand before promoting me, in addition to insisting I go to business school now that I was weeks away from getting my bachelor's degree.

A few cocktails in, my dad's requests were nothing but silly semantics.

Who the hell was he to tell me who I could love?

Bexley looked gorgeous. The sides of her dress had these cutouts, revealing tanned skin and subtle curves. Her long, lean legs looked fucking delicious in those pumps. As I downed my fifth or fifteenth drink of the evening, I imagined running my tongue up the back of her calf, making my way to the inside of her thigh.

It didn't help that she ignored me for most of the evening, drinking champagne and laughing with her friends. But I caught her near the bar.

"Aston Prescott," I said with my hand extended.

A million emotions flashed across her face—disbelief, anger, confusion, lust, and finally, happiness.

"Bexley," she said, slipping her hand in mine like when we first met.

"Nice to meet you, Bexley…?"

She laughed. "Stop. You already know me, Aston."

I pulled her into my side, and her head dropped on my shoulder, her hair cascading all around her face and mine.

"I was just remembering when we first met," I said as I kissed the top of her head.

"Aston," she whispered.

"It's good to see you." And it was better than good.

"I thought you were moving on. You said it yourself—your dad needed your full focus, and that included not being with some washerwoman's daughter."

"I hate that you heard that." I couldn't stop breathing her in, with her cherry lip gloss and drugstore perfume.

"I thought you were driving me back to school. I waited and waited, and you never showed. What else should I have done? I came to your office—"

"Enough. I don't want to talk about it anymore. You look too gorgeous tonight to be sad. Plus, I'm a partner at Federal now. Nothing my dad can do."

That was definitely the alcohol talking. When it came to my dad, nothing stopped the power-hungry, money-grubbing man.

"You are?" Her eyes lit up like the buzzers on top of slot machines.

I had no clue how she could be so excited over something that had led to so much pain for her.

"Yep. Come on, let's have a drink and celebrate."

We did a little more than that.

I ended up back at her mother's house, fucking Bexley on her small bed. It was the skin-slapping, aggressive, it's-been-too-long kind of fucking, not the languorous making love we'd once done. I assumed she was still on the pill, and I didn't ask any questions before diving into what I still considered to be mine. What would always be mine.

I marked her neck, and she bit my nipple, running her tongue along my chest. My skin smelled like her when we were finished. Afterward, when I dragged my clothes back on, I decided not to shower.

I had to go…her mom couldn't find me there. Not after I broke her heart.

Bexley called a cab for me, and I was gone before the sun came up or I could question my actions. As I dragged myself into the carriage house behind my dad's mansion, he sat waiting for me, questioning enough for both of us.

Of course he'd been watching me. He knew what I'd done, and threatened to take away what was mine—my partnership at Federal, and any chance at ever taking over the company.

When he demanded that I end it with Bexley, once again, I agreed. I owed it to my mom. She hadn't endured all his bullshit for me not to get that damn company. No way in hell was he going to give it to his new kids.

A month later, I heard Bexley had married Seth, the jerk she'd been seeing. They'd gone down to City Hall and made it official. At least she didn't go to Vegas.

chapter
Twenty-Six

Aston

Present day

"I have another daughter," I said to Aidan, sitting across from him at his overpriced law firm.

"We know this already, Aston. We're taking care of all the paperwork you requested, setting up a trust fund and college-saving accounts. But we really do need to talk about the case. You're wanted for some very serious crimes. The fact you're walking around a free man is a small miracle, a gift of having money and status—"

Kicking my feet out in front of me, I stared at him. "Look, I didn't do anything. We've been over this. Someone planted that shit there and then called in the Feds. I'm out on bail because they don't have a case against me, and they fucking know it."

My hair tickled the back of my neck, and I reminded myself for the millionth time to schedule a haircut.

"This new piece of evidence definitely helps. Do you think you can get them to testify?" Aidan asked, still talking in vague terms because it was a delicate situation.

"Yes. I'll handle that. More importantly, I have a kid. A daughter. I want the prick to give up his rights, and I want visitation. I'll pay whatever Bex wants."

Aidan shook his head. "I'm pretty sure Bexley isn't going to limit visits. I'm not even sure we need to be so formal with all the paperwork, which is odd for me to be saying. Do you need to really poke the bear when it comes to this Seth guy? He could take you for a ride."

Leaning forward, I squinted. "Give him whatever he wants. Get him out of my daughter's life."

"Pardon me for saying this, Aston, but you knew she existed. You could have waded in a long time ago. What's the big push now?"

"Because she's mine and the time is right. I had to wait. My life was a mess."

"And it's not now?" Aidan stared at me, and this time it was his turn to squint.

"You know I'm working on all that other shit. But I'm free of Cass, and it's time for me to be with Bexley."

"You're a piece of work, Aston."

"Yep." I stood and gave him a salute before walking out.

Snatching my phone out of my pocket, I saw a missed call from the star witness in my case. I texted that I would call later, when I had privacy, and made my way to my car.

Aidan knew I'd wrap this up in a bow for him. Christ, look what I'd done with Piper. I had everything wrapped up tight before meeting her.

Speaking of her made me think of her mother, and I swiped my finger across my phone.

"Aston, I'm at work."

"We're going to have to work on how you answer the phone, Bex."

"Unlike you, I don't have a family business."

"I might not soon either." Smiling, I leaned against the driver's door of my car.

"Not funny."

I could sense her glaring at me through the phone. That's how it used to be with Bexley. *Easy.* She said what she meant with no care for who I was or the differences between us. We were two equals. These days, though, I could see a line that divided us. My dad made me painfully aware of that, but I let him. Now it was my time to erase it for good.

"How's Piper?" I asked.

"She's okay, more worried about Tyler than herself. That's Piper. Also worried she'll hurt Seth's feelings."

"Fuck that shit," I grumbled into the phone.

"Aston, he raised her. When he didn't have to, mind you. You have to let her come to terms with this. She's only thirteen."

I felt my brow furrowing and ran my palm against my forehead, staving off a headache. "I know. Don't you think it haunts me?"

"Look, this is all new, and she's a kid. I know you want to make up for lost time, and I'm sure you will. But you have to let her decide how and when."

Thinking about what Bexley said, I nodded.

"Are you still there? I have to get back to work, so I can grab the kids. Tyler has karate."

"Yeah, I'm here. Leaving the lawyers. If it matters, Piper is going to be well taken care of."

Bexley sighed. "I'm not sure she even knows what that means. She might think it means a limitless budget for makeup. Which I don't let her wear, for the record, so don't get any ideas."

Of course she didn't, because she was a good mom. The best. I wished my other kids had someone like Bexley, but Cass was still their mom. She'd done her best. Which reminded me . . .

"Oh, my kids are having a visit with Cass later. Denise is going to take them and stick around. Any chance we can get dinner?"

"Um, Tyler has karate. I'd have to see if I can find someone to stay with them. Are you sure?"

"Yeah, I'm fucking sure, Bexley. If I hadn't made it clear yet, I want you back. All the way back. I should've never lost you, but that's on me. This time I'm doing shit my way."

"Okay. I need to text a neighbor to look after the kids."

"What?" I ran a hand over my face. "I don't like a random neighbor coming over. Why don't I have Denise send a friend? Someone she knows."

"Aston, if you want to have dinner with me, we have to do it my way. I'm not going to bend to your rich ways. My kids have stayed with plenty of neighbors. They're fine."

Slipping into my car, I decided to take what I could get, which was a dinner out with Bexley. I'd worry about taking over matters with my kid later.

Kids. Piper and Tyler were a package deal, and I was okay with that.

"Your way, Bex, I've got it. But I'm making a reservation somewhere decent. How's eight?"

"Eight's fine. I'll deal with all of this while I'm waiting at karate."

"Looking forward to it. Be prepared for a good time. You know I don't disappoint."

I disconnected before she could respond. Knowing this version of Bexley, she wouldn't so easily accept a five-star steakhouse, or my paying, or whatever else I decided to do.

chapter
Twenty-Seven

Bexley

Present day

A ston knocked on the door, skipping the doorbell, and Piper ran through the house shouting, "I'll get it."

When I'd mentioned my getting together with Aston, an avalanche of questions had spilled from her mouth.

Is it a date?

Are you going to marry my dad?

Do you still love him?

Will we be rich?

I assured Piper it was just a dinner between two friends. I knew Aston didn't think of it that way, and we'd already had sex, but I wasn't ready to go there with him again yet.

Am I?

Tyler, worrying his lower lip, looked at me while Piper ran to the door. "What about my dad?"

"Like I said, this is a friendly dinner. Your dad is still your dad. I promise, no one is going to take that away from you," I said, pulling him in for a hug.

"Do you love me?"

For a beat or two, I considered not going to dinner. This whole situation was ripping my son apart.

"Mom? I know you do. I just want to hear it, 'kay?"

"Baby boy, of course I love you. And you'd better know it. Never forget it. You hear me?"

He nodded.

"And you need a shower. Rosalie can smell you all the way at her house." My neighbor from two doors down was going to come over as soon as she cleaned up from dinner.

"Mom, Aston's here!" Piper yelled from the hallway.

"Wanna come say hi?" I asked Tyler, but he was already on his way.

"Hey, Aston," I heard him say.

"Hey there, buddy. Little A said to ask when we can all go to the arcade again."

"Really? Can we?"

"Of course. Maybe over the weekend…if your mom says it works."

He put the last part in there for effect. I knew this because he looked up and winked while saying it. I also knew Aston and the way he loved to be in charge.

"Sunday. You're staying with your dad on Saturday."

Tyler nodded, looking somewhat disappointed. I'd have to talk with Aston about not trying to buy his affection.

"Ready?" This time it was me rushing to go.

"Where's your neighbor?" Aston asked, looking around.

"Oh, she's coming as soon as she cleans up from dinner."

"When is that?" Aston's eyes narrowed, a good sign he was about to dig in his heels.

"Soon. Five or ten minutes. She's a nursing student, so she's going to bring her work over. Kids don't need too much."

Aston blew by me and sat down on the sofa. "We'll wait. Come on, Piper, tell me about school today. You too, Tyler."

"We can stay by ourselves for five minutes," Piper said, her gaze darting between me and her newly discovered natural father. *My fierce little protector.*

"We do it all the time," Tyler said, not knowing he wasn't helping.

"Well, not anymore," Aston said sternly.

Lifting my palms, I tried to reason with him. "Aston—"

"No, this is unacceptable."

"I'm thirteen. Old enough to babysit," Piper said, undeterred by Aston's firm tone.

"We'll wait," Aston said, digging in. "Tyler, do you have a game system? I want to get a new one for Little A to keep at my place. Do you have a favorite?"

Out of nowhere, Piper said, "Aston, you're my dad, right?"

"Yes, but can I ask Tyler a question?" Aston took off the sport coat he had on and laid it over the back of the chair behind him. Most people looked uncomfortable in a crisp white shirt, but not Aston. He looked comfortable as fuck.

"That's not what I meant." Piper dug in equally as hard, crossing her arms stubbornly over her chest. "Well, I know you just met me, but I'm old enough to babysit. I passed my certification at school. Mom has Rosalie come over for her own peace of mind, but you don't have to worry too. I'm good."

Sometimes in the past when I looked at Piper, I'd find myself thinking, *Where the hell did she come from?* Now I knew.

Nodding thoughtfully, Aston said, "Okay, if you say so." Then he stood and put his jacket back on.

Pretty certain he would have debated the issue with anyone but his own daughter, I picked up my purse as Aston turned back to my son.

"Tyler? Do you want to think about it some more?"

Tyler shook his head. "No. Xbox. Definitely Xbox."

"Thanks, buddy. Let's go, Bex. Piper, you'll call if there are any problems?"

"We have a landline," I said, answering for her.

"She needs a phone."

Giving him a warning look, I said, "Later, Aston." I kissed both kids on their foreheads and walked toward the front door. "Okay, 'bye."

This isn't awkward or anything.

"You look gorgeous," Aston whispered for my ears only as I started to lock the door.

"I'm here, Bexley," Rosalie called from behind us.

We both turned and found my neighbor making her way up the walkway.

"Oh, hi," she said as she took in Aston.

"Aston Prescott," he said, and then he went and did it. As soon as he extended his hand to Rosalie, she was Jell-O for him. The guy got everyone with his charm.

Including me, even watching him *give it* to my neighbor. I was such a goner.

"Okay, we shouldn't be late," I told Rosalie. "Tyler has to shower. You just need to remind him."

"Have fun." She took in the two of us, her gaze darting between Aston and me as if she were trying to put the puzzle together.

Certain she recognized him from his recent bout of publicity, I tried not to squirm. In my heart, I didn't think Aston could do what they said he did. He might be power- or money-hungry, but drugs had never played a role with him. But there wasn't time to dwell on that.

There we were—me in a red sundress, sleeveless, but not spaghetti straps. I needed a bra these days. Aston in jeans, white shirt, sport coat, and loafers. He looked like money, and smelled like it too.

"Rosalie," Aston said, "can I give you my number? In case you need us."

"She has mine—"

"Well, I'd feel better if she had both," Aston said, interrupting me.

"Sure." Rosalie gave in, which wasn't a shocker. She whipped out her phone and was ready to input the number before I could protest again.

"'Bye," she said a few seconds later, running up to the house with new digits in her phone and a big smile plastered on her face.

"Shall we?" Aston's hand was on my lower back as he led the way to his car.

"We can just do something casual," I said. "You don't need to impress me."

"No and yes," he said while opening the car door.

"Aston . . ." I paused as I slipped into the car, not knowing what to say to that.

He shut the passenger door and made his way around the front of the car. As he settled in the driver's seat, he said, "Bexley, let's have a good night. My life is a mess, and right now, reuniting with you and meeting my daughter are all that I have."

"Don't say that," I said as he started the engine and shifted into gear.

"Why?"

"What about your kids? Please don't say what you just said, because your kids matter." When he side-eyed me, I explained. "Your other kids. The ones you've raised so far. You know what I mean."

"Mara and Little A are always a bright spot for me. Except for having to share them with Cass."

"I don't want them to hear you say that we're making you happy. They should hear that they're making you happy. They'll resent Piper, and I don't need her to have that. She's dealing with enough."

"Stop it, Bex. Seriously. No one is going to resent anyone. I love *my other kids* and they love me. They will love Piper and Tyler…and you. And they'll still see their mom because they need to do that too."

"And Tyler and Piper will see Seth. That is, if this all works, and we somehow figure it all out," I whispered as we sped down the road.

"You know that's not an option, this not working out. You know me."

"I used to," I said, staring out the windshield.

"Come on, don't do that." He didn't look at me, though. Flicking on his blinker, he exited the freeway and made a left at the intersection.

"It's the truth. We knew each other once, and then you abandoned me."

A moment later, Aston pulled into the parking lot for an exclusive steak place. I'd never been there, but I knew better than to argue in this moment.

We stopped when a valet attendant gestured us to, and Aston was out of the car in an instant, not allowing the stranger to open the door for me.

"I didn't abandon you." Aston had his hand on my lower back as he spoke into my ear, leading me into the restaurant. "Yeah, I made the wrong choice, but I thought I had time on my side. I'm here now. It's a little too late, but I have to live with that."

There was no time for me to reply because we were being ushered to a corner booth, the hostess all smiles for Aston and sneering for me.

"Janie will be right over to take your drink order, Mr. Prescott."

We were left alone to slide into the booth next to each other, thigh to thigh, heat radiating between us and menus spread in front of us. But it was impossible for me not to stare around and take this place in.

"Come here a lot?" I asked, not turning to face Aston.

"I do. Usually for work. Here or the club. My dad still lives over there, on the golf course."

"Oh. Good for him," I said, unable to hide my sarcasm.

"He's not going to bother you. I made sure of it. I swear, Bex."

"Whatever. I got over him a long time ago. Right about the time he judged me, thought of me as being a lesser person, all because I didn't have seven figures in the bank. Long before he tried to buy my silence over Piper. I didn't need his money to raise her."

"No, you didn't, and I don't mean that in a derogatory way. You did what any decent, good mother would do to protect her daughter. *Her child.* Look," he said, taking my hand in his palm, his smooth, well-manicured hand enveloping mine. "I was an ass. I can't deny that. But I've lived for years being miserable. Other than the kids being born, my smiles were all fake. I'm here to make this right. For you. For Piper."

"And Tyler."

"Absolutely, he's part of all this. And my dad doesn't get to be a part of any of it."

"Does he even want to meet Piper?" I swallowed the lump in my throat. *Why did I ask that?*

"It's off the table, even if he wanted to. I wouldn't permit it, Bexley, you have to know that. The company is mine in a few short months. And no, don't bring up this bullshit charge against me. I'm about to get out from under it. My dad is done, retiring soon. I fulfilled my duty, and now Federal is mine to do with what I want. And what I want is for him to be out of there and out of my life. C'est la vie, finito . . ."

Aston flicked his wrist in the air, signaling the end of this conversation. "Now, we're here to have a good time. What do you want to drink?"

"Wine? White, please." My head hurt from trying to keep up with all the nuances and major changes that had come into my life in the last few weeks. I needed wine more than ever.

"Good. Let's get a bottle."

"You're going to drink white wine?"

"No, you'll drink what you want, and then we can leave the remainder for our server. The bottles are better selections."

"That's a little crazy. I'm fine with a glass." I eyed Aston, and he dismissed my judgy perusal by burying his face in the wine list.

Our silence was interrupted by a young brunette, all cheery and bubbly. "Hi, I'm Janie. Welcome to Saddlebrook's. Have you been here before?"

Aston said, "Yes, you know I have, Janie."

Feeling out of place, I simply shook my head.

"How about this bottle of chardonnay? Bin number forty-three," he said, glancing at her as he pointed to a line on the wine menu. "And a Lagavulin, straight up, for me." Turning toward me, he asked, "Are you good with the chef selecting our dinner and sending it out in courses, so we don't have to be interrupted anymore?"

In absolute disbelief that this was my current life, I nodded.

"Great. Now we can get on with our evening." His full attention and blue eyes on me, Aston took my hand and kissed it. "Aston Prescott."

"That doesn't work on me anymore."

He leaned close, his thigh singeing mine, his lips tickling my ear. "If I stuck my hand inside your panties, would you be ready for me? My guess is you're dripping for me."

As I squeezed my legs together, I shook my head, smirking.

"Yeah, you would."

"Aston," I whispered. "We're two grownups now, with four kids and two marriages between us. We have to act like it."

Tucking a lock of my hair behind my ear, he said, "We can have some fun, Bex. An evening out. You look so beautiful, even more so than when we first met."

"Older, maybe a little wiser?" I said, but considering where I was sitting and the fact I'd already slept with Aston, probably not so much.

Janie appeared with the bottle of wine and poured it quietly, then served Aston his Scotch. She'd obviously received the DO NOT DISTURB message.

"Tell me what I've missed when it comes to you, Piper, and Tyler." Aston held his glass in the air and waited for me to clink glasses with him.

"From what I gather, not much, with your guy following me around."

"Ha. I'm sure there's been plenty. For the record, when Piper had her appendix removed, I almost stormed the hospital."

After taking a gulp of my wine, I answered honestly. "That was a brutal time. Seth confirmed that she wasn't his, something he long believed to be the truth. He knew it somewhere deep down, but she's easy to fall in love with. Believe me, Seth isn't an easy man. He comes across that way, but he isn't. Piper softened him."

"She looks exactly like me, Bex. Pretty hard not to know she's not his," Aston said with a wink, dismissing any discussion of Seth's character.

"Yep, she was a daily reminder of you. Every time I looked at my daughter, I was reminded about your being gone. In reality, this was hardest on me, like I couldn't move on. Seth knew it. I know you'd prefer not to talk about him, but Piper not being his was a bitter pill for him to swallow."

Aston nodded, holding back his snark this time.

"She got the best of us, Aston. She really did," I said, feeling my eyes get misty.

"She's spectacular, from what I can tell."

"She really is."

Aston turned my face toward his with the tip of his finger. "Go on. Tell me more."

"She's so marvelous. Pragmatic, deep thinking, caring like you...when you're not being forced to choose between your lifelong goals and someone you fell in love with. Someone you shouldn't be with," I said, feeling compelled to throw the last part in. It had burned in my chest for so long.

"She's a better person, I'm sure. If I teach her one thing, it will be not to sacrifice her own happiness for some stupid family business. She can build her own empire."

"You could have too. Built your own," I said, swallowing close to fifteen years of resentment. "Plus, Piper's wise beyond her years. I'm sure most parents say that, but I mean it. She's pretty inside and out. The way she cares for Tyler. All of her. She's the best. She'll find her own way," I quickly added, not giving Aston a chance to argue.

"Which is why I don't want my father anywhere near her. Don't ignore what I said, Bex. I will tell her to find her own happiness."

I nodded more for appearance's sake and took another sip of wine.

Our first course arrived, a cold soup. Vichyssoise. I knew what it was from my time working at the club.

For Aston, it was another dinner out, but for me, it was a special night. Here we were, sipping soup in silence, his warm palm on my thigh. I tried to reconcile it all.

A Caesar salad was made tableside a few minutes later.

"This is better than the soup," I said. "I love Caesar."

"Good, I want you to enjoy yourself. You deserve it and more, Bex, and I'm going to use all I've got to make sure that every day is magnificent for you, going forward."

There was no rebuttal to that, so I ate my salad.

"By the way, is that job of yours safe?" he asked. "Do you worry about it? Did Seth?"

And here we go with Aston taking over. I knew it would only be a matter of time.

I did my best to skirt around the issue and move the conversation to lighter, easier topics. As the courses arrived, wine flowed, and we laughed more.

"Milly's kids are wild," I said, grinning. "She got her payback, definitely."

"Yeah, Mike's mentioned they're a handful for her. He does pretty well with them, and he was no angel either."

"Like you were."

"Hey, my kids are pretty dang good."

Noticing a sadness creeping into his tone, I asked, "What's wrong?"

"They're good because of Cass. And despite her. She's a mess because we're always fighting. I've done my fair share of shit. They think they need to behave so we love them, or some bullshit like that. It's what the therapist says."

I took his hand and rubbed my thumb over his. Sparks always flew between us, but this was more. A river of feelings flooded the space between us. We'd cared about each other for way too long. It wasn't in my DNA to allow him to be sad.

"I think being with you now will be good for them," I said, not knowing what the hell I was saying. After all, Aston could be taken away from them at any moment.

"I have my limitations, I know. I spend too much money, spoil them, and depend on Denise and other sitters she knows, but I'm stable when it comes to them. Someone is always there for them. Food is ready and available. I don't embarrass them in public. Shit, other than the accusations. But you know what? I love them."

"Sometimes that's the best thing you can give. Love. Unconditional love."

Our fingers entwined, he squeezed my hand, then reached over and tucked a strand of hair behind my ear. His lips ghosted my cheek, my ear, and back to my cheek.

"I like this. Talking with you. Hashing things out. I probably shouldn't say this, but Cass and I never did this. Never saw anything the same or even listened to each other. I threw money at every problem, just like my dad always does."

"We always listened to each other," I said, wishing his lips were back on me. Instead, I drank some more wine, took a bite of filet, and continued to listen.

"We did. And I don't want you to think that I'm doing the same with my kids. Throwing money at them, like my dad. I just want them to have fun, be kids, not worry. I try to give them attention and affection too. I'm learning."

"You're doing just fine. And like you said, you're going to beat all these allegations. They will be fine too." As I said it, though, I knew I was saying it more for myself than for him.

His lips found my cheek again. "Thank you."

And then we went back to laughing until dessert.

"Milly's up to no good," he said over coffee.

"What do you mean?"

"You don't know?" He raised an eyebrow.

"No, I don't. How would you know? Through Mike?"

I truly had no idea what Aston was getting at, but he'd never liked Milly much.

"Eh, forget it. It's probably just club gossip."

"Now, I remember your PI saying something . . ."

"It was nothing."

I was liking my chocolate cake too much to think about it anymore. After all, club gossip was only true about ten percent of the time.

Later, we pulled up in front of my house. Instead of getting out right away, we sat in the car, the engine idling and our minds racing.

"I want to come in," Aston said, speaking the words of a teenager with the determination of a grown man.

Shaking my head, I said, "We can't."

"Denise will stay with the kids. They're fine for one night."

Turning to face him, I was brutally honest. "This has nothing to do with your kids, Aston. How dare you?"

"Piper and Tyler will adjust. We have to move forward."

Throwing my door open, I wanted to get the hell out of the car and forget this night ever happened.

"Wait," Aston said, taking my arm and holding me in place. "Tell me what I said wrong."

"You're so goddamn presumptuous. Always have been. Yeah, I fell into bed with you at the engagement party, and look what that got me."

"What? A beautiful daughter? Now I'm here, wanting to be a permanent part of your life. Can't see how that's a bad thing, Bex."

Moonlight shone softly into the car, lighting his perfectly blue-blue eyes, his white shirt as bright as the moon itself.

"Forgive me for questioning this all," I said sharply, "and not being a sure thing after an expensive dinner."

"Don't do that. You always go to money."

"Well, your dad ripped us apart once. And now you might go to prison."

"I told you I've got that covered."

"And there's this little thing…Piper's a young woman," I shrieked, and then lowered my voice as I shut the car door to give us more privacy. For all I knew, she could be watching from the same window I'd waited in not too long ago. "She can't see me hooking up with men. I don't bring men back to my bed when the kids are home. Scratch that—I don't bring men home to my bed, period."

"I'm her father, for fuck's sake." Aston pinned his gaze on me. His stare was hard, the complete opposite of his gentle palm caressing my thigh.

"No, just no. Aston, accept it. Kiss me good night and let me go inside."

If I were being truthful with myself, what had me going was how much I wanted him to come in. To take charge of my body, in my bed, both of us sweaty and sated, falling asleep in each other's arms.

"That's what I want," he said. "More than anything."

"What?" My eyes flew open wide. "Did I just say that out loud?"

He nodded. "Look, I hear what you're saying. I didn't get it…I've only been a parent to a teenage girl for a few days. I don't know all that involves. Right now, I'm going to kiss you, go home and smoke a cigar, and go to sleep. Probably after handling my own business, which I'm too old for. But know this, Bexley. It's not going to be long before I'm in your bed every night."

I tried to formulate a response, but Aston didn't give me time. He leaned over the console and placed his lips on mine. His kiss scorched my mouth and my body, sending past memories colliding with more recent ones. With his tongue teasing mine, he gathered me closer, making me believe in a future together.

"I've loved you all my life," he murmured. "If it takes me forever, I'm going to earn your forgiveness." He pressed his lips more firmly to mine, and I reconsidered not allowing him to come in.

"We have to stop, or we won't," I finally said.

"That would make for an interesting sight."

"Uh, yeah. I don't think so. Thank you. Don't worry about walking me up. Let's leave this casual with the kids and all that," I told him as I got out of the car.

"Bexley," he called to me, and I turned around on the sidewalk. "You don't have to say it back. I know you still love me."

I simply turned back around and walked to the door. There wasn't any response I could say to save face. He was right.

chapter
Twenty-Eight

Bexley

I'd stopped at the store on the way to school pickup from work, filling my trunk with frozen waffle fries and hamburger patties, yet I still felt the need to ask the kids for permission.

"Hey, guys. Aston, Mara, and Little A are going to come for dinner. Is that okay?" I said as Piper and Tyler slid into the car.

"Yeah, Mom. You don't have to ask," Piper said. "We know you like Aston. Dad said you've never stopped liking him, even when you were married to him."

Mentally, I growled, but I kept a smile plastered on my face. Seth had settled into a one-sided game of backhanded warfare. Problem was, he wasn't lying, so I had no right to argue with his stance.

"Guys, this is uncharted waters for all of us, and already unusual. We don't have to make it more difficult. Let's try to get along. I'm doing this so you can get to know Aston and your half siblings, Piper."

"Mom, we all get along. I'm getting to know Aston, and I know Dad doesn't like it. It's fine, okay?"

Wishing my hair wasn't pulled back, I plucked the ponytail holder out, allowing my hair to shield my face from the passenger seat where Piper was sitting. "You have every right to get to know him. Seth can be hurt, but it's not his place to judge you. Only me. I mean, he can only judge me."

"Are you going to be a witch when it comes to video games later?" Tyler said, interrupting me. "Can we go to Aston's? I bet you his house is bigger, and he probably doesn't care how long we play."

"Sorry, bud, we're hosting, and I don't plan to be a witch except when it's time to sit at the table for dinner."

With Piper sufficiently distracted, playing a game on her iPod, I drove us home in silence. I hadn't wanted to go to Aston's. Piper still hadn't resolved her "are we rich?" issue, and I was certain seeing his house would only stir up those feelings again.

Also, I wanted Aston to have a taste of what our life was like. His kids would probably be shocked and hate it. For a second, I wondered if I was self-sabotaging…and then we were home, and I had too much to do to worry.

With the table set and fries in the oven, I was prepping some veggies to go on the grill before the burgers when the doorbell rang. Of course, Piper yelled she would get it, and before I knew it, four pairs of feet were running through the house, and a deep voice greeted me.

"Hey."

"Hey, you." I looked up from slicing veggies.

"I wish you would have let me host. Denise could have helped, and you wouldn't have had to go to all this trouble." Aston came up behind me, pulling me away from the cutting board into his warmth, his lips traveling the nape of my neck.

"Aston," I whispered. "Stop with the PDA."

"No. I've waited all day to say hello to you properly."

He spun me to face him and kissed my lips. Tenderly at first, and then harder.

"Piper took Mara to her room so she could braid her hair, and the boys are probably halfway to catatonic in front of a video game," he mumbled against my mouth. "Kiss me."

So I did. On a breath and a sigh, my mouth opened, and his tongue slid in. With my back cutting into the counter, we kissed like long-lost lovers.

Oh, right, that's exactly what we were.

Aston broke free first. "How was your day?"

For a second, I was sad he ended the kiss, even though I'd initially fought it. "It was good. Busy. Yours?"

"Great. I'm back to working big deals, and about to close a partnership with the largest cruise line sailing. We would handle all their business on a five-year contract."

"Wow." Taking in the sparkle in Aston's eyes, I said, "You know what? You were made to do this. Seeing you excited like this, I don't regret you picking the company over me." And I think I actually meant it.

"I could've done both."

"Maybe. Maybe not."

"I also got a huge break in the case. We're going to be in court next week in front of the judge for a preliminary hearing. I'm hoping he'll dismiss the charges. Make it all go away."

"I don't think I even want to know," I lied, but I really did. My body and mind craved some type of assurance that Aston was going to beat this.

"When I'm all freed up, I'll tell you everything. Promise. But now, are you sure I can't sneak you into a bathroom and take care of you? I'll put my hand over your mouth to cover your moans."

"Aston." Not sure if it was a need-filled moan or a scolding one, but his offer did sound appealing.

"Come on. Let's chop these vegetables." He gave me the out and made his way toward the cutting board.

"You cook? The surprises keep coming."

As he skillfully sliced the squash, I grabbed a pepper. For a few minutes, we worked in silence side by side, and I imagined this was what it would be like if we really ended up together.

"One sec," I told him. "Let me light the grill."

Making my way out the back door, I flicked the gas on the in-ground grill, watching the grates burst into flame.

"Of course you know your way around a grill. You were always a girl with many talents."

"Um, we have to eat, Aston. The kids and me."

"Did Seth ever cook for you?" His question might as well have been plucked from the sky. Aston might be a lot of things, but jealous wasn't one of them.

"This was his," I said, pointing at the grill. "Sadly, he didn't use it much because we only got it shortly before he moved out. But no, he didn't cook much. He worked."

I took in Aston, wearing another white shirt, dark jeans, pristine Adidas sneakers, and quickly glanced down at my jeans with the hole in the knee, and my black off-the-shoulder tee. We were a mismatch. I was grilling burgers, and he would probably call for delivery or hire a caterer.

"Don't do that."

"What?" I asked.

"Mentally calculate all the reasons we don't belong together. I can see your mind churning, Bex." He didn't get in my personal space, rather looked me dead-on, and waited until I settled down.

Blowing out a breath, I finally spoke. "I can't help it. This is so surreal."

"Enjoy it. Let's toss those veggies on—"

"I can do it."

"News flash, so can I. Let someone take care of you, Bexley."

Later, I yelled for all the kids, and they came tumbling out of wherever they were hanging out and gathered around the table. Mara stared with wide eyes at Piper, taking in every movement, every syllable spoken. To say she was smitten was putting it lightly. Little A and Tyler laughed and joked while wolfing down burgers.

"These are good," Little A said with a mouth full of French fries.

"Hey, buddy, chew your food," Aston said sternly.

"We're just boys," Tyler said, defending his new friend.

"Who should chew their food," I said, chiming in.

After swallowing and taking a swig of soda, Little A grinned. "The fries are good, though."

"We never have these at home," Mara said. "It's always broccoli, and more broccoli."

"Broccoli is important to stay healthy and grow. Tonight's just a fun night. Like if we went out for pizza," I said, defending myself.

Aston squeezed my knee under the table, and if I weren't so nervous, the squeeze would have made other parts of me flutter. "Mara, Denise always makes you a healthy meal. If you want fries, we'll plan to get some, but I think you probably have enough when you're at the mall."

Mara's mouth dropped open. "Dad, that's supposed to be a secret between Denise and me."

"Then tell Denise not to put it on my credit card."

This made Piper laugh, and I watched Aston take it all in. Her happiness appeared to consume him, and the smile stayed on his face. Then she proceeded to launch into a huge discussion about the mall—her favorite stores, the smoothies at the food court, and a jumpsuit she'd been wanting, but she was waiting for it to go on sale.

This time, it was my turn to squeeze Aston's knee when he leaped into asking where it was from. He'd buy it for her at full price, right this second, if he could.

"American Eagle," Piper said.

"Never heard of it," Aston said.

"Oh, it's jeans and shirts and sweaters and socks. Ya know, everything. All the cool kids wear it. It's expensive, though. Mom took me for my birthday last year because I got a gift card."

Aston pulled out his phone. "What's it called again?"

"We don't usually have phones at the table." Piper looked at Aston, then me, and back to Aston.

"I'm sure we can make a quick exception. I want to make a note of this store. I'm getting to know Piper," he said, turning to appeal to me.

"American Eagle," Piper said again.

"Do you know it?" Aston looked at Mara while he typed.

She nodded. "Denise goes there for her niece."

"Where have I been? I've never heard of it. Now that problem is solved." He turned his phone so we could see he'd pulled up the website.

"Piper, why don't you show Mara the jumpsuit?" As he passed the phone toward Piper, I made a mental note to speak with him later.

"Oh, that's pretty." Mara sighed at the screen once Piper had found the jumpsuit, and Aston reached for the phone.

"Let me see."

Tyler rolled his eyes. "Mom, can we go play games? This is so boring."

"Let them," Aston said. "They ate. Loved it."

"Clear your plates," I said to the boys, and Little A gave me a confused look. *Uh-oh.*

"Come on, let's toss our dishes in the sink." Tyler stood up, either not noticing Little A's confusion or was pretending not to.

Little A watched Tyler, following suit, and off they went.

"Done!" Aston exclaimed, and I realized I'd missed the whole phone interaction while stalking Little A's movements.

"Oh my God! Thank you!" Piper jumped up from her seat and threw her arms around Aston's neck from behind. She leaned forward and planted a kiss on his cheek, the messy bun on top of her head falling forward, meeting Aston's mussed hairline.

Aston closed his eyes as soon as her lips met his skin. A moment's peace rolled over his face, smoothing all the lines in his forehead. He'd waited years for this. At least, that's what I imagined.

Deciding to let the impulse purchase be for the moment, I told Piper, "I can't wait to see it."

"Mom, I can wear it to the dance! Misty Crawley is going to be so jealous."

"Piper, that's not a reason to be excited." This type of attitude I wouldn't tolerate. "Remember what I told you? I grew up wanting for everything, and it's never fun to be that person."

"Yeah, but Misty isn't even nice."

"Yeah, yeah," I said, giving Piper a disapproving look. "You don't know what's going on in her life, so take it easy."

Piper nodded and went about gathering her plate and Mara's. "Bring the glasses," she told Mara, who complied, although I suspected she'd never been told what to do.

"Let's go paint your nails," Piper said to Mara, and then turned to Aston. "Can we?"

"Sure," he said. "Let them dry, Mar."

With all the kids back to their earlier pursuits, Aston and I were left alone with the dirty dishes. I headed for the sink and turned the water on, and was rolling up my sleeves when he came up behind me, his arms sliding around my middle for the second time this evening.

"Let me do it," he said, his voice rumbly.

"When was the last time you did dishes?" I turned to face him, and he swallowed my words with a kiss.

"It's been a while, I admit," he said, his lips brushing mine. "I'd like to get you someone to help here. This is all too much for you."

"Stop. This is my life, my kids' lives. Pitching in is how we do it."

He brushed a strand of hair off my face and stared at me. "I don't deserve you. I know I don't. But I want you, all of you, nonetheless. And I'm going to have you."

"Aston . . ."

"You're good for me," he said softly. "Great for my kids. I know you can't or won't replace their mother. But you're all good, Bex. I want to be as good for you."

He didn't allow for a reply on my part. He kissed me, close-mouthed, making a promise to be good or better without saying it. Then he simply said, "Move over," and loaded the dishes in the dishwasher.

It was a sloppy and imperfect job, but it was done while I sipped the rest of my wine. It had been a while since I'd been cared for, and this small action plugged a hole in my heart I didn't know was there until this moment.

"See? You gotta let someone do something for you sometimes. Now I'm going to take my kids home to get ready for bed with Denise, and then I'm coming back to get you ready for bed."

I opened my mouth to argue, and Aston held up his hand.

"I'll be discreet."

chapter
Twenty-Nine

Bexley

My hand shook as I opened the front door. Here I was, a living and breathing cliché, getting ready to sleep with the former love of my life while my kids were asleep down the hall. My long-lost ex-boyfriend stood in my doorway, waiting for me to invite him in for a secret late-night rendezvous. A freaking booty call.

I was everything I'd never wanted my daughter to be—other than in love. I'd truly been in love with Aston for forever, and in this moment, I didn't care how long we lasted. I needed to feel him, give myself to him, even if for one last time.

My job was to console him, to take away his hurt and ease my own. My happiness should be first, but at the moment, I was all about him. My heart beat *Aston, Aston, Aston.*

With the door closed behind us, Aston spun me toward the banister and worked his mouth over mine again. His left hand held me still as the right traveled down my back and up again. On its second descent, he tugged at the hem of my tank and pulled it over my head.

"Adore this, missed it so much," Aston said as he dropped to his knees in front of me.

He kissed my stomach while his hand came over my breast, his thumb moving slowly over my nipple. His tongue lingered around my navel and then journeyed south. He used his free hand to unbutton my jeans and toss off his jacket. Guiding me toward the third or fourth step, he gently set me down and shimmied my pants off, and I heard my flip-flops fall to the floor. My panties followed next.

Dazed, I sat there, the carpet rough against my bare ass, thinking I'd never done anything like this with Seth in the house we bought together. Not even remotely close, even though we'd been sort of happy at one point.

Giving my head a slight shake, I pushed thoughts of Seth far out of my mind as I watched Aston shrug off his shirt. He knelt before me, revealing a tattoo of a crest covering his heart.

That's new. With a trembling finger, I traced the outline. It was filled with ancient symbols and letters within letters, but in the center was what looked like an A and a B entwined.

"For you," he said when he saw me staring at it.

"Aston . . ." A tear fell from my eye.

"Don't," he said. "Not now."

With a stroke of his thumb, the salty drop was gone, and his lips were back on mine.

His mouth began to move down my body for a second time until he was crouched between my thighs. He covered me with his hot breath before bringing the tip of his tongue to my most sensitive spot. I nearly shot off the step on a long moan. I'd definitely never done this before—on the stairs, bare for anyone to see. The kids could wake up and want a glass of water. Unlikely, considering they slept like the dead, but still.

"Shh," he said, stilling me with a hand on my hip and continuing his assault on my most sacred part.

I came fast and hard, a long-awaited moment of ecstasy after over a year with just my vibrator and hand.

I needed to remember this, savor it, because it might never happen again. Aston could disappear from my life as quickly as he'd reappeared. Prison. His father. Everything was stacked against us, but I couldn't bring myself to care. I'd held out long enough.

I'd wanted to draw out my release, but as soon as he slid a finger inside me, I was nothing more than years of want and desire bursting, huge waves of ecstasy and emotion roiling inside me. The stair digging into my back was nonexistent, didn't matter. My mind only calculated how many hours we had until the kids woke up.

There wasn't enough time to get my fill—not even close. There never would be.

Aston kissed me, my taste on his tongue, and I found myself wanting him all over again. I needed him inside me. Everywhere, touching every nerve, stretching and filling me.

"Let's go to my bed."

I tried to stand but wobbled when I finally made it to my feet. Aston steadied me, his hand on my hip, and took my hand to lead me upstairs.

"On the left," I told him.

In my room, I heard his zipper being undone and then his pants hit the hardwood. My back landed on the bed, and I watched as he squeezed his length, pumping his hand up and down before sheathing himself.

And then he was inside me. Deep, perfect, snug…it was as if he'd never left.

He knew what I needed, and he did it without prompting. Our bodies moved in sync, finding all the spots and the exact speed we needed, loved, and had discovered years ago. My hands ran down his back and scratched their way back up as he pumped into me. He sucked on my earlobe and moaned words meant only for me.

I wrapped my leg around his waist, digging my heel into his ass. He braced himself on one hand and dove deeper, taking long, leisurely strokes in and out. His pace quickened, and my heel dug harder, encouraging him. Sweat lined his brow and gathered in the small of my back.

The room swirled with lust and smelled of passion. Moans cascaded against the walls, and we came. Hard, together, as one, like we had so many times in the past.

It was a while before Aston stilled on top of me, still pulsing inside me. When he tried to slowly pull out, I kept my foot in place, digging a little harder.

"One more second," I asked of him. "Stay."

I didn't know if I'd ever feel this satiated again. Whether Aston wanted to face it or not, he was in trouble. Not to mention, I was sure his father was about to freak the fuck out. If he wasn't on his way here already, ready to tear us apart. He might do it himself or send someone. Who knew how many people he had watching us?

Aston kissed my lips tenderly and muttered, "Beautiful, let me clean up, grab our clothes, and I'll be back." He didn't take his eyes off of mine as he slid out of me, keeping his hand on the end of the condom.

I watched as he padded off to the adjoining bathroom, only closing my eyes when he was out of sight.

I couldn't question what I'd done. It was as if a force larger than us drew us together. It had been perfect, special, earth-shattering. I couldn't allow my overactive mind to ruin it.

I only feared a force was working against us at the exact same moment.

chapter
Thirty

Aston

Being with Bexley was more than I expected. Or deserved.

The way she held me—it was if I were the only man she'd ever wanted to hold on to. That did something to me, especially since it had been way too long since I'd been held in a meaningful way. Probably since I was last with Bexley, to be honest.

It made me want to roar and puff out my chest, but there wasn't time for that. Past shit, ghosts from years ago, haunted us, and we needed to escape them for good.

Her hands, fingers, toes, everything belonged to me. And there was no denying Bexley owned me.

After I tossed the condom in the wastebasket, I grabbed our clothes and two waters, and made my way back to her. She was curled on the bed, her eyes closed, drifting off to sleep. I crawled in on the other side and curled up behind her, pulling her close and whispering, "Beautiful Bexley," in her ear.

She sighed, and her breathing evened out. She must have been exhausted. I never remembered a round of sex knocking her out. It didn't matter if she was older…she was ragged with emotion and overworked.

I closed my eyes, curled up close behind her, and must have drifted off to sleep myself.

"Aston, wake up."

I felt someone shaking my shoulder.

"Aston."

My eyes opened, and I found Bexley seated on my side of the bed, her ass next to my dick.

"It's almost six," she said. "Your phone's been buzzing up a storm for the last hour, but I let you sleep. You have to go. The kids get up soon, and I need to get them to school and myself off to work."

I pulled her down for a kiss, murmuring, "I don't want to go."

"You have to. Plus, you have to check your phone. It's been going nuts."

She stood and went over to the vanity and combed her hair. It was the type of domestic bliss I was sure she'd always imagined for us, just not under these sneaking-around circumstances.

I rolled out of bed, semi-erect, willing myself to go down. Snagging my pants, I checked my phone. I'd missed three calls from my assistant and one from Doug Pyle. He'd also texted *Call me.*

I shoved one leg into my pants and then the other, taking my time watching Bexley slip into a pair of flats. She'd already put on sexy-as-fuck pencil skirt and a white button-down.

"Everything okay?" she asked, her words coming out shaky. I didn't say it wasn't okay; that I wanted to get back in bed and rip her skirt to shreds, enjoy my morning . . .

"Why are you nervous, Bex?"

"Because the last time I slept with you, you disappeared, and I…I ended up having a baby. Alone."

"And that's because? You what, didn't tell me?"

"Forget it, forget I said anything. I was lost back then, feeling dejected. I thought I was doing you a favor. I knew the score. I'm just worried about now."

She thought she could blow off my questions, and I let her believe it.

"Well, this time I'm not going to disappear. I'm going to be back again and again until I'm with you all the time. You won't be lost ever again."

"Aston, I'm a big girl now, a grown-up. I can't afford to get lost with two kids."

"I get it, but I'll be damned if you do anything alone ever again."

Ignoring my threats, she walked out of the room without asking me to clarify what I meant, which was good. I didn't know what I was threatening. Or promising.

Stumbling down the stairs, I followed Bexley to the front door.

"I don't think we should say or do anything radical until you get your life cleared up," she said as I stood in the threshold.

"More bull. I'm not waiting much longer."

"We've slept together once, Aston. It hardly gives you reason to boss me around."

"Go have some coffee," I told her.

"Don't change the subject." She tried to look at me defiantly, her eyes squinting, her hair a wild mess all around her face. Instead, she looked ethereal.

"You fell asleep in my arms, Bexley. Felt like you hadn't slept that hard or content in a long time. You did that with me, and I'm pretty sure you haven't done that with anyone else. So I'll tell you again, go have some coffee."

She scowled and stared out the window.

"You know I'm right, so I'll gladly take charge of what I should've done a long time ago. You hear me?"

Her head swung back toward me. "What about your kids?"

"They'll adjust. All of them. I told you, kids are resilient."

"What does that mean? Were you?"

"It means exactly what I said. All the kids will be fine. And yeah, I was. I was just stupid."

"Go," she said, lightly shutting the door in my face.

Yeah, she wanted to slam it, but the kids were sleeping. *Thank fuck.*

chapter
Thirty-One

Bexley

Much like the summer of my eighteenth birthday, Aston stealthily crept into my heart and my bed with little to no coercing. Despite my attempts to be strong, to stick to my firm resolve, he enraptured me…mind, body, and soul.

Or perhaps I never let him go.

Inside this older man—slightly more distinguished, complete with laugh lines—was the same younger man I fell for. Yes, he was still bruised from his parents' divorce, beholden to his mom in some ridiculous sense of duty, but this version was trying to allow himself to love fully, something he didn't let himself do way back when.

We lay in my bed, our bodies twisted and spooned together, our limbs tangled as weak moonlight seeped through the window. His fingers walked down my back, touching each of my vertebrae, sending chills down my spine.

"You need to get over this Seth thing," I said, feeling the need to clear the air. For me, and for Piper.

Aston pushed up against the headboard. "Um, I'm pretty sure you're not supposed to bring up a strange man when you're in bed with a different one.

This one, may I remind you, being the one. The only one."

I sat up next to him and took his hand in mine. "First, Seth isn't a strange man. He's my ex-husband, so you need to get good with that. Second, we have to talk about this at some point, because if we don't, Piper will feel it, and she won't like the strife. She's a sensitive soul, wise beyond her years. She'll internalize this, analyze it, and will come to nasty conclusions. And, may I remind you, I tried to discuss this at dinner."

Tyler and Piper were at Seth's for a movie night. Piper had arranged it, mostly to make Tyler happy. Mara and Aston Junior were at their mom's with Denise. This was my new reality, as surreal as it felt, and I had to adjust to all the logistics.

In reality, Seth didn't care whether the kids slept over, and Aston's kids didn't care about going with Cass, but we were doing what was right. Or at least what we believed to be right.

Aston turned his head toward me and his lips met my temple. Sliding his hand behind my rumpled hair, he pulled me close and kissed me.

"You can't just ignore me," I mumbled against his mouth.

"I know," he said, looking into my eyes. "I'm reminding you that I'm the one. I don't like Seth because he took my love away from me. It's an ego thing."

I scoffed. "You gave me away."

"Okay, okay. But he also had my daughter for thirteen years when I didn't, and I don't like that. You have to understand, Bex."

My lips fused to his forehead, where I gave him a long kiss full of promise for years to come. In typical fashion, I comforted Aston. It was a role I couldn't seem to shake, no matter how independent a woman I became.

"Look," I said, "I'm trying to do right by him. He's not been the best recently, but he was mostly there, and had a lot to accept when it came to Piper. Somewhere inside him, he's a good guy, but he lost some of that along the way. Maybe because of me, I don't know, but I have to be sensitive to it."

Aston's mouth turned up into a half smirk, half smile, and he took my cheek in his palm. "Didn't we have such a great night? Dinner, un-fucking-real sex, and I get to sleep over. Let's not ruin it."

He tried to kiss me, but I pulled back.

"No, it doesn't work that way, Aston. You can't sweet-talk your way out of the hard discussions. Especially now, with all these kids. Who, by the way, you think are going to be just fine. Yes, dinner was amazing. I love DeGiorgio's. The wine, the homemade pasta, and the sex, all of it was decadent, but we need to talk about this. You need to bury your feelings when it comes to Seth. Piper needs to know you support him, because he's not going anywhere. He's Tyler's biological father. He raised Piper until now, and he took care of me."

"And now I take care of you. You get that, right?"

"Aston! Come on, get with me here. Say you understand what I mean. This is about your daughter."

"If I do, can we have sex then?" Aston was smiling, and I knew he was joking, but I needed him to pay attention.

"Ouch!" He yelped when I pinched his arm.

"Say it," I said. "We need to be clear on this. I need to be transparent, and you're joking."

"I hear you. I'll be nice to Seth. I'm only joking because this fucking hurts. This cracks my chest in half, Bex. All this disappointment and destruction was because of me."

"I get that, but when it comes to the kids, we have to put that all aside. Even if Seth's not nice to you," I said, needing to cover my bases.

"As long as he's nice to you, I'll be nice to him. I swear. Deal?"

"Deal." Without waiting for him to ask again, I kissed him.

"I love you. Always have," he murmured. "You know you're going to get anything you want for the rest of my life," he said, stalling the kiss.

"I don't want much, and I don't need a lot. You have to get that it's not me. I understand why you needed the business, and keeping the life you were used to, but I wasn't used to that."

"It was foolish. I sacrificed my happiness for my mom's…I know this. All I'm left with is a shit show."

The palm of his hand grazed my naked back. We were front to front, bared to the depths of our souls. It was the most honest moment we'd ever had.

"I'm sorry you felt you had to do that," I said, running my hand through his rumpled hair. I loved that he left it a little longer. It showed his boyish side, but I had to remind myself that he was accused of a serious crime.

Addressing the elephant in our lives, I said, "Scratch that I don't want much. I want you to be free of this. I feel like I'm loving you on borrowed time."

"I didn't do it," he quickly said.

"I know you didn't. In my heart, I believe you wouldn't jeopardize something you've given your whole life for. Your happiness, your being, everything."

"Exactly," he said before fusing his lips to mine. "I knew you believed me."

"But what are you going to do? Yeah, the media has died down, but this is serious, Aston. How are you going to beat this while you're wasting your time and resources on me?"

"Hey." He squeezed my butt. "I'm not wasting shit. I told you, I have a key person who's going to clear me. I was going to share, but I can't. It will compromise you and them. I'm not keeping secrets, but my lawyer and my PI are the only ones who know the details, and I need to keep it that way."

"Because your PI has so much free time now?" Now it was my turn to joke. It was similar to nervous laughter—if I didn't make jokes, I was going to fall apart.

"Yep. I get my intel on you firsthand now. It sure beats hearing from him."

"Ha-ha. Seriously, I hope this works. For your kids' sake, and for Piper."

"And you," he said. "It will, Bex. It will. Now, let's try to focus on something good, like being in bed together, me staying the night, the kids all being busy so we don't need to sneak around."

Our mouths found each other's, and our hands busied themselves with exploring each other's naked bodies. I felt Aston's moan into my mouth all the way to my core.

Raging with desire, I slid my hand under the blankets. Finding his already hardened length, I grabbed him tightly, firmly, the way he liked it, and jerked him.

"Ugh, this is so fucking sensational," he said, his head hitting the headboard. "Just like that…God, that feels…so fucking perfect."

Our lips fused tightly again, his tongue sneaking into my mouth, curling around mine, until his hand stilled mine. With his other palm on my shoulder, he urged me to get on top of him. I did as he wanted—after all, his wants mirrored mine. I seated myself on him, relishing the burn, the friction, the desire curling in my belly.

Moving slowly, Aston buried himself as deeply as he could possibly be inside me. I tipped my head back and let out a long moan. I didn't know how badly I'd missed this type of passion and human connection.

Yet, despite it feeling incredible, small anxiety butterflies flitted in my chest. I sat up and watched the two of us connecting, Aston sliding in and out of me as I moved.

I was falling hard—incredibly hard—for this man again, and besides the kids and exes, the criminal charges still loomed. Even though he'd said to relax, that he had this, I couldn't. He kept saying he had a plan, but I didn't know what it was.

"Bex, don't think so hard. It's all going to work out, babe. Ride me, make yourself feel good," Aston said, reading my thoughts.

"How do you do that?"

"I just do. It was what I was meant to do."

He pulled my face down for a kiss, and I let myself get lost in him. He was meant to be with me—I wholeheartedly believed this. If not, we wouldn't burn so brightly. We wouldn't be so intimately connected.

My body moved faster with his, sliding up and down his length.

Aston was pushing up into me, friction setting a fire between the two of us. Of course, he was hitting all the right places. It had been years since we'd innocently groped and learned our ways around each other's bodies. As an adult, Aston seemed to know exactly what to do with me, which buttons to push.

Within moments, I began to unravel, my entire body shaking with pleasure. "That's right, Bex, let yourself go."

Aston didn't need to encourage me. I wanted this. Needed this. Had to have this.

When I fell apart, Aston drove furiously into me, finding his own release. I'd never loved anyone's pleasure as much as his. Seeing him climax and then come down was a secret pleasure I didn't know existed.

Once again, we lay sated and sweaty in each other's arms. This time, we lay there quietly, enjoying the moment.

Until Aston's phone rang.

"Get it," I told him. It was after one in the morning—only emergencies happened then.

My heart raced as fast as my runaway thoughts. What if it was his lawyer? Something happened with the witness? He was being taken from me again . . .

"Calm down, Mara. Tell me slowly," Aston said into the phone.

My pulse began to calm, and then I mentally slapped myself. How selfish was I? My heart only calmed when I realized nothing was going to happen to Aston. If he'd dismissed my children, or just Tyler, in that way, I'd be furious.

Moving closer to Aston, I wrapped my arm around his back as he listened, nodding and murmuring *uh-huh* into the phone.

"What did Denise say?" he finally said. After more nodding and murmuring, he said, "Let me speak with her...Hey, Denise...No, no, she can call anytime...I know you have things under control."

He spoke calmly, but I could feel his body tensing.

"I think that's fine. Yes, you definitely should, if that's what they want. I'll call Aidan in the morning and let him know about this."

He listened a while longer, nodding to himself, taking my free hand in his and squeezing. If he only knew how insensitive I'd been, dismissing his kids and worrying about myself. Shaking myself free of those thoughts, I pulled Aston a little closer to me.

"Yep, that's good. I'll be on my way in a few...No, don't worry. You didn't ruin anything."

I tightened my grip on his shoulder. He was leaving, but for his kids. Not running.

"Oh," he said. "I could, but maybe I shouldn't. I'll check and text you, okay? In the meantime, you get on your way."

He listened for a beat longer and then disconnected the call.

When he turned to me, he looked pained, his brow furrowed and emotions rippling over his face. I'd never seen this side of Aston before, the emotionally wounded one. The last time his kids called, he'd grown angry and frustrated, but this was something entirely different.

With his fingers pinching the bridge of his nose, he blew out a long breath. "This isn't going to work," he mumbled.

I jumped away from him so quickly, I became light-headed. Bracing myself on the night table, I looked directly at Aston, resolving to be strong.

"Not us," he said, looking ashamed. "That came out wrong. Not us. We're going to work. I meant this thing with Cass. Trying to have her in the kids' lives isn't working."

"Oh," I said, sheepishly crawling back onto the bed.

"Come here." He sat up and pulled me into his arms, kissing the top of my head.

"I'm sorry," I said into his chest. "You shouldn't have to comfort me now. Tell me what happened."

"Cass was good at first. Had dinner with the kids, pretended like she was happy they were there, in that big house I let her keep. Whatever, it was the right thing to do. Anyway, she sent them to watch a movie and then proceeded to get rip-roaring drunk. Denise put them to bed anyway, but a little after midnight, Cass started tearing through the house, yelling at them."

Placing a kiss on his temple, I ran my hand down the back of his hair, pulling him tight.

"Same old shit. It was their fault that I left. Kids cramp my style. I'm a playboy . . ."

A little giggle escaped me. "Shit, I'm sorry. It's nerves."

"No, it's okay. She's not wrong. I did go down a bad path when we first separated, but that's behind me. And before you ask, I've been to a doctor and I'm okay health-wise."

I hadn't thought of it, but now that he mentioned it, it gave me pause. I'd jumped back in bed with him so easily. "It can't be good for Mara and Little A to hear all that, though," I said, getting back to the more urgent matter.

"No. Denise tells them otherwise, and so do I, but Cass gets twitchy with it. Anyway, they want to go home, and I told Denise to go ahead and take them. I'll need to call my lawyer in the morning. I tried to avoid taking visits away from Cass, but it's time. Denise has some video evidence."

"Poor babies. I hate that they had to deal with that. I understand you want them to see their mom, but this doesn't seem good for them. But I'm not qualified to make that decision." I kissed along the side of his face, watching his brow smooth out.

"I know. I don't mean you're not qualified. You're a mom, a good mom. Look, just an hour ago, we were discussing Piper. You were sticking up for her with every bone in your body, even when it meant taking sides with your ex."

"She's my daughter. That's my job," I said, defending myself now. "To watch out for her."

"You don't have to explain yourself. I admire it. I wish my other kids had that. Piper is lucky to have you. Damn lucky."

A tear trickled down my cheek, despite my demanding the waterworks stay in.

"I tried, but Cass isn't going to be a present mom. Nan said it, even though she was the one to introduce us. I guess I'm shit when it comes to evaluating moms. Look how I fell for my own. Her dying wishes still haunt me."

"She was your mom. She did her best—"

"If she didn't insist I go after heading up the family business we would have been together all these years, Bex."

As much as it hurt me to think about it, I had to grant Aston some peace.

"Shoulda, coulda, woulda. We're here now. You need to do right by your kids. My mom did her best until she died, but you already know that."

"I did, but right now, this…it just means more work for me. More to tackle. I have to get out from under these charges. I want to make this work with you. I need to protect the kids. Denise will help, but…this is all on me. My dad is a piece of shit. Nan is busy. My mom is gone, and Cass is helpless."

"Look, go now. And we'll worry about all the rest in the morning."

"Denise said for me to stay. She knows how much this night means to us. The kids are tired, and she's going to put them back to bed at my house."

"Are you sure? I'm not going to be mad," I said, and it was the truth. Worried, yes. Mad, no.

"I'm staying," he said. "I'll text Denise, and then let's take a warm shower and sleep. I need this few hours of calm before I tackle the rest."

He tapped at his phone while I rubbed his back, and then I took his hand in mine and led the way to the bathroom.

chapter
Thirty-Two

Bexley

A few days had passed since our sleepover date night that started out full of promise and ended with tension. Since then, I'd busied myself with work and near constant worry over Aston. He'd texted that the witness he procured was going to speak up in court in two days at a preliminary trial.

This whole thing was surreal—with deep pockets, Aston was still walking around a free man and tackling full custody with his kids. I had no clue what type of alternate universe I'd entered, but it wasn't one I'd grown up in.

Especially when my phone rang, and I swiped ACCEPT CALL.

"Mom!"

Piper had called from some unknown number—lucky for her, I'd picked up. Call it a sixth sense, or one of my hunches, but I knew it was important.

"Mom! Are you there?"

"Piper, calm down, what's wrong?" I tried to steady my voice. Her shrieking was freaking me out, but I had to be the strong one.

"I'm stuck in the Italian restaurant in the Village Shopping Center. Come get me, please. Hurry."

"What? Why? What happened, Piper?" I shrugged off my robe, letting it fall to the floor, and stood stark naked in my closet as I grabbed clothes. "Piper? Are you there? What happened? Why are you stuck? Where's your dad? Aston?"

A million questions ran through my head at lightning speed.

Aston had taken Piper for a daddy/daughter date, trying to give her some individual attention despite being pulled in a million different directions. I'd planned to take a hot bath and relax.

Aston wanted to get to know her, look out for his other kids, be kind to Tyler, deal with Cass, exonerate himself, and care for me at the same time. He'd murmured something about me doing some self-care while kissing me, his tongue teasing mine. There were promises about him sneaking into my bed later, with a piece of tiramisu and a crème brûlée, about feeding me and licking whipped cream off of me.

Christ, I need to concentrate on what's happening.

"Dad's gone. Aston, I mean. Mom, hurry! The police were here."

"What?" I shrieked.

Shaking, I put the phone on speaker and shoved my legs into a pair of jeans, forgetting underwear, and tossed on an old bra and a ratty white T-shirt. My flip-flops were on my feet before Piper spoke again.

"He…he…I mean, we were eating. Aston and me. Everything was great. He's so nice, the best. Then his dad, Peter, you know who I mean? Aston's dad came up to our table and stared me down. Marched right over . . ."

"Take a breath, Piper. I'm coming." Unsure how I could ask her to do something like breathe when I couldn't, I grabbed my purse.

"He said all these mean things, Peter did. Then I remembered you told me he's not nice, so I tried to ignore him. But then he said something about Dad—I mean Aston, not Seth, okay? He said Dad better get rid of some evidence he recently found, or—"

"I'm coming, baby," I told her, turning on the car, grateful that Tyler was at Seth's place.

"Mom, he said *or he would get rid of me*. Peter said that. What does that mean? Mom, are you there? He wants to get rid of me. I didn't do anything. And what does that mean?"

I was speechless. My heart cartwheeled in my chest as my daughter shrieked on the other end of the line.

Thank God I was on autopilot, backing the car out of the carport.

"I'm here. Don't worry about what that means, honey," I told her, and then told myself to not worry either. Aston was there…he would protect her, right?

He hadn't stood up to his dad in the past, though.

"Mom, listen. I'm trying to tell you what happened. Dad got so mad, he stood up and punched Peter in the face. Blood sprayed everywhere. I think his nose is broken. Dad's fine, though, but the restaurant called the police, and they took Dad with them after Peter said he was going to press charges. What does that mean?"

"I'm on my way, sweetie. Sit down and order a Coke. I'll be right there. Promise." My voice was steady, but I was anything but calm.

What kind of person told their granddaughter they would get rid of them?

And what would happen to Aston's witness now that he was in jail? His preliminary hearing was in thirty-six hours.

Just as I was pulling into the shopping center, my phone rang through the Bluetooth.

"Hello?" I said without glancing at Caller ID.

"Bex, it's me."

"What the hell, Aston?"

"I'm sorry. Things got carried away. My dad's a prick, you know."

"Um, yeah, I can't talk. I'm parking now at the restaurant to get Piper. She's scared half to death because your father said he's going to get rid of her. Do you understand what that does to a young girl?"

"Fuck, Bex, that's why I'm sitting where I am. I wanted to kill him with my bare hands. It's because of the witness. He's trying to quash it."

"You know what, Aston? I don't care."

I'd spent the better part of a week worrying, and then Aston hauled off and acted like a testosterone-filled teen. And how the hell did his father get off talking to my daughter like that? Rationally, I knew Aston couldn't control Peter, but my mom guard had shot up and wasn't going down.

"You go deal with your own mess of a life, Aston. And I'll deal with the monsoon of disappointment that, once again, you left in your wake."

I disconnected the call and tossed my phone in my purse, determined to rid myself of Aston Prescott for good.

Part 2

chapter
Thirty-Three

Aston

"Listen to me!" I pounded my fist onto the desk.

"Aston, that's not helping anything," Aidan said, grabbing my arm, and I shrugged him off me.

"Look," I said to Dan, the police officer. "Do you have kids? Because I'm not a violent man. But my father threatened his own granddaughter. Do you hear me? And that's not called for—that's wrong in anyone's book."

Stuck in an interrogation room this time, I stood up and paced, but at least I wasn't going to a holding cell like I did before.

"I understand my father wants to press charges, but that's because he wants to silence me. I have a key piece of evidence in the trial against me, and he doesn't want me to use it. We need to secure that first. Then, do what you want with me—"

"Let me talk," Aidan said, interrupting me. "Dan, let's have the chief come in, and we'll discuss this. Aston was defending his daughter, and he could also press charges against his father for threatening a minor. The man is unstable, for sure, perhaps not totally right in the head. Anyway, I spoke to the chief on the matter of our evidence, and he's dealing with this, and then I'm sure he'll be in. In the meantime, let's all calm down."

"Oh yeah, I'll calm down," I said, pacing. "The woman I've been in love with for fifteen years is mad at me. Again. The daughter I only recently got to know is accosted by my father and then witnesses me pummel him. And, oh yeah, I'm on trial for drug trafficking. Sure, I'll calm down."

I leaned against the wall and looked down at myself, my Polo wrinkled, my jeans tight and hot. I was a mess. Taking a deep breath, I tried to control myself. I had to get a handle on things, because I might have just blown everything.

Fuck, I whispered to myself, flexing my aching hand. *I shouldn't have done that.*

"Okay, Mr. Prescott," the chief said as he walked into the room, stealing all the air. "I used to see you once a year when you donated money. Now I see you all the time. No offense, but I'd like to stop seeing you."

I nodded. "Me too. This is all a misunderstanding."

"Your father's broken nose says differently."

"I can explain that, and if he wants to press charges, then so do I. He harassed my daughter, his own granddaughter, intimidating her and threatening her with bodily harm."

"I hear you," the chief said, motioning for me to sit across from him.

Wanting to be a good boy, I did.

"My daughter, who I only just met, and I were getting to know each other." My whole body shook as I spoke. "My father had the nerve to tell her he was going to get rid of her. She's a minor, and that's a viable threat, Chief."

"I understand, Mr. Prescott, but we learn in preschool not to use our hands when defending ourselves. We use our words."

"Chief, you know if it were your kid, you would do the same. Be honest, would you let someone threaten your kid?"

"I'm not the one sitting here wanted for drug trafficking, and then picked up for breaking his father's nose. In a public place, no less."

"Alleged drug trafficking," I said.

"About that. I spoke with your lawyer." The chief cocked his head toward Aidan as if they'd just met.

In reality, they grew up together. They went to the same local prep school, both two years behind me, and both from money like me. The chief hailed from a longtime family legacy in law enforcement, a dynasty that lined their pockets with healthy donations from businessmen like me.

"Let's cut the crap, Brad," I said, addressing the chief by name. "You and Aidan go way back. I've been donating to your campaigns since I was old enough to do so. I need to get out of here now, and you need to attend to the more pressing matter at hand. I have a hearing on Friday, and my goal is to get this whole fucking thing thrown out."

Brad leaned his elbows on the table in front of him. "Your dad's a powerful man. You sure what you're doing is a good idea?"

"Fuck off. Yes. I'm getting my life back together."

"Okay, fellas, let's not get off track here," Aidan said, then turned toward Brad. "Did you take care of what I needed?"

The chief nodded. "It's done, and I don't think you'll need to worry, come Friday."

"Can I go now?"

Once again, the chief nodded, and this time he stood. "Only because of your girl, Aston. I'm sure she had to be scared."

"Thanks. I'm sure by now she wants nothing to do with me. Her mother probably doesn't either." Hurrying past them, I told Aidan, "See you Friday. Be ready."

When I got outside the police station and belatedly realized I didn't have a car, I muttered, "Shit," and pulled out my phone to call Mike.

"Can you stay out of trouble for one day?" was how he answered the call.

"Fuck off." Seems that was all I was saying these days. "Listen, I'm at the police station and I need a ride. Are you in town today?"

"Lucky for you, I am."

"Good. Come and get me," I said, leaning back into the wall.

"Are you going to ask why I'm in town today?"

"Yeah…why?"

"Look, Aston, you're not the only one with problems. My fucking life is on the rocks. Milly's running around, says I don't pay attention to her, that I don't jump when she says to jump. As freaking luck would have it, tonight she got a frantic call from Bexley…who, by the way, hasn't called in weeks. You screwed her over, Piper was a mess over your dad, and Tyler was out with Seth, so she didn't want to bother her ex."

"What the fuck does she need her ex for?" Squeezing my eyes shut, I wanted to slam my fist into the brick wall.

"Is that all you can focus on? Seth? Maybe because he's been there for Bexley for years, when you weren't. And now you weren't again."

"Just get here and finish your story then." I didn't have the patience to do this with Mike over the phone. I should have called Bill, my PI, or even Cass, but for some stupid fucking reason, I wanted to talk with Mike. Maybe because he knew Bexley and Piper, and was one step closer to them?

I disconnected the call before Mike could protest, wishing for a cigarette or a bottle of Scotch.

I didn't open my eyes until I heard a car pull up and stop in front of me. Looking up, I saw Mike waiting in his Hummer. Not one for the environment, and always wanting to make it clear he had the biggest dick in the room, Mike bought a car that personified him.

After rolling down his window, he said, "Get in."

Happy to comply, I jumped in. "Talk," I said when I was seated in the passenger seat.

"Well, I'm actually just coming from Bexley's. A month ago, she hated my guts. Now she says I was right all those years to keep you two separated."

"What the hell?" I blew out a long breath. "Did you tell her she was mistaken?"

"I didn't get a chance to say much. By the way, you self-centered prick, did you hear me say Milly's cheating on me?"

I nodded, feeling the burn in my eyes. "We all knew. My guy, he knew."

Mike slammed his hand against the steering wheel. "Christ, do you ever do what's right? Do you ever think of anyone else?"

"I try. It's not my strong suit. My life was fucked up—"

"Enough of that shit, Aston. Grow the fuck up."

"I'm trying. Really."

"Look, man, you're a good dad. You were way better to Cass than she deserved. You lived your whole life for your mom. But your dad is pure evil, and I don't want to see you become him."

"That's what I'm trying not to be. Look, I'm sorry about Milly. She doesn't know what the fuck she's doing. She has a good life, and she should wake the fuck up and realize that. You're not some robot."

"Try telling her that," he said, glancing at me for a second as he drove toward my house. "She says I'm not there for her. Christ, I have to make money, and a lot of it, to support her and our lifestyle. She thinks it's easy."

I huffed at him, rolling my hand in the air to tell him to get on with it, and he glared at me but continued.

"Anyway, she calls me tonight as I'm finishing up a work dinner. Says Bexley needs help, and I need to go right away. That's our new reality. Milly says jump, and I say how high…and Bexley is fucking furious with me since the last time I saw her. Why? Because I told her you had someone watching her and knew about Piper."

"Did you go help her? What did she say?"

"She was hysterical, consoling Piper. Told me I should have never let you close, that this was my fault. I should have stopped you from intruding on their lives."

"Did you tell her I meant well? That I want to be with her, and Piper?"

"I told her how fucked up you are, confused and misguided, but you love her. Always have."

"Good. Maybe I should go there?"

"I don't think so."

"Why?" I swiveled my body to stare at his profile.

"Seth brought Tyler home, and Piper told him what happened."

"That fucking ass. She's my daughter. And that's my woman."

"For a minute, Aston. Seth's taken care of them for a long time."

We pulled up at my house, and Mike put the huge beast of an SUV into park. "You stink and you look a mess. Go shower, hug your kids, and go to bed."

"Nah, I'm going to do all of that and then go see Bexley."

"I don't recommend it. They're quieted now."

"Are you saying that to defend yourself? You put yourself back in Bex's good graces, and you don't want to ruin it? Milly is waiting to hear a good report on you? This is my life too. You've had it good for years, and now it's rough. It'll be good again. Milly will get her head out of her ass."

"No, I'm telling you to go to bed. That's all."

"Huh-uh. I'm not," I said, whipping off my seat belt once I remembered I had it on.

"Don't go there, Aston."

"Why?" I practically growled at him.

"Piper asked Seth to stay. First, she asked me, but I can't. I have to go home to Milly."

"Fuck!" I roared, slamming the dash. "Forget the shower. Take me to Bexley's. Now. I'm too fucking mad to drive."

He set his jaw and shook his head.

"Mike, you know me better than this. I'm not getting out of this damn fucking car until you take me."

Cursing under his breath, he put the Hummer back in gear, and we sped off.

chapter
Thirty-Four

Bexley

"You don't have to stay. She's asleep now," I said to Seth, my back to him while I steeped a mug of tea at the kitchen counter.

After crying on my shoulder, then Mike's, and finally Seth's, Piper wore herself out. She vacillated between being scared of and mad at Peter. Mostly, she was worried for Aston, but I wasn't. He made his bed.

Once again, Seth did the right thing. Despite being mad at me, he comforted Piper. Told her she was going to be okay, that no one was going to hurt her, saying all the right things.

"Hey," he said, tugging on my shoulder and turning me. "It's going to be okay. Piper's young. She'll get over this."

Looking at him, I wondered if I could love him again. "Yeah, but I don't know if I'll get over this."

He lifted my chin with his finger. When Seth looked at me like he did when we first got married, with caring adoration, I wondered if this was the same guy who'd refused to meet me recently for a cup of coffee.

"You need to forget about Aston. He's haunted you for too long. It's time to give him up."

"I know, but it's not that easy." As I stepped back, Seth held on to my arm. "This is weird. I don't want to talk about him with you."

"It's too late for that now," Seth said, stepping closer. "He's in Piper's life now, and I'm smart enough to know he isn't going anywhere. I'm forever connected to the guy because I care for Piper. Love her like she's my own, and she was for a while. This hurts me too."

"Ugh, Seth. This is a mess." I sighed and stepped into his arms, my tea forgotten.

Of course, at that very moment, my back door burst open and a haggard Aston appeared, ready to tear Seth to shreds.

"Get the fuck off her, dude."

His hair unruly, eyes wild, clothes rumpled, I'd never seen Aston look this disheveled.

"Sorry, Bexley, but there was no stopping him," Mike said as he begrudgingly trailed behind Aston.

"Listen, calm down." Seth stood tall, but he was no match for Aston's six-foot-plus frame.

"Don't you fucking tell me what to do." Aston stomped toward me, and I regretted not checking to see if the back door was locked. "Where is she?"

"Who?" I asked, playing dumb.

"Don't be coy."

"She's asleep, and if you don't stop stomping around here, you're going to wake her. It took us a long time to calm her down, and may I remind you, it's almost midnight?"

"I want to see her. I won't wake her."

"Why? Because you feel guilty exposing her to the asshole who is your father? Or because your childish outburst led to someone calling the cops?"

Aston didn't answer, and I dropped my face in my palms and took a long breath.

When I looked up, I said, "You all need to go. All three of you. Mike, go home to Milly. Seth, call me in the morning, and we can work out when you'll see the kids next. Aston, just go."

"No. You two can go," Aston said while waving his hand in front of the other two men who were just standing there, bearing witness to our private battle.

"I don't want to do this right now, Aston. Please."

"We're not doing anything. I'm here to see my daughter, and these other guys are leaving. I won't wake her. I'm just going to look in on her. Then I'm going to set her mother's mind at ease and take care of you. Why? Because you're mine now." Turning toward Seth, he said, "Not yours."

"Don't, Aston. It's not necessary. Seth was here tonight, and he's a part of Piper's life. He always will be, because he was there when she was born."

Seth shook his head, walking toward Aston. "Christ, you don't have to defend me, Bexley. I took care of Piper tonight because I wanted to, because it was what she deserved. I changed her diapers, bathed her, held her when she had a fever, gave her a brother, took her to her first day of school, while you," he said, glaring at Aston and pointing a finger at him, "built a business and a different life. You weren't there, and I was. Yeah, I got the shit end of it, learning she's not my daughter, and getting a divorce. I may be bitter, but you know what? I do what's right when it's needed."

"You son of a bitch. I didn't even know she existed," Aston growled out. "And that wasn't my fucking fault."

I worried this was going to escalate quickly as I watched Aston's fists clench and unclench. The last thing I needed was for him to break someone else's nose tonight.

"This is all my fault," I said quickly. "The blame is on me. Listen to me, both of you."

Aston and Seth continued with their stare-down, not bothering to even glance my way.

Frustrated, I shrieked, "Look at me!" and then clapped my hand over my mouth. I didn't need to wake Piper. Lowering my voice, I said to Aston, "Don't disregard me and my feelings. I loved you, and I thought I could love you again. Or maybe I never stopped loving you."

This got his attention, his wary eyes turning on me.

"And I loved you, Seth, very much at one point. Cared for you very much, I should say."

Seth shrugged. "I'm over the hurt, Bexley. Truly. Now I do what's right, and none of that has to do with my feelings for you."

"Look, guys, I love Piper the most. I'm her mom. I've always been there for her, and she doesn't deserve this, all this fighting between the three of us." God, I was bone tired, and I didn't have the time or patience for temper tantrums from grown-ass men.

"This isn't a debate over who loves her the most," Aston said, then spoke with authority. "Mike, leave."

Mike shook his head as he turned and walked out the back door. When he was gone, Aston turned to me.

"This is about a girl who has a lot of people who love her, and me, who was shut out of her life. I want back in."

"Not everything is always about you, Aston," I shot back, and he looked at me like he'd been punched. "Don't look at me that way. I mean it. That's the whole point…you can't punch someone in front of your daughter."

"And expect me to pick up the pieces," Seth said.

"Dude, get out," Aston said to Seth. "Seriously, get the fuck outta here. Thanks for helping. I mean it. When I calm down, I'm sure I'll appreciate it even more, but just go home."

Aston glared at Seth until he started walking toward the door.

How does he do this? Always get his damn way?

Aston turned his focus on me. "Bex, look at me." Moving to stand in front of me, he said softly, "I'm sorry. I fucked up."

I shook my head. At what, I didn't have a clue.

"I fucked up, Bex. You know how messed up I am when it comes to my dad, but the fact that you turned to him—Seth, I mean, not my father. Seth, your fucking ex." Aston spat out the name like he was choking. His expression anguished, he said, "I can't handle it. I love you. I'm sick over you turning to him. Please, listen to me."

He tried to gather me close, but I pulled out of his arms.

"Aston, please. I'm begging you, just go home. Go home to your other kids. They need you right now. Take a shower, get a good night's sleep, and deal with this drug shit. I don't need anyone to rescue me. First, Milly sent Mike here, then Piper called Seth over here, and then you showed up. For God's sake, I'm a big girl. I can handle myself."

"Can you?"

"Screw you, Aston. Yes, I can. I want you to go. Really."

"Not until I at least set my eyes on Piper."

He crossed his arms in front of his chest, his expression formidable, and I knew I wasn't getting rid of him until he got what he wanted.

"Come on and be quiet. And then you're going," I said firmly, then turned to pad my way toward Piper's bedroom.

Gently, I opened the door and motioned for him to peer inside. Piper was in a much-needed deep sleep, burrowed under the covers, her hair tangled all around her face. As quickly as I allowed him to look, I swiftly shut the door and stalked back toward the kitchen.

"Don't do this." Aston came up behind me and slid his arms around my middle.

"Aston," I said, turning and finding myself caught in his sneaky embrace.

"Please, Bex. I have a plan. My dad was messing with it, and I can't let him do that."

"Oh, you and your mysterious plan. I meant what I said, that I loved you. Love you, Aston. But this can't go on."

"It can't be over," he begged, pleading with his eyes.

So typical when it came to Aston, I found I couldn't say no to him.

"It's on hold," I told him.

I didn't move away from his arms. I couldn't. Aston was home to me, but I had to separate myself from him. I needed space. We needed a breather.

"This will be over in a couple of days. Please, Bexley."

I pulled out of his hold. "Go. Go to Mara and Aston Junior. This isn't fair to them. Relieve Denise, and take care of them."

His head hung low, and I was desperate to comfort him.

Shoving that need away, I pointed to the door. "Go."

"Will you have Piper call me tomorrow?"

I nodded. "If she wants to. Remember, Aston, this isn't about you."

I pulled the door open, and he walked out without another word.

chapter
Thirty-Five

Bexley

After a mostly sleepless night, I sat in the kitchen, drinking coffee.

"Morning, sweetie," I said to Piper when she came into the kitchen, and swiped her messy hair out of her eyes with my free hand.

"Are you okay, Mom?"

She's asking me?

"You don't have to worry about me, Piper. I'm the mom. Let me do the worrying for both of us." Setting my coffee mug down on the counter, I gathered her in for a hug.

"I was scared," she said into my chest. "But I'm not now."

"That's good. You don't have any reason to be scared. Peter's just a lot of hot air and mean words."

"Yeah, he's not so nice. I'm glad I don't have to be close with him," she said, pulling back from me.

"Do you want to stay home from school?" I asked as she opened the fridge and pulled out the juice.

"No. We're doing a project in history class, and I don't want to have to make it up."

I nodded. I didn't know where I got this levelheaded kid, but she was amazing. "I'd better go wake Tyler."

Moving across the kitchen, mug in hand, I wasn't looking forward to going to work. I needed a martini instead of coffee.

"I'll be ready," Piper called after me.

"Oh," I said, turning toward her, trying to act nonchalant. "Aston wants you to call him. Only if you want."

She simply nodded, and I let it be. It wasn't my job to force him on her or push their relationship.

I went through the motions—dragging Tyler from bed, getting myself ready, and taking the kids to school.

Finally settled at my desk, I texted Seth.

> BEXLEY: *Thanks for helping with Piper. She went to school this morning. I thought you'd want to know.*

He didn't respond other than to thumbs-up my text.

I knew better than to beg him for more. Honestly, I didn't want to get tangled up with him again, any more than I already was.

Of course, as soon as I started to do some charting and look at the day's agenda, my phone pinged. Thinking it was Seth again, I looked at the screen.

> ASTON: *How is she? When does she want to talk with me? I want to be available. I'm spending the day at Aidan's office, prepping for tomorrow. Then this will all be over.*

Cocky as always, Aston never considered Piper might not be up for talking, or that he might not have this whole case-being-dropped thing in the bag.

I didn't feel like getting tangled up with his rhetoric either, so I left the text unanswered.

The rest of my workday went by relatively quickly and easily. At three o'clock, I went to get a coffee down the street, and was met on the sidewalk by Peter Prescott as I pushed open the door to the coffee shop.

"Bexley," he said, his tone stern.

"No, don't talk to me. Go away."

"You know me better than to think I will walk away from what I want, and what I want is to talk with you right now."

With his hand on my back, he guided me to a table inside the coffee shop. He was that much of a bully, and confident to boot.

"Get your hand off of me," I said through gritted teeth, then added in a hushed tone, "Screw off."

"Not until I get what I want," he said, his voice slightly over a whisper but firm. He had the nerve to motion to a chair.

"What is it you want, Peter? Or should I say Mr. Prescott, sir? You ruined your own son's life. You've made mine miserable, and I hardly know you. Should I go on? I think I will. You scared the shit out of your very own granddaughter. What else could you possibly want?"

He sat down across from me like we were two people happy to meet up for coffee, gently splaying his sport coat behind him. "I need a favor."

"You want me to do a favor for you? Are you serious?"

He nodded as if this wasn't the most outlandish conversation. "I want you to call your boyfriend off the road he's going down. He acted poorly when it came to our business, and he needs to accept the consequences. End of story. I need Aston to accept all this."

"You've gotta be fucking shitting me. First off, I barely know you. Oh, wait, I already said that," I hissed as I leaned forward, my eyes narrowed on Peter Prescott. "I met you when I was a teen, and it sucked. You judged everything about me, and then you took away the one person I ever loved, the one person who made me believe life may be a little better for me. Later on, you came after Piper when she was a baby, and now you've terrorized her." I continued to whisper when I wanted to scream.

"Look, Aston's going to get what's coming to him," Peter said through gritted teeth. "There is no second chance for you two, and the sooner you realize that, the better."

"I don't know what Aston's going to do, but I'm done with this whole scenario. I'm throwing in the towel." I stood, talking loudly enough for a few people to notice. "What I do know is that I'm done talking with you."

With bystanders' eyes on us now, Peter acquiesced and nodded while he watched me walk away from him.

What was it with these Prescott men demanding what they wanted? Granted, Aston never meant to hurt people the way Peter did. Clearly, Peter meant to hurt Aston in some way with this drug allegation. I couldn't help but think he was involved or at the center of it.

But why? Why else would he be threatening Aston?

By the time I ordered my coffee and was ready to go, Peter was gone. On my walk back to work, I decided to put all Prescott men out of my mind for forty-eight hours.

Slipping out my phone, I noticed three more texts from Aston asking if I saw his first text. I switched the phone to DO NOT DISTURB and went to pick up my kids.

I needed a break from all of it.

chapter
Thirty-Six

Baxley

"**H**ey, sweetie," I said to Piper when she jumped in the car. "How was your test?"

"Okay," she said. "I'm glad it's over. And guess what? I made the soccer team! They posted today."

"Oh, wow, baby, that's so awesome."

Just then, we were interrupted by Tyler getting in the car. "What's awesome?"

"Piper made the soccer team."

"Great, can we go for ice cream? To celebrate, right, Piper?"

Memories of running into Aston at the ice cream shop filled my mind. "Maybe this weekend?"

Piper nodded, and Tyler whined.

Pulling away from the school, I told the kids I was going to get pizza for dinner, and their mood changed dramatically. It was mostly smiles and laughs all the way home. I wished my mood could improve at the mere mention of pizza.

"I need to call Dad," Piper said as we walked into the house.

I didn't know which dad she meant, and honestly, I didn't want to ask for clarification.

"Can you give me his number?" Piper said, answering my unasked question, and I pulled out my phone.

"Sure."

"I want to tell him about soccer. Maybe some good news will cheer him up."

I pulled my thoughtful daughter in for a hug, smushing her to my chest, unable to look into her blue eyes, so reminiscent of his. She shouldn't have to be such a grown-up.

"Here you go." I handed her my phone and watched her press the CALL button.

"It's me," Piper said into the phone.

Of course Aston knew who it was. Even worse, he knew it wouldn't be me.

"Yeah, Mom said when I get to high school, I can have my own phone."

I shook my head. He was angling for her to get a phone. The man had been in jail twice in the last month, was wanted for drug trafficking, was in the middle of a divorce and trying to reconcile with me, getting to know his daughter, and now he was worried about buying phones?

"Tyler will be so mad."

Oh, he will.

"Yeah, I'm fine," she said. "I understand. You were mad." She sat down on the floor, her back to the door, and continued to listen. "Yes, I know we shouldn't do that."

Aston talked for a moment, and then Piper spoke.

"I'm sorry that I called my other dad, Seth, you know? Today in school, I thought about it. I don't think you would want him to know what happened. I'm really sorry."

The air whooshed out of my lungs.

"You don't have to do that," I whispered to Piper.

She shook her head at me, her palm in the air, silencing my words with her version of *talk to the hand*. "It was wrong of me. But you know, I just met you, and I wasn't sure what to do. And I've known my other dad all my life…Uh-huh…Uh-huh. Right. It was wrong, though."

Whatever Aston said put her mind at ease, and she gave up on the apology.

"Well, I wanted to tell you I made the soccer team!"

A smile brightened Piper's face, and I couldn't help but think even ice cream wouldn't have that effect.

"I thought you'd be happy to hear…Yeah, I worked really hard…Sure, when we get the schedule."

There was a little more chitchat, and then Piper said, "Yep, she's right here."

Before I could protest, she shoved the phone at me and ran off, saying she was going to practice outside.

"Hey," I said into the phone.

"Thanks for having her call," Aston said.

"I didn't. She's Piper. She wanted to call." I slid into the same place Piper had occupied only moments before.

"Listen, Bex, I fucked up. I can't apologize any more—"

"Your dad visited me again today. Told me to call off my boyfriend."

"What the fuck? Aidan, get in here," Aston yelled.

"I don't think it's necessary to involve your lawyer."

"It damn fucking is."

Cradling my forehead in my palm, I tried to stroke away the stress headache coming on.

"Bexley, listen to me. Nan is going to testify against my father."

"What? He's her husband…how? Why?"

"Because my dad set me up, and he wants me out."

Leaning my head back against the door, I asked, "Why?"

"I'm not sure we'll ever know the why, babe. He's mad I divorced Cass. Her family's wealth and power are more important than the well-being of my kids and me."

"That's crazy. All you've ever done is please him. Ever."

"I know. Didn't do me much good, did it? I'm a miserable son of a bitch."

"Aston, don't do that. What will Nan do? What does she know?"

"Well, my dad wants me to call this all off, making it easier on him. He won't go to Nan, because then it's as good as admitting it's true. Basically, he wants to make it look like I'm lying. I had to make sure Nan was safe."

"Is she?"

When I first met Aston, he wasn't sure about Nan. He didn't really like her, but that was baseless.

"Of course. That's why I kept this quiet. Look, my mom never liked Nan, and neither did I when I first met her. But she's been an ally to me. Yeah, she set me up with Cass, but she thought it would make everyone happy. She never knew how it would rip everyone apart. I guess this is her way of making it up."

"But how?"

"I don't want to say over the phone. I'll tell you everything. She's a good person, though. Nan, I mean. Look how she connected the kids with Denise."

"Okay. I get it." I wanted to know, but I understood his reasoning. I also wasn't in the mood to see Aston.

"I can't see you right now. We're working overnight on this."

"It's fine."

"Are we okay? I need to know, Bex. I need you in my corner."

"I told you I needed some space. This is too much. I'm in your corner, no matter what, but I still need my space."

"You have one day. Then I'm coming for you." Aston hung up before I could protest.

chapter
Thirty-Seven

Aston

"We did it." I slapped Aidan on the back, and he blew out a long breath. "I'm raising my rates for you."

"Nah. You love me," I said, walking into his office with him.

"Okay, your charges have been dismissed," Aidan said as he sat behind his desk. "Your dad was arrested immediately on a whole host of charges from the district attorney. He'll need to pay a hefty bail, and will probably be required to turn in his passport. Naturally, he's been asked to step down as CEO by the board. I'm sure you can force his resignation there."

Too restless to sit, I paced his office. "My only priority right now is protecting Nan. Let's make sure she gets what she needs, financially and house wise, and all that. Oh, she and her kids, my stepsisters, need to get a buyout package for their shares in the company, and a letter to sign to give up any and all rights to be a part of Federal. They're both happy in their fashion internships in Paris—no doubt Federal's connection with the fanciest hotel in Paris helped land them a spot with designers. Maybe Nan should go there and enjoy herself for a while."

"I don't think it's a bad idea." Aidan leaned forward on his desk, making notes.

"My dad is temporarily down, but that won't stop him. He has a long reach. We need to act fast on behalf of Nan. She put herself on the line for me. Can you take care of all of this? I have to get back to Bexley and let her know what happened."

"Oh, I forgot to mention. Seth agreed to all your terms."

"Of course he did. Sucker. Listen, don't ever mention the money to Bexley."

"I hear you," Aidan said. "Now, get out of here and see your girl, so I can finish working and go home to my family."

"Bexley, open the door. Please," I begged, standing at her back door. I'd texted on my way over, saying that the charges were dropped and that I wanted to tell her everything.

She'd left my message on READ but didn't reply, and I'd gone straight to her house.

"Please." I knocked again. As the door swung open, I muttered, "Bexley," only to realize my daughter had answered the door.

"Oh, Piper." I gathered her close, belatedly remembering to ask, "Is this okay?"

She nodded into my chest.

"I have so much to tell you, sweet girl, but I'm so glad to hold you right now."

Pulling back, Piper asked, "Are you going to marry my mom?"

I wasn't sure where this was coming from. Of course I'd like to marry her mom, but I didn't think Piper and I should be discussing it.

"Can I come in?" I asked, figuring it was best to start with something innocuous.

Piper shook her head. "Mom said she's not up for company."

"Listen, Piper. You know I loved your mom very much a long time ago. That's how we got you. Here's the thing…I never stopped loving her, and I really need to see her now."

Piper crossed her arms over her chest. "She told me you chose not to be with her. She told me today, when I asked why she didn't tell you about me."

"It's complicated," I said, leaning against the door frame.

"Well, she said she needs time. She also said you need to go home and see Mar and Little A. I think so too."

"Why do you think so?"

"When I don't see my mom or dad, Seth, for a while, I worry. I'm sure Mar would like to see you. I don't know about Little A, really. I don't get Tyler most of the time."

"Oh," I said, taking in my daughter. "Were you always this wise?"

"Yep. Mom says I'm an old soul."

"I'd really like to see her, just for a quick second. Maybe we could sneak-attack her? I could see her, and then go do what you recommended?" Look, I wasn't against a little subterfuge.

"She'll probably get mad."

Smoothing my hand down Piper's hair and looking into her eyes, which were so much like mine, I said, "I'll take the blame."

Reluctantly, she relented, moving aside to let me in. "Okay."

"Where is she?" I whispered when I was inside the house. I knew I was pushing it, but I had to see Bexley.

"Her room," Piper whispered back. "Hey, you didn't say if you were going to marry her."

Stopping, I turned back to Piper. "What do you think?"

"Well, I think you guys are getting along for me, but Mom would like to get back together."

"What about me? What do you think I want?"

"I don't know." Her words came out hushed. "You have kids and a life. Maybe I can be a part of it?"

For an old soul, she didn't know everything.

For the second time today, I pulled my teenage daughter close, this time kissing the top of her head. "Piper, you are a part of my life, and you will always be. I'm sorry I missed those years. But don't think for a minute that I don't want it all with your mom, 'kay?"

"Okay . . ."

But our moment was interrupted.

Bexley stepped into the hall and let out a huff. "Ugh, Aston. You had to weasel your way in, didn't you?"

Piper threw her hands up in the air. "Mom, I tried."

"I know, baby. He's like that." Bexley turned her glare on me.

"I needed to see you for one quick second."

"Piper, go hang with Tyler. We'll eat when I'm done."

"Tacos?" Piper asked. "Only because I know Tyler'll ask me."

"Tacos," Bexley said.

"But it's not even Tuesday," I said when Piper left the room.

"Aston, I told you I need time."

"I know," I said, walking close. "I had to see you, tell you it's over. My dad set the whole thing up. He was mad about my divorce. Son of a bitch expected I'd try to get with you. Nan knew about it, and quite frankly, she was sick of his bullshit. She wanted out."

I took Bexley's hand in mine. "I know I should go see the other kids, but I wanted to see you first, and then I'll do what you and Piper want."

"So, it's all over, just like that?"

"Yep. Nan went to the judge, and when he heard what she had to say and looked over the evidence she had, he dismissed the charges against me and had my dad arrested. Now I need to decide if I want to press additional defamation charges against him. Personally, all I care about is his surrendering his shares of the business and calling it a day. What I'd really like to do is break more than his nose . . ."

Tugging her hair loose from a messy bun, Bexley tilted her head, providing herself shelter with a fan of hair, distracted me from my wayward thoughts.

"Don't hide," I told her. "This is good. Really good."

Bexley shrugged one shoulder, not looking at me. "Your mom would be happy."

"I don't care. For the first time in my life, I'm worried about my happiness. And yours, and all the kids', and even Seth's. I'm ready to move forward."

"I still need time." She stood on tiptoe and kissed me on the cheek. "I'm happy for you, but I need some time to get my head straight. I've been swept into all this, and it's been a lot."

"I still want to see Piper, but I'll give you a week or two. Then I'm coming in hard."

"Go," she said with a smile while shoving my chest. "Start by listening and go."

A few days later, once Nan was safe in Paris, and my dad had been released from jail after paying a huge bail, I drove by his house.

The sight of the FOR SALE sign outside made me smile. I told myself not to park, but I couldn't help it. After parking my Porsche into the driveway, I stepped out and walked up the pebbled path to the house for the last time. We were done, my dad and me, but that didn't mean I didn't have a few choice words for him.

Using my key, I let myself in and found my dad wearing one of our company's luxury robes as he sat at the kitchen counter. Rather than drinking coffee, which you'd expect at eight in the morning, he was working on a cut-crystal glass of what I suspected was Macallan.

"What do you want? My kidney too?" he had the nerve to ask me.

"No, I just want to make sure you're going to stay away from my family. The law will make sure you never step into Federal again. Who the fuck sabotages their own business? Takes a lifetime to build something, and then sets it on fire with the careless flick of a match?"

"Oh, there was nothing careless about what I was doing, son. If it weren't for that scheming woman I married, I'd be in the clear. She and her brat daughters didn't have it good enough?"

Gritting my teeth, I clenched my fists. I wanted to break his whole face, not only his nose. "Listen, I don't care what you did, how you did it, or why. My life is too full to worry about it. What I do care about is how you intentionally tried to ruin my life, to make sure I had nothing, and I'm your *son*. So, fuck you, Dad." I spat out the last part. "Stay away from me, and stay even further away from Bexley and all the kids. Hear me?"

He looked up at me and sneered, his normally coifed hair a mess, the lines in his face deeper than I remembered them. "It was always about that little poor bitch. I knew she'd eventually trap you and your money. Or I should say, your money and you."

"Good-bye, Peter. Good-fucking-bye," I said, more furious than I'd ever been in my life. "You have enough legal trouble, so keep your distance."

If I stayed much longer, we'd come to blows, and a third trip to the slammer wouldn't serve me well with Bexley. So I walked out of his house on the golf course for the last time, feeling like a huge load had been lifted from my shoulders.

chapter
Thirty-Eight

Bexley

Saturday morning, I took an extra-deep inhale. Enjoying the quiet, I sat in my kitchen, a steaming-hot cup of coffee in front of me.

Then my phone rang.

"Bex, you okay?" Milly yelled into the Bluetooth in her car. I envisioned her driving on the freeway with her windows down, her professionally dyed hair blowing all around her.

"Yeah, I'm fine. Are you okay? You sound like you're in a wind tunnel."

"Well, first you call me for help, so I send Mike over, and then I hear nothing. He says you made him leave, and Aston stayed. What the heck?"

"Me, what the heck? What's going on with you? You've been MIA—"

"We'll talk about that later."

"Mill, what's going on? Tell me."

"Bexley, did you hear me? You first. Mike says Aston stayed, and then I never heard from you."

A horn blew in the background, and I figured I'd better answer, or Milly was going to cause a five-car pileup.

"He stayed for a bit, saw Piper sleeping, and left. Honest."

"That's it?"

"I told him I needed time. I'm still telling him that. By the way, the charges have been dismissed."

"What?"

"Don't you talk with Mike? I can't believe that he doesn't know. Aston told me last night."

"I thought you were keeping space...Jesus," she yelled, laying on the horn.

"Where are you, Milly? It's Saturday morning. Why aren't you home with your family?"

"Look, I'm trying to do something. End something. I told Mike if he tried, I would do this."

"What?" All of a sudden, I remembered Aston's comments. Milly had secrets, and I had no clue what was going on with her.

"Our marriage has been shit. Mike with all his money and bullshit things, and me too. I need and I want, but there are no feelings, no sex. So I found that somewhere else, and Christ, it was good."

"Milly!"

"Don't judge me, Bexley. Don't you freaking dare. You found a good guy, made a life, and then you didn't want it, so you got out. That was your choice. You have a freaking job, that's why you can make it. You have freedom."

"I'm not judging you, Mill. I just don't understand why you never said anything to me. That you weren't doing well. That your relationship was in trouble." I stood up and paced my kitchen, feeling my brow furrow, wrinkles forming.

"Can't you see? You always lived with this fantasy that it really could have worked between you and Aston. Happily-ever-after between the have and the have-not. I'm here to tell you, it doesn't work that way. The haves and have-nots shouldn't mix. Ever. Look at me—I'm nothing but arm candy. But I forced the issue back then, really believed I could make this happen, and I transformed myself into a richie. You could never do it. Why? Because you have morals."

I wasn't sure when I lost touch with my good friend in this way. A way that I had absolutely no clue what the hell she was talking about.

"Mike got in a snit. Liked me the way I was when we met. Liked me for me. Whatever. I told Mike that if he wants me to himself, he needs to make me the center of his world."

"Mill, you've always been the center of his world. Why did you think you're not?"

"Work and more work. It's always work-work-work with him."

I gulped down my coffee, although with the way this conversation was going, I didn't need any waking up. I'd be better off with a sedative.

"He was working for you, Mill, and the kids. He never wanted you to do without. I'm sure you knew that somewhere deep inside. You couldn't live the way you were doing without him working."

"No. He was working for him."

I shook my head. Knowing better than to try to convince Milly otherwise, I said, "Okay, but you need to move forward. You're ending whatever side thing you have?"

"Sadly."

I didn't like her answer, but again, I knew better than to argue. "Good. Then make it right with your husband. All the way right, Mill. You have a family. Don't destroy it."

"Why? Because you're gonna make a go with your baby daddy and we'll all be friends? It can be like a redo of one of those rom-coms you love so much."

"Listen, you're one of my oldest friends, but I don't deserve this. I'm not sure when you became so jaded, but you need to snap out of it. I really appreciate you sending Mike to help me the other night, but you need to go focus on you right now. Not me."

"Don't be that way."

"Look, let's talk next week."

Another horn blared, and she said, "I gotta go."

"'Bye, Mill. Be careful."

Blowing out a long breath, I poured a second cup of joe and thought about what Milly said. I think somewhere deep inside, I knew it would never work out with Aston. Maybe that was why I let him go so easily? Let him off the hook when it came to Piper?

Mike was a good guy. A great one. He didn't deserve what was happening to him. No one did. In a way, I understood how Seth must have felt. I wasn't physically cheating on him, but my heart betrayed him.

Life was certainly messy, and I had no idea how to fix it.

Part of me wished I could go back a year or two in time. It would be so great to wake up, unaware of the problems Aston was having, no intuitions or sneaky suspicions about my ex, only my simple life I'd crafted around me.

To make my life even messier, Aston didn't want to give me the space he'd promised. He texted and begged, but I forced the issue.

I worked more, picking up an extra day a week. I busied myself with grocery shopping, lunch packing, and cooking new and exciting dinners.

When I could, I sent Piper to have dinner with Aston, Mara, and Little A. Aston didn't like me sending her by herself, but he took what I gave him. When it came to Piper, he was desperate to make up for lost time, maybe even more so than with me.

He was always gracious—even genuine—and invited Tyler. At first, Tyler was in his own way, usually wanting alone time with Seth. I didn't realize it at that point, but it was the beginning of an end for Tyler and his dad. Now they seemed to chat a little on the phone, go to dinner once in a while, but Tyler started spending fewer whole weekends at Seth's and wanting less and less contact with him.

When I wasn't working or cooking, I was either cleaning or organizing closets or going to Piper's soccer games. Aston was always there, but between my warning looks and not wanting to upset Piper, he kept his distance, cheering for her and her team.

"Mom, you need to be nice to my dad," Piper said one night while helping me make a Greek salad.

"Which one?"

"Don't be stupid. Seriously, Mom," she said while raising an eyebrow at me. "I'll always be close with Seth, but he's not my dad-dad, and you know it. Seth and I talked, and we want to be tight, but he knows I need to get to know Aston. Plus, he's dating someone seriously, and she has a son and he needs to get to know him. *Quid pro quo*, or whatever he called it."

"Wait. That's a lot of information to unpack. He said that? Back up." Setting down my knife, I grabbed a glass of wine, figuring it was needed, and told Piper to sit on the stool next to me. "Okay, slow down and tell me when all this happened…who said what, and all that."

"You've been busy. I get it. You needed time to yourself, or whatever. That's what Dad said. By Dad, I mean Aston. I'm calling him Dad now. We're close. Texting all the time."

"Wait," I said, pulling my hair off my neck where I was starting to sweat. "Texting? How?"

"Uh, he got me a phone." Her cheeks reddened. "He told me to keep it secret and to only use it to text him, and I listened. Honestly, I'm not doing any apps. But I want to be able to talk with my dad. And you're always listening or rushing around lately."

"He can't buy you, Piper."

"Mom! Don't you know me? Jeez—"

I pulled her in for a hug. "I'm sorry, baby. You're right. I'm being unfair. So, where were we? Aston got you a phone, and you text and you call him Dad. You could have told me. And when did you talk with Seth?"

I rambled, mentally berating myself for being so preoccupied and self-centered these last few weeks.

"Mom, look how you're freaking out. That's why I didn't say a word about Dad…I mean, Aston."

I rolled my eyes. "Seriously, I'm not freaking out."

"You are. Anyway, when I went to dinner with Seth and Tyler, Tyler didn't want to go alone because Cherry—that's his girlfriend—was bringing her son. His name is Chad, and he's super cute. He really likes Seth. His dad died. Isn't that horrible?"

"Yes, just awful. I wouldn't wish that for anyone," I said.

"Sometimes Tyler is sort of jealous of him, and honestly, other times, I think he likes his time with Little A better. Aston Junior looks up to him and wants to do everything he does. Anyway, when Seth drove us home, Tyler popped his headphones in and watched something on his iPad, and I mentioned how lucky I was to have two dads and Chad has none. I told Seth I'd be okay with giving him to Chad."

"Piper, that's not necessary."

"Seriously, Mom, you have to stop interrupting me. Look, Seth knew what I meant. I'm taking time to get to know my dad-dad, and he's making a life with Cherry and Chad."

"Jesus Christ, I don't know when things got so complicated. Pardon my French."

Inside, I was torn up for Tyler. This couldn't be easy for him, and I decided to schedule a mom-son date to discuss it this week. As soon as I finished this chat with Piper.

"Christ, sorry," I said, repeated myself.

"It's fine," she said, her hair springing free from a messy bun. "Dad swears a lot too. He also said not to tell you that, but I knew you wouldn't care. Look, I'm sorry about the phone. I can show you. I only use it to text Dad, and there are no apps. Maybe I can get some now that you know?"

She smiled at me, and I couldn't help but giggle.

"You're just like him, you know? Always have been. Equal parts stubborn, a heart too big for its own good, and the drive to do everything you want. It used to keep me awake at night, thinking about nature versus nurture. Do you know what that means?"

She shook her head.

"It's the debate between your personality being crafted from your genetic makeup, who your parents are, or from the environment where you were raised. I'd think over and over in my head that you were a prime example of nature. Not only your eye color, but everything about you."

"Oh. Dad did say I have a lot of him in me."

"You do," I said, laughing again.

"Which is why you have to give him a chance."

"Did he put you up to this?" I eyed my daughter.

"No. All he said was he wanted a chance. And I agreed."

"Piper—"

"He may have encouraged me to talk with you. To mention this."

"I don't think it's a good idea for you to be in the middle, baby," I said, brushing some hair off her face.

"I'm not. I swear. I asked Dad if he's going to marry you when he first came by a few weeks ago. I know he wants to…is all I'm saying."

"Piper." I blew out a deep breath before continuing. "Look, this can be confusing, I'm sure. You're reunited with your dad, and I'm glad, but that doesn't mean this is some fairy tale where he whisks me away. We have to think about Tyler. And me. And Aston's kids. And maybe he doesn't want to marry me . . ."

I rambled until there was a knock at the door. Based on the guilty look on Piper's face, I realized my thirteen-year-old daughter was running the show.

"Shoot," she mumbled.

"What now? Please, God, don't say what I think you're going to say," I said, looking down at my worn denim shirt and jean cutoffs I'd changed into after work.

"I kind of forgot to mention that I invited Dad to eat. Mara and Little A were going with Denise to see their mom, and he was all alone," she said, giving me puppy-dog eyes before she ran to the door.

"Piper," I said through gritted teeth, and then plastered a smile on my face.

Her dad walked through the door like he owned the place. Holding out his hand to me, he smiled and said, "Aston Prescott. Nice to meet you."

I was a goner.

"Hi, Aston." I pulled my shit together. "Good to see you."

"Not as great as it is to see you."

I never understood the expression "he drank me in" until this moment. That was exactly what he was doing…I felt myself pour into his body.

"Piper invited me, so I couldn't say no."

I nodded. "And the phone? You couldn't say no to that either?"

"Let me explain," Aston said, coming close.

"You don't have to. No worries, seriously. Plus, I need to finish this salad."

The closer he got to me, the more I felt myself caving. I wanted him to hold me. I needed him to tell me everything was fine. Better than fine. Good or great.

My heart beat furiously at the idea of the two of us really being together.

"Are you starving, Pipe?" he asked.

"Piper," I said, correcting him.

"Pipe's okay, Mom."

When did I lose control?

"Um, I have homework. 'Bye," she said, slipping out of the kitchen.

I turned toward Aston and gave him an accusing look. "You two are in collusion."

"We are. Why? Because my daughter is smart, and she knows what's best. I want to be with her mother, and she wants that too."

"Aston," I said, unable to come up with a better response.

"Don't. I've given you space, and now it's time to let me back in," he said while his finger traced its way up my arm, stopping to tap over my heart. "In here."

"You've always been there. You never left," I said, having a weak moment.

"I know. We were meant to be together, and now we are. We will be."

"What about your dad?"

"Fuck him. I'm done with him."

"You can't just say that. You did whatever he wanted for years."

"I did. My mom told me to, and I jumped. It was wrong of me. I should've made you the priority."

"Whatever. I can't have this same discussion again. It happened."

"Know this, Peter's out of our lives. We'll keep in touch with Nan, though, if that's okay?"

"Don't be ridiculous. She just saved your behind. Of course."

"Exactly, and here I am. I want to start over, but with all these feelings. Let them grow."

"Well, there are a lot of kids between us . . ."

"Pretty sure Mara and Little A are happy about us getting together. They love your kids, and they're down to one visit per month with Cass. It's all she wanted, and it hurts them a lot."

"What?" I felt the blood drain out of my face. "What kind of mother does that?"

"Cass. And Tyler is part of the gang. He's dealing with Seth moving on, so we're an island for him."

"Does everyone know about that but me?" I asked.

"You've kind of been off doing your own thing. Taking space and all, babe."

I shrugged. "I needed it."

"I get it." He tugged me into his embrace and placed his lips on mine. "I want you, all of you. You, your kids, my kids, and maybe a pet," he mumbled into my mouth.

Rather than answering, I kissed him back.

We stayed like that for a while…kissing, taking our time exploring, our feelings growing, just like he said.

Finally breaking away from the kiss, I said, "Um, but we're still going to discuss the phone."

"Bex, I have a lot of money—"

"It's about parenting together, Aston."

"But you weren't talking to me."

I sighed. He had a point.

"Still, you should have waited until we could discuss it."

"Again, I'm sorry. But I have the money to do it, and they're my kids to spoil, and I will. I'm going to spoil you too. Seriously, you need to get over this. I know you work, and I'm proud of you, but I can do what I want."

"Oh God, stop, and let me go make this salad." I couldn't get into this debate with him at this moment. He'd go right for my work, its safety, et cetera.

"Go right ahead, but know this. I'm smoking a cigar after we eat, and then I'm spending the night." His hand brushed my wrist, and he pulled it up to kiss it. "Got that?"

"Maybe," I said.

He shook his head and winked, signaling he didn't fall for my hard candy-coated exterior.

chapter
Thirty-Nine

Aston

We ate dinner as a foursome that evening, but Little Aston and Mara's absence weighed heavily on me. They should have been there, enjoying this with us, instead of worrying about their mom. I might have tons of money and all the things that come with it, but they hadn't been dealt a good hand when it came to unconditional love. Cass was a bitch, and they knew it.

"Hey, Tyler, want to go four-wheeling with Little A and me this weekend?" I asked over dessert.

"Me? Really? You want me?"

I knew Aston Junior needed it, and Tyler deserved some extra attention. That prick, Seth, had done a number on his own kid, and I wasn't going to stand for it.

I also knew better than to argue with Bexley about it. It was time for me to take matters into my own hands. She would pussyfoot around how we had to be nice to Seth. Everyone might think he was a good guy, but he wasn't. Plus, this made me feel a bit better about my other kids missing this dinner.

"Yeah, you," I told Tyler. "We like to get in a ride or four and then grab pizza. Sound good?"

"Yes!" The kid practically shot out of his seat and through the roof. "Mom, can I? Please?"

Bexley looked straight at me, and all I did was smile. I had her.

"Of course, baby," she said to Tyler, who scowled at that.

"I'm not a baby."

"I know." Bexley smiled at him, her eyes crinkling a tiny bit.

I loved the way she adored her children. *Our children.*

"Aston?" Piper said to me. "I mean, Dad?"

"What's up?" I said casually, not wanting to admit how it cut me like a knife when she called me by my first name, and how it made my heart pound when she called me Dad.

"Do you think Mara could hang with us? I mean, if you have Denise set up, maybe she can take a day off?"

"Would that be okay with you?" I asked Bexley.

"Of course," she said with that same comforting smile she reserved for the kids.

I grinned at Piper. "Of course, then."

"Fun! Mom, can we go to the nail place? I want to get my soccer team colors, and Mar would love that. Please?"

Bexley turned to me. "Is that okay?"

I held up my hands. "Look, let's stop with all the *is it okay*s. If it's okay for your kids, then it's okay for mine. Let's be honest…they're all my kids."

Tyler's hopeful gaze landed on me.

"You too, bud," I said to him, then looked at Bexley. "You get the nails taken care of, and I'll pay. Done. Is it time to clean up?"

Bexley glanced around the table. "Everyone full?"

They all nodded, and we started clearing dishes.

"See? That was great," I said to Bexley, who had a glass of wine in her right hand, and her left hand in mine. The kids were both in their rooms, tucked safely in bed, and we were sitting in the kitchen.

"I didn't like that Aston and Mara weren't here," she said, and I fell for her for the millionth time.

"Yeah, that sucked. But when I planned to come over, I wasn't sure what would happen, and so I had Denise take them to see Cass."

Sipping her wine, Bexley looked at me, her brow furrowed, and I could tell she wanted to say something.

"What?" I asked.

"I shouldn't say it, but I think they would have been happier being turned away from here than going to see Cass."

"You can say whatever you want to me, and you're not wrong. They would've been happier here."

Her fingers ran over mine, drawing small shapes. "So, from now on, we'll all be together?"

"Yes, if that's what you want."

She nodded, a small tear forming in the corner of her eye. "I'm sorry I wasn't there for you during these last few weeks."

Gathering her close, I encouraged her to set her wineglass on the counter. My lips found her forehead, and I spoke quietly. "I deserved you shutting me out, but I told you I was going to fight for you. Now I did, and I want you back. All of you. Tyler and Piper and my kids as one."

Her lips found mine. Our mouths lingered together as she said, "It's always been you, Aston. Always." She didn't give me a chance to answer, kissing me harder, opening her mouth to me.

"Slow down," I told her, bringing our foreheads together.

"Why? Did I do something wrong?"

"No, absolutely not. I just need to slow for a minute to tell you it's always been you for me too. Always." I repeated her words to her, but it was the truth. "I love you. I know it was my fault that we were cheated out of many years, but we're here now, together, and I want this. More than anything."

"Me too." Her reply was soft, but urgent in tone.

As her eyes ate up every inch of me, I felt myself morphing from nice guy to caveman. I wanted that look to be for me, and only me.

"How will this work?" she asked.

In my mind, we'd all move in together, and I'd provide for the family we were meant to be. The family my dad almost denied me. But I didn't say any of that.

Instead, I said, "Don't worry about that. It will."

Without any more words or plans, we kissed, our tongues exploring each other's mouths, my palm running the length of her back.

Bexley stalled the kiss. "It's okay if you have to leave and head home to the kids."

"No, Denise is there. I told her I'd be home in the morning."

Tilting her head back, Bexley said, "So, that's the way it is? You were that cocky?"

"Maybe," I said on a wink, then murmured in her ear, "Aston Prescott."

"Stop," she said, pretending to protest with a smile on her face.

"You know you like it. It turns you on," I said softly, my lips tickling along her earlobe.

"It does." She ran her hands down my arms, staring at me.

"Can we go to bed?" I asked, more than hopeful.

Bexley nodded and took my hand, her glass of wine forgotten on the counter. I turned off the light and followed her.

Inside her bedroom, she held up a hand. "Let me check on everyone first."

By the time she was back, I was naked and in her bed.

"Everyone is out," she said, pulling her shirt over her head, revealing a lacy black bra.

"Come here. Let me do that," I demanded, my gaze never leaving hers.

She obeyed, and straddled me on the bed, putting a little pressure just where she needed it.

"Oh God." She moaned and her head fell back, allowing me access to the front clasp of her bra.

Once I quickly unfastened it, the straps fell down her arms, her breasts coming loose of the cups. I leaned forward, taking one nipple in my mouth, the other between my index finger and thumb. She continued to moan, her hair spilling down her back, the prettiest sight I'd ever seen.

"Let's get you out of those clothes," I said, pulling free of the covers and shoving down her shorts.

She rolled to the side, landing with her head on the pillow, and I tugged her panties and socks the rest of the way off, settling right where I'd dreamed of being, my mouth at her core. I felt the heat coming through her panties, and decided to get rid of them too.

"Just relax," I told her, and she listened a second time, her head pressing back into the pillow.

My tongue ran its way over her heat, up and down, finally finding the place where she was most sensitive. I took my time, gentle licks and nips, driving her wild, until she begged, "Please." Only then did I pick up speed and give her the release she wanted. I dragged out every moan, savoring each taste and sound, until Bexley was wrung out underneath me.

After climbing my way back up her body, I fused my mouth to hers. She'd never minded tasting herself on me, and it was good to see things hadn't changed.

"Want you inside me," she said, "but I also want you in my mouth."

"We have plenty of time to fool around later. Right now, I want to be deep inside you."

When I started to get up, she asked, "Where are you going?"

"Condom."

She shook her head. "We don't need it."

"Is that so? This coming from the woman who works at the health clinic?"

"Stop, get over here," she said. "I'm clean, on the pill."

"It's been a while for me . . ."

"That's good enough for me," she said, and I didn't wait.

With one push, I was inside her, and this time it was me doing the moaning.

"Feels so fucking good," I whispered, my lips ghosting across her cheek.

Catching her hands in mine, I raised them above her head and drove into her. With her eyes open, she took me in, watched me pump in and out of her.

"Faster," she demanded, and I obeyed. "I want to feel you let go. Please, Aston."

She didn't need to ask again. I did as I was told, climaxing just as Bexley went off for a second time.

Coming down from what felt like a major high, I rolled to the side. "I should get something to help you clean up, but I think I'm dead," I murmured. "You know, I'm a lot older than when we met."

Bexley laughed. "Wait here. I'll use the bathroom and take care of all that. Rest up for round two."

She slipped out of bed, and I snatched her wrist. "Hurry back. I like how you're thinking."

Her giggle was the best thing I'd heard all day.

chapter
Forty

Bexley

"This is fun. Thanks, Bexley," Little A said to me over a bright red snow cone.

We'd gone to a craft fair in the desert, and now we were sitting having a snack. Originally, the boys had fought me on it because they'd wanted to go to the arcade, but we all needed some outdoor time, and Piper had recently gotten into making papier mâché. Soccer had ended for the season, and she was in full-on craft mode.

"You're welcome," I told him, tapping his red nose. "You look like Rudolph. By the way, you know you can call me Bex like your dad does. Or B, if you want."

"What about Mom? I don't have one anymore, you know?"

It had been six weeks since Aston had wormed his way back into my life. Since then, we'd been spending most of our free time together, sharing dinners and outings with the kids, and going on dates. But for the most part, we stayed the night in our separate houses.

Occasionally, Aston spent the night at my place, leaving Denise with the kids. Of course, Cass had thrown a major fit when she found out that Aston and I were dating again, and landed in some chic rehab center for two weeks. Once she was out and clean, she decided that being a part of the kids' lives—and subsequently Aston's—was too much for her to handle.

I couldn't even begin to unpack my feelings when it came to that woman.

"That's up to you, buddy," I told Little A.

The sweet-talker he was, he took my hand in his. "Well, I asked Dad. I don't want Tyler to be mad, because you're his mom. But I think Dad is going to marry you, and then you'd be my mom too. Since my own mom doesn't want to be mine anymore."

"Aston . . ." My big guy growled at his son by his full name while still listening with one ear to Piper go on and on about papier mâché.

"It's okay. He can tell me and ask me anything he wants," I said, rushing to Little A's defense, scowling at Aston for getting mad at his Mini-Me for being honest.

"I know that," Aston said, side-eyeing me. "I meant what else he was going on about. Getting—"

I shushed him. "It's fine. Kids have overactive imaginations. Piper, did you sell Little Aston on a fairy tale?" I joked, because the reality of it all was frightening. I'd wanted to spend the rest of my life with Aston Prescott since I was eighteen years old.

"Mom, stop. Really—"

I took a look around, realizing all eyes were on me.

"Yeah," Mara said. "We had a meeting last week when you were in the shower, and we decided you should get married."

"What?"

"After you quit your job you don't need," she added.

"Mar," Aston quickly said. "Remember, that was between us?"

"Why would you have a meeting?" I asked. "And I do need my job. I like it."

"Okay, gang," Aston said with a sigh. "Looks like we're going to do this at the fair, rather than over a steak dinner the way I'd hoped."

This got a major eye roll from me.

Aston sat next to Piper, his elbows on his knees, and those gorgeous blue eyes focused solely on me. "Bex, tonight I was going to have everyone clean up, and we were going to go out to dinner. There would have been candles, champagne, and sparkling cider. I was going to get down on one knee and ask you to marry me in front of all the kids, since they're all part of this now. Mike and Milly were going to join us for dessert."

"What?" I asked, running through the whole scenario in my head, especially the part about Mike and Milly.

Aston stood and came close, his unruly hair falling in his face. "I called Milly. Told her she needed to make amends, apologize for her actions, her secrets. Mike told me all about your words with her. They're getting help and working things out," he said as if he could read my mind.

"But what? You were going to ask me to marry you?"

"Yeah, of course. I love you. Didn't you think that would happen?" Just like his son, he took my hand in his. "Aston Prescott, and I'd like you to be my wife."

"So you want me to quit my job?"

This got me a big chuckle. "No, because I love you and so do my kids—all of our kids. And I want to make up for all the years we should have been together."

I nodded.

"Is that a yes?" he asked.

My heart in my throat, I nodded. "Yes, it's a yes."

"Can we still go to dinner?" Tyler asked while the girls were jumping around and Little A clung to my waist.

"Of course," Aston said, grinning. "We need to celebrate and also talk to your mom about hiring her for our new business venture."

"We're opening hotels!" Tyler jumped up and down this time. "A big hotel with a pool and a game room. We may live there sometimes like the kids do on TV!"

For a second, I closed my eyes, cooling my temper. I was getting married to the man of my dreams, despite the fact he did crazy shit like this. Aston would have to learn to not throw his money around, get the kids all excited about grandiose ideas.

"It's a good thing, Bex. We're going to take Federal and do something bigger, change shit up. Do our own thing, create our own legacy—for our kids. They can have it one day, no matter who they fall in love with. And I need you with me."

"Tyler, we'll discuss it later, okay?" I said to my son, blowing him a kiss.

"Gross." He ducked, pretending to avoid my affection.

Coming close, Aston ran his palm down my cheek. "Bex, let this go. I want this for us. For them."

"I'm a social worker, Aston. I can't work with you."

"Babe, you can. Plus, I need someone in charge of human resources, and who better than you? You believe in me, right?"

"Later." Totally overwhelmed, I decided to defer that conversation. "Did we just get engaged? At the fair? With all these people and our kids around?"

"We did. But just to be clear, I have a ring back at my house. Our house, I should say."

"Mom, guess what? Dad said we're going to move in this week," Piper said, joining the conversation.

"I must have taken a really long shower. This sounds like it was a really involved convo," I said to my kids, one eyebrow arched.

"We asked," Tyler said. "Don't be mad at Aston."

Aston gave me his version of puppy-dog eyes. "Look, I have the room. Eventually, I'd like to get a bigger place, but I was thinking that this works for now. For all of us. We're not going to be apart."

"What else were you thinking about? I'm afraid to ask."

"We could sell your place and put the money in a college fund for Tyler and Piper. You won't need the money to live on now, and this will be good for them. I assume you got it in the divorce."

I dropped my head on Aston's shoulder. "Oh God, let's go to our celebratory dinner first. My head feels like it's going to explode from how much you thought this through."

Mara ran in place, glowing with excitement. "Wait until you see the ring, Bexley! I love it! Dad let me try it on. It's soooo sparkly. Can I call you Mom like Little A does? Can I?"

I felt my heart grow larger, so big it felt like it was going to burst out of my chest. "Sure, Mar. Anything you want. If it makes you happy, then you can do it. You know why? I love your daddy and you and Little A."

"And Piper and Tyler," she said, nodding.

"Of course." A bittersweet shiver ran through me. I wouldn't want my kids choosing a new mom, but I wasn't Cass. That much was clear.

Aston pulled me into his side and kissed the top of my head. "Come on, gang. Let's go home and change."

The kids bopped excitedly in front of us as we left the fair. Mara held Piper's hand, and the boys were busy trying to trip each other.

"Getting married," Aston said close to my ear. "Can you believe it?"

"You think this is smart? It's been quick, you know?"

Aston stopped in his tracks. Turning me to face him, he tucked his index finger under my chin. "I'm sure. I've been waiting too long for this."

Then he kissed me in broad daylight, for the world to see. The richie and the girl from the other side of town were finally getting their happily-ever-after. It was a sweet, chaste kiss with the kids impatiently waiting nearby.

"I forgot to mention," Aston said, breaking free from my lips. "Movers are coming in the morning to pack up your stuff."

"Oh my God, Aston. You don't give a person a chance, do you?"

"No, I don't. Come on."

Two nights later, I climbed into Aston's ginormous bed, which he'd told me was new since he divorced Cass. In fact, all the furniture was new.

"Thanks, the kids loved that," Aston said to me, his eyes crinkling at the corners.

"It was pizza dough. Seriously, no big deal."

"Well, they've never done that before. We've never done it."

"I think you're going to need to adjust your life a bit. We can't be fancy all the time. Plus, Denise doesn't have to work twenty-four/seven. She needs a vacation."

Gathering me in his arms, Aston settled me on my side, turning to face me. His palm ran over my cheek, tucking my hair behind my ear. "Whatever you want. But that job, it's not safe, and I need you with me on this project. Please?"

"Aston, I've been at the job a long time. They depend on me. I'm good at helping those women."

"Give them notice. Help train the next person."

Tilting my head to look at him, I spoke quietly. "Look at Milly. She gave up everything about herself to be some new person, and she wasn't exactly happy. I don't want to be that person. I'm not a society lady."

This got me a laugh from Aston. "I'm not asking you to plan parties. I need your expertise, your good judgment when it comes to hiring people. I don't want you to be anyone else."

"I'll think about it."

"Good. Now let's think about something else."

His hand traveled down my side and into my pajama bottoms—we had four kids, there wasn't any racy lingerie. His finger quickly found my heat and slipped inside, bringing me to the brink at lightning speed. When I was close, he put pressure where I needed it, and over the edge I went.

"Shh," he warned me and then shoved my pants all the way down.

Yanking the shirt over his head, he turned to glance at the door, making sure it was closed, and then he was inside me. Slowly stroking inside me, he pulled off my tank top and took my nipple in his mouth. My head tipped back, and he picked up speed.

"Aston," I said softly, his name a whispered plea.

"I got you," he said, and rode me faster.

Our bodies moved in sync, looking for release until we were both covered in a fine sheen of sweat and panting. After we finished together, Aston told me he loved me, and then hurried off to get a washcloth. By the time he returned, and I was cleaned up, there was a knock on our door.

"Come in," Aston called out, making sure I was covered.

Little A peeked in. "Dad, can I sleep in Tyler's room?"

"Sure, but don't stay up all night. Hear me?"

"Yes. G'night," he said, and went running off.

Aston chuckled. "We're going to have to get those two bunk beds."

"But we don't need to get anything else."

"Shh."

He silenced me with a kiss, which only lasted until Piper burst into our room crying, showing us pictures on her phone of a sleepover she wasn't invited to.

"This is a great life," Aston said to me.

I nodded over a teary-eyed Piper and went back to consoling my daughter.

Epilogue

Aston

Three years later

It was late. The sun had set long ago, but I didn't feel like going inside. Not yet.

Mainly because the house was a fucking zoo, not that I minded it. Actually, I loved it, and was learning not to try to control the chaos. It was so different from the way I was raised, yet so much better.

Tonight was supposed to be different, though. Tonight had been meant for Bexley and me, but our night would have to wait. No big deal. I'd already waited a lifetime to get her back. I could wait a day or two for a special date night.

When I'd had enough of the hysteria inside earlier and went to step outside on the expansive wrap-around deck, Mara stayed inside, determined to feed baby, Olivia, and Bailey, the beagle, a mashed-up banana.

Yep, Bexley and I couldn't help it…we had a baby, pretty much right away. Apparently, we were fertile. We also got a puppy for the kids when we moved. We were gluttons for chaos.

As I'd slipped out through the back door, I noticed there was more banana on the dog's back, on the floor, and on the wall than in Olivia's belly, but I let it be. The housekeeper would clean it up in the morning, and I'd be damned if Bexley didn't leave it for someone else to do. She would argue, and I would shut her up in my own way.

Little A and Tyler were battling it out on the PlayStation, screaming and yelling at each other over whose football team was better.

They didn't even hear me shout, "Quiet down, you punks," so naturally, I gave up and let them be too.

Then there was my beautiful Piper—the real reason tonight was different. My baby girl was upstairs in her room, crying over Jensen Danvers. God, I hated the little prick. I did *not* want to let him be. Never had I wanted to beat the crap out of a tenth-grader before.

The little jerk had wooed her all goddamn year, even when I told her not to fall for his shit, and invited Piper to the homecoming dance. Of course, now the cocksucker was shacking up with some senior and had ditched Piper for the dance.

I had every reason to head over to the Danvers' house on the sixteenth hole and give those parents a talking-to. The only thing keeping me home was Bexley. She'd given me a death stare that clearly told me if I crossed her on this, I'd be jacking off from here to eternity.

Unable to control myself and my mouth, I'd retreated to the deck. Of course, Bexley thought she should handle Piper on her own.

Feeling helpless, I texted Mike and checked in. He and Milly were heading out on a date, like I should have been. They had a nanny, though, and we didn't.

Denise's husband took retirement right after Bexley moved in with me, and they took off to explore the country in an RV. Most recently, they fell in love with an area along Cheat Lake in West Virginia, said they would be back for Christmas to see the kids.

I explained to Mike that Piper, who was supposed to have been watching the other kids tonight, was out of commission. Plus, Mike and Milly were setting things straight and needed the night out. Even though I was pretty certain that our date wasn't happening any fucking time soon, I had what I needed—Bexley. Forever.

And I couldn't fault Mike for putting his marriage back together.

Taking in deep breaths, I was trying to remember what it was like when I had my first crush, my first love, when I heard the sliding door open. I braced myself for whatever type of catastrophe might interrupt my Scotch and me.

"Hey."

Thank God it's Bexley.

She slipped into my lap with something hidden behind her back.

"What you got there, young lady?" My lips brushed her temple as I breathed all of her in.

"Kiss me, and I'll show you."

For the record, she didn't need to bribe me to kiss her. I set my drink on the ledge and covered her mouth with mine, my hand wrapping behind her neck, pulling her as close as she could be. I wanted to devour her.

Trying to distract her with my tongue, I tugged on her arm, pretending I wanted her to wrap it around me.

"Huh-uh, no way," she said before breaking free with a smile.

"Come on, Bex. I've been sitting out here by my lonesome. I deserve some happiness," I said with a wink. She knew I was happy as fuck.

"It's nice out here," she said, tilting away from me as she stalled.

"Yep. That's exactly why I'm out here. Inside, it's a loony bin, and I want to grab Piper and drive her over to Jensen's house and let her slap the asshole across the face. But somehow, I don't think you'd like that idea."

"That's not a solution. And you love the craziness. You never had anything like this, and neither did I." Speaking the truth, she smiled even bigger.

"I do love it, but I still think we should hire someone to help." What I didn't add was that I planned to hire someone full time to run the house, not these part-time housekeepers. This I knew she didn't agree with me on.

Proving me right, she said, "We don't need anyone. The kids are happier when we're here, or just being together themselves."

"I feel ya, Bex, but what I want is to really feel you inside and out. Feel you up, if you didn't know what I mean. Feel myself buried deep in you."

She laughed, her giggle rising into the night sky. "That's how we got Olivia."

"So? We love Olivia. We could have one more kid. We're already outnumbered."

"Okay, enough of that crazy talk. Look what I brought you." She pulled a fat cigar out from behind her back and ran it under my nose.

I breathed in the bold cinnamon and nutmeg scent. "Mmm." I moaned, a Pavlovian response. "You're too good to me."

"I know we're supposed to celebrate tonight, but Piper's not doing great, and I feel bad leaving."

"I know. Don't worry. Rain check?"

Bexley nodded, touching her forehead to mine. "Remember that night we sat out on the seventeenth hole and shared a cigar?"

It was my turn to nod. "Feels like a lifetime ago, and maybe yesterday, all wrapped up in one."

"Sometimes I wish we could get the years back. The ones I wasted not being with you."

"Don't, Bex." I ran my hand through her hair and pulled her tight to my chest. I knew this haunted her. I didn't like thinking of all the time she spent with Seth either, or the years I wasted on Cass. But all of that was behind us now. "Don't ruin today with that crock of shit."

"I know. Today's awesome."

"Pretty much." I kissed her, this time not letting her pull away. We stayed like that until we couldn't breathe.

"Wanna share this?" I waved the stogie in the air.

"It's all you, AP. On to the next. Time to celebrate."

"I can't wait."

"Me either," Bexley said, snuggling into my chest.

For a moment, I'd forgotten the reason for our date night. With Bexley, the why never mattered when it came to celebrating together. I'd been biding my time, but I'd finally penned a deal this morning to buy another small resort in Tahoe, and now it was all mine.

Well, ours. We planned to add a luxury spa to the five-star gaming hotel we'd already started. It was a little slice of perfection for travelers who wanted it all.

Federal Stars Hospitality Supplies was no more, and my father was alone to stew about it all by himself. Together, Bexley and I were making a new family legacy. Now the Bexley Brand was quickly becoming a well-regarded line of small luxury resorts.

The thought made me grin as I snagged a lighter from by the grill and lit up my cigar.

It might have felt like a hundred years since we first sat on the seventeenth hole together, but my heart always knew there was only one love for me.

The End-ish

Acknowledgments

These are increasingly difficult to write. With every book, I realize the effects of the romance world on my daily life. There is no separation between who I am in my daily life and when I step into Romancelandia. These people are my family.

Thank you to my fabulous betas: Michelle, Jenn, and Virginia. I'm sure you have me on Do Not Disturb at this point. Queen V—when are we going to another signing again? I hope soon.

As always, Sarah Hansen created this beauty on the cover. This time around, I said work your magic. I didn't say one thing. This is what she gave me on the first try.

Pam Berehulke, where would I be without you? Together since the beginning, we have gone through so many of life's ups and downs. I appreciate your editing expertise more than you know.

Emily Tippetts and gang, without you, I can't upload a thing. Thanks for making it all work.

Jenn Watson and everyone at Social Butterfly, thanks…times a million. Jenn, thank you for standing up for this community and your advocacy to make it a better place.

Nic, my PA. Three babies and a sprained tailbone, and you're still better organized than me.

Christy Pastore. My daily text, call, yell for help—you always answer me, and if you don't, I find you. Thank you for being part of my personal and professional life.

Fabi, glad you're back after disappearing into the social media black hole. Our lives are better with you in it. Thanks for channeling my inner cowgirl.

To my family. Just thanks for being you.

To THE ELECTRIC READERS, I love you eternally.

And to YOU, for reading.

About the Author

Rachel Blaufeld is a bestselling author of Romantic Suspense, New Adult, Coming-of-Age Romance, and Sports Romance. A recent poll of her readers described her as *insightful*, *generous*, *articulate*, and *spunky*. Originally a social worker, Rachel creates broken yet redeeming characters. She's been known to turn up the angst like cranking up the heat in the dead of winter.

A devout coffee drinker and doughnut eater, Rachel spends way too many hours in local coffee shops, downing the aforementioned goodies while she plots her ideas. Her tales may all come with a side of angst and naughtiness, but end as lusciously as her treats.

As a side note, Blaufeld, also a long-time blogger and an advocate of woman-run anything, is fearless about sharing her opinion. To her, work/life/family balance is an urban legend, but she does her best.

Rachel has also blogged for *The Huffington Post*, *Modern Mom*, and *USA TODAY*, where she shared conversations at "In Bed with a Romance Author" and reading recommendations at "Happy Ever After."

Rachel lives around the corner from her childhood home in Pennsylvania with her family and two beagles. Her obsessions include running, coffee, basketball, icing-filled doughnuts, antiheroes, and mighty fine epilogues.

When she isn't writing, she can be found courtside, tweeting about hoops as her son plays, or walking around the house wearing earplugs while her other son, the drummer, bangs away.

To connect with Rachel, she's most active in her private reading group, *The Electric Readers*, where she shares insider information and intimate conversation with her readers:

Tunnel VIPs

As well as:

www.rachelblaufeld.com
Twitter
Facebook
Newsletter

If you liked this book, feel free to leave a review where you bought it or on Goodreads. Send me an e-mail when you do, and I will thank you personally!

www.ingramcontent.com/pod-product-compliance
Lightning Source LLC
Chambersburg PA
CBHW060543260626
47161CB00003B/1023